The Mirror Man

First Edition, August 2022

ISBN-13: 9798986259109
ISBN-10: 8986259109

Published by Somerton Press | Philadelphia, PA

The
Mirror Man

J.B. MANAS

SOMERTON
PRESS

ACKNOWLEDGMENTS

First and foremost, I must acknowledge my dear friend Dawn Mahan, whose generosity with her time and insightful intuition made such an important contribution to this book, especially around the characterization of Lela Mars. Dawn was a huge help in bringing Lela to life.

I must also thank Paula Berinstein for her continued wisdom and encouragement; Eric Miller for his keen editing eye; my brother Dr. Eric Manas for his scientific insights; and Dave Bellamy and Michael Myers for validating that the depictions of police procedures were reasonably realistic.

I'd be remiss if I didn't acknowledge my stellar cover designer, Kirk DouPonce, whose work always boggles my mind.

Thanks also to my amazing team of beta readers, whose feedback was so helpful in the editing process: Carmen Harris; Jen Abrahamson; Bob Abrahamson; and Felicia Martin, and to fellow authors Roland Hulme and Gabriel Rabanales for their generous feedback.

Thanks to Donna Frankel; Diane Vilches; Maggie Mullen; Guy Dorian Jr. (my fellow writer on the COR series); Ed Miller (my co-author on The Kronos Interference), and

Marvel legend Guy Dorian, Sr., for their everlasting support and encouragement.

And of course, last but not least, thanks to my wife Sharon and daughter Elizabeth who had to stare at the back of my head for months on end as I wrote, not to mention listen to me ramble on about story elements completely out of context.

Praise for The Mirror Man

"A stylish and engaging crime tale... The well-developed characters and their intriguing powers help set this thriller apart from the pack... Manas generates an insistent sense of momentum that makes the reading experience tense and enjoyable."

- Kirkus Reviews

"Manas has married a modern spy thriller with speculative elements and old-school hints of Hitchcockian crime noir to establish a genre-busting, white-knuckle novel that will keep you turning the pages."

- AgentPalmer.com

"THE MIRROR MAN includes all the essential elements of successful suspense story writing—high stakes, conflict, drama, quick pacing, red herrings, cliff hangers, and a satisfying ending... A complex and intriguing plot, an abundance of action and outstanding characterization make THE MIRROR MAN a compelling read."

- Indie Reader

"An epic supernatural spy thriller that may be the first entry in a blockbuster franchise... Highly recommended."

- BestThrillers.com

PROLOGUE

FORGET ME NOT

Brussels Airport – February 18th, 2013

They would have twenty minutes to steal 130 bags of diamonds worth fifty million USD from one of the busiest airports in Europe. Everything had been timed to the minute, which is why Ivan Petrov knew he had precisely two minutes to get the black Mercedes police van to the Zurich-bound Fokker 100 aircraft once the cargo door was ready to be closed. He scanned the tarmac through his Steiner binoculars. Right on target, the Brinks armored vehicle was pulling up to the awaiting Helvetic Airways plane. The Transport Security agents were already there.

He watched as the Brinks van stopped and the drivers loaded the coveted parcels into the two cargo doors of the 109-passenger jet. The adrenaline rushed through his veins as he observed the workers in action, his unsteady hands making it difficult to focus through the binoculars. It felt as if the Brinks men were moving in slow motion, a long, opening ballet before the main event. He could hear Strauss's Blue Danube playing in his head, and soon began humming it to himself. Before he knew it, his hands stopped shaking.

He lowered the binoculars for a moment to wipe the sweat from his eyes with his sleeve, even though it was the middle of winter. No matter how many jobs he'd done, he still got nervous before the action began. Anyone who said they didn't was a liar. But once things got going, he took comfort in operating to a good plan. And this was a good plan. He made a mental note to congratulate the orchestrator when this was all done, whoever it was.

After taking a deep breath, he lifted the binoculars back up to his eyes just as a Brinks driver was shutting one of the cargo doors.

It was showtime.

"Hoods up," said Petrov, as he lifted the black federal police hood over his head. "Remember, we have eight minutes till that plane starts taxiing. Six minutes once we get there."

Without hesitating, he turned on the blue police lights and hit the accelerator, pushing through the prepared hole in the security fence. He glanced in his rear-view mirror to make sure Schmidt was right behind him in the Audi.

"Look, they see us coming," said Gerardi from the back of the van.

"I don't think so," said Kamal, who was next to Gerardi.

"We stick to the plan," said Petrov. "As far as they know, we're *Police Fédérale*." Petrov wasn't accustomed to working with others, let alone seven complete strangers. But Hans had assured him everyone was properly vetted. They may have been younger and thinner, but Petrov doubted they had anywhere near his experience on major heists.

As Petrov and the others approached the plane in the two police vehicles, the Brinks drivers and security agents gawked at them in confusion. Once parked, Petrov wasted no time. He grabbed his Galil assault rifle and rushed the Brinks drivers and the agents, who instinctively backed up with their hands raised. Two other armed teammates joined him, while the others worked on retrieving the parcels.

"Five minutes," announced Petrov to his team. He ordered the security agents to kick over their weapons to him, which they did without a fuss. They weren't about to risk their lives over precious gems that were protected by insurance. After all, it was protocol not to resist in such cases.

Petrov surveyed the situation. Even though he'd rehearsed this job in his head a thousand times, his heart was pounding. While Gerardi, otherwise known as *Il Meccanico*, or *The Mechanic*, broke the two cargo doors open, Schmidt organized the transport of the jewelry into the two vehicles. As per the plan, Kamal stood at the front of the plane to prevent the pilot from moving. As far as the pilot was concerned, this would simply look like police activity, perhaps an inspection of something in the cargo hold, which wasn't unheard of. The passengers, barring any official police announcement, would not be notified and would have no clue what was going on below them.

"Two minutes," said Petrov as the men were still transporting parcels to the police vehicles. Time was of the essence. If the plane didn't begin taxiing when instructed by flight control, attention would be coming their way. The last thing he needed was for the pilot to report he was being delayed due to police activity.

As the seconds began to evaporate, he watched like an expectant father as the men raced back and forth with the bags. Now he was beginning to sweat again. A lot could still go wrong.

"Thirty seconds!" he shouted. "We need to go. Leave the rest."

He ordered the security agents and Brinks drivers to head toward the nose of the plane and not look back. Then he walked briskly back to the Mercedes van, looking around for any signs of incoming police. He spotted Schmidt trying to grab the last of the bags, just as several of the security agents turned around to observe what was going on.

"Now!" yelled Petrov. "We're out of time."

Petrov climbed into the driver seat of the Mercedes van and honked the horn for the others as he started the engine. Schmidt finally gave up and trotted back to the Audi. The rest of the men followed suit and climbed back into their respective vehicles.

In less than a minute, they were through the security gate. Petrov breathed a temporary sigh of relief. They had done the job in nineteen minutes and thirty seconds. With luck, they'd have ten or fifteen minutes before police caught up to them. He floored the gas pedal and headed for the dirt road.

Once on the bumpy dirt road, he headed to the rusty yellow construction sign marked *Port Obligatoire: Personnel Autorisé seulement*—its illustrations indicating the obligatory helmet, goggles, and boots—and turned left. As soon as he turned the corner, he pulled behind the same abandoned construction site they'd hidden in for three hours beforehand. The tractor-trailer was there waiting as planned, its loading ramp open and ready. He drove carefully onto the rickety double ramp and pulled all the way into the truck's shadowy cargo space to make room for the Audi.

That's when he heard the police sirens.

Wiping the perspiration from his forehead, he glanced in his rear-view mirror and watched as the Audi slowly pulled in behind him.

"Dammit, Schmidt, hurry up," said Petrov.

Just then, he felt the Audi hit the rear bumper of the Mercedes, and his car alarm went off.

"Idiot!"

While Petrov fumbled with the keys to figure out how to turn the alarm off, Schmidt and the others ran out to remove the loading ramp.

This was taking way too long.

He frantically pressed the buttons on the key fob and studied the endless dials and controls on the Mercedes dashboard while the shrill sound rang in his ears. The police sirens seemed to be getting closer, though the noises were beginning to blend.

He once again wiped his sleeve across his forehead and then resumed pressing every button on the key fob before throwing it across the car in frustration.

Somehow, that did the trick and the alarm stopped. Hurriedly, he opened the driver door to join the others. The door didn't have room to open fully, and he cursed his oversized gut as he tried to squeeze himself out of the van. It must've looked like a rhinoceros giving birth.

Once he wedged himself out and angrily kicked the van, he ran out into the chilly February air to lend a hand. The police sirens grew deafeningly loud and were almost upon them.

"Get in the truck!" yelled Petrov. "Just leave it."

"Have faith," said Schmidt, as he worked on folding the ramp.

"Remind me to tell you that in prison."

Petrov paced as he watched the dirt road that led to the construction site, expecting the police to arrive any second. He could barely breathe.

Just then, four Belgian police vehicles went racing past.

Petrov exhaled slowly.

"We're good," said Schmidt, winking.

"We're lucky," said Petrov.

After they all piled back into the semi-trailer and secured the ramp and the tailgate, the truck was at last moving.

Petrov and the others sat quietly in their dark, cold, vehicles while the truck continued its journey for the next hour. He could see his breath as he settled back into his seat, Gerardi and Kamal behind him. He could hear Kamal snoring.

"How could he sleep at a time like this?" said Gerardi.

"He's a rich man now. He's getting practice."

"We're not rich yet," said Gerardi. "I, for one, will not rest till I know who we're meeting and I have those diamonds in my hands."

During the next thirty minutes or so of bumps and turns in pitch blackness, Petrov tried to settle his mind, which kept wanting to drift to the various possible outcomes. He tried a method he'd learned in the military that had usually worked for him—silently naming as many cocktails as he could. It kept him grounded and decluttered his mind. Tom Collins… Manhattan… Gin and Tonic… Bloody Mary.

Finally, the truck pulled off the highway. It seemed to be slowing down and the terrain grew rougher; it sounded like they were driving on a dirt road. Then it came to a stop with a squeal and the engine shut off. The sudden silence was deafening as he waited to see where they were and who would be greeting them. This was the part of the journey they weren't told about—only that the truck would take them to an undisclosed location where the parcels would be divvied up.

After about a minute, the tailgate opened, and the winter sunlight flooded the cargo space.

Petrov exited his vehicle, leaving his weapon in the car as instructed. In the back of his mind, he wondered if he was walking into an ambush. He reached in and grabbed his Beretta, tucking it into his pants as a precaution. At least this time it was slightly easier to maneuver his body out of the van and catch up with the others.

As he stepped down from the truck's tailgate ladder with the team, he could see they were in the middle of a barren field, its dried grass and dirt hardened from weeks of ice and snow. The truck driver, a portly, bearded man with red hair, was there waiting for them. Two identical metallic-blue 3

Series BMW sedans were parked several yards ahead.

Within seconds, a well-dressed, fit, dark-haired man in his thirties stepped out of the driver side of the left sedan. He was wearing a finely tailored, double-breasted gray herringbone overcoat, a black scarf, and Wayfarer-style sunglasses. Having come from a family of clothiers, Petrov knew high-end sartorial savvy when he saw it. The man glanced at his watch, which as far as Petrov could tell, was a rare Rolex Daytona variant, which was worth more than the two BMWs combined. Clearly, this man was accustomed to the finer things in life, which made him wonder why the man was driving a mid-class BMW and not a Bentley or Aston Martin.

He watched as the other sedan's driver-side door opened, and a tall, blond-haired man stepped out, dressed in all black attire. Petrov recognized Hans immediately. It was hard to miss the pale skin, flaxen hair, and the scar that ran down the side of his face.

Meanwhile, the man in the sunglasses and herringbone coat approached them casually, while Hans walked slowly behind him, remaining at a distance.

"I must congratulate you all for a job well done," said the man, who spoke with a slight British accent. "You're practically right on time."

"Ah, you're the planner," said Petrov. He should've guessed by the authority of the man's gait and his casual demeanor, but he was expecting a middle-aged man like himself.

"Sebastian Blaine," said the man, cheerfully. "But call me Sebastian. We're all friends now."

"We get thirty percent, as agreed," said Schmidt, confirming the deal.

"Gunther Schmidt," said Blaine. "As efficient with your tongue as you are with your driving. Hans was right. But I wouldn't have it any other way. Yes, twenty percent to me, fifty to the house, and thirty to be split between the eight of you. That's nearly a million pounds for each of you. Not bad for a day's work."

"Not bad at all," said a female voice in the group. Petrov nearly forgot about her, as she'd been in Schmidt's car. She was the only female among the eight thieves. A real looker too, with strawberry blonde hair and icy blue eyes. Shame she had the personality of a reptile.

"Helena Petrovitch," said Blaine, with apparent admiration. "It's a pleasure to meet you in person. Your reputation precedes you. Which reminds me…"

Blaine reached in his jacket pocket and pulled out a small bouquet of blue flowers and offered it to her.

"Nice," said Helena, offering a slightly crooked smile before returning to her usual poker face. "Now let's get it done, shall we?"

"We shall," said Blaine.

"You forgot something, Blaine," said Schmidt. "How do we get out of here once we divvy everything up? We can't leave in the police cars."

"Ah, the question I was waiting for," said Blaine. "It's quite simple, really. You're going to leave in those." He pointed to the two BMW sedans. "Hans and I will take the truck. After unloading your share of course."

"And you're just going to give us the BMWs," said Petrov. "Just like that."

"Consider it a bonus for you and Schmidt as our expert drivers," said Blaine. "It's a gift from one of the beneficiaries of our haul today."

"Who?" said Schmidt.

"A certain car dealership. Now, let's shake hands on a job well done and then get those police vehicles out here, shall we?"

♦

Sebastian Blaine eyed up the eight thieves—all vetted and approved by him and referred by Hans. He knew his plan was solid and was pleased to see it executed flawlessly. Once he dropped off the haul, he'd be paid his portion in cash through the usual methods. The balance would be distributed to a vast network of backers, ranging from a luxury car dealer in the French Riviera to a Swiss real estate agent, several top attorneys, a surprising number of international celebrities, and about forty others. Whether or not the goods would eventually be traced to the thieves or anyone in the network was none of his concern. His job was done, and none of them knew he was involved—only his benefactors did, and even they remained well insulated from the backers at large.

"Nicely done," he said to Schmidt as he shook his hand.

He moved on to Gerardi next. "Il Meccanico. Excellent work," he said, shaking the man's hand vigorously.

When he took Helena Petrovich's hand, he leaned in and kissed both cheeks. "Till we meet again," he said.

She smirked. "We won't."

He glanced back at Schmidt and Gerardi, who, as expected, had a glazed look in their eyes. Then Helena developed the same familiar look, as the smirk evaporated from her face. In seconds, she went from coldness to confusion.

It seemed Petrov noticed it too, so Blaine quickly grabbed Petrov's hand and shook it. "Splendid driving," he said. Petrov looked down at his own hand and squinted. It was clear he suspected something was up.

After Blaine shook hands with the remaining four, he could see they all were groggy. He took a deep breath as he felt the usual wave of emotions flood his mind—for he knew that the eight thieves' memories from the events of the day: the nervous race across the tarmac to the awaiting jet; the frantic scurry to load the parcels into the two police vehicles; the adrenaline rush as they made their way to the construction site and the awaiting truck; and the uncertainty they surely felt once inside the cold, dark cargo space would all be evaporating this very moment. Though he couldn't see their memories, he could feel them, the way a blind man senses somebody is nearby. Any second now, their trepidation at meeting him, wondering if they'd been double-crossed, or even ambushed, would be completely forgotten. All their recent memories of the last few weeks would be a blur. In fact, they'd have no recollection of his involvement at all.

As if to will the cluttering of their minds, he said the words to himself that he had said so many times before.

Erase.

Erase.

Erase.

Erase.

With his mind at ease, he knew that theirs was as well. That was his gift in life, and his curse—to be able to make people forget with just a touch of his hand. And he'd managed to put it to good use over the last couple decades, though some would argue that point.

With the eight thieves still dazed, he nodded to Hans, who climbed into the truck's cargo space and opened the trunk of the Audi. The bearded truck driver returned to the cabin.

"Looks good so far," said Hans, inspecting the trunk.

"Good, throw me down eight bags," said Blaine.

"You're leaving them diamonds?"

"I'm feeling generous. Besides, they earned it."

Hans threw him the parcels and he caught them and tossed them on the ground in front of his groggy subjects.

He walked up to Helena, whose eyes were still glazed over. "Oh, and you can keep the flowers," he said. Then added quietly to himself, "Isn't it ironic?" With that, he trotted to the passenger side of the truck's cabin and climbed up.

Within seconds, the truck was on its way and the field of dreamers was far behind them—the dreamers in question likely just coming out of their fog.

Blaine picked up his disposable phone and pressed the familiar numbers. A silent party picked up on the other end.

"It's done," said Blaine. Then he disconnected and threw the phone out the window.

◆

Petrov had the strangest feeling. He was standing in the middle of a desolate field with seven people who seemed familiar, but he couldn't quite place where from. He had no recollection of how he got there. It was clear the others felt the same way. And there were two empty BMW sedans parked just ahead.

"Why do I know you?" said Schmidt.

"I was going to say the same thing," said Petrov.

He gazed down at the eight bags and picked one up. He opened it and peered inside.

"Diamonds," he said.

"Eight bags," said Schmidt. "There's eight of us. That's convenient."

"Were we drugged?" said Gerardi.

"Seems like it," said Petrov. "Either that or it's some kind of social experiment."

"I don't know any of you," said Kamal. "How did we even get here? Someone has to remember."

"Who cares how we got here?" said Schmidt. "We have eight bags of diamonds and two cars."

"I'm with him," said Gerardi.

Petrov looked over at Helena, who was holding a bouquet of flowers and examining them.

"Are they your flowers?" he said.

She shook her head. "I don't think so. But it's the type of flowers that has me spooked."

"What kind of flowers are they?" he said.

She crinkled her forehead and turned to look at him.

"My favorite kind. Forget-me-nots."

CHAPTER 1

JUST LIKE CARY GRANT

Philadelphia — Nine Years Later

J ulian Black was in his element, his headset drowning out the real world while he roamed the virtual streets of Paris looking for his target. Spread seamlessly across the three large computer monitors on his desk was the most beautifully rendered 3D version of the hilltop village of Montmartre he'd ever seen—not that he'd ever been there. He wandered among the countless artist tables, cafés, and street merchants at Place Du Tertre, marveling at how real it all seemed—the sights and sounds of the bustling, open-air, village square he only knew from watching *An American in Paris* a dozen times. Despite his aching desire to peruse the colorful canvases and study the chalkboard menus, he had to remind himself he wasn't just playing tourist. After all, he had a job to do. Here, he wasn't Julian; he was Jericho Stone, part of a covert group of international operatives hunting down Bergeron Krupp, assassin supreme, believed to be targeting the visiting British Prime Minister. According to today's Stealth Invaders file, Krupp was spotted in the Montmartre area, possibly to meet

13

up with one of his associates.

"I have him cornered," said the familiar female voice through his headset. "He's heading into Sacré-Coeur."

Natalya Bush was a fellow operative and former KGB agent, but he knew her as Cassie from New Jersey. About the only thing she had in common with her alter ego Natalya was that they were both twenty-seven. He had even less in common with Jericho Stone. But none of that mattered *in world*.

He raced toward the famous Sacré-Coeur Basilica at the summit of the butte Montmartre, the highest point in the city and a stone's throw from Place du Tertre. In front of the cathedral was a sprawling observation area where tourists would gather for magnificent views of Paris. From what he'd read, even more spectacular views could be seen from the dome at the top of Sacré-Coeur. He got to the basilica just in time to see Natalya chasing Krupp into the building and followed them inside through the large bronze doors on the left. When he got inside, he scanned the area. They were nowhere to be seen.

"Where are you?" he said.

"Chasing him up the stairs," said Natalya. "They're in the back left of the building."

He headed to the left and saw the signs pointing to the Dome. He darted up the narrow, dark, spiral staircase which seemed to go on forever. If this were real life he'd be out of breath by now. Every so often he'd see them up ahead, and then they'd disappear around another spiral.

When he finally emerged from the staircase, he tried not to be distracted by the spectacular views of Paris from what was quite a dizzying height. He moved around the observation area until he saw Krupp wrestling with Natalya behind one of the stone pillars that lined the observation area. As he got closer, he could see Krupp was trying to push her over the edge.

Fortunately, Krupp hadn't spotted him. He took aim with his rangefinder, trying to make sure he hit Krupp and not Natalya.

With a single shot, he hit his mark. Krupp staggered and fell between the pillars and over the edge, plummeting about 300 feet—landing just in front of the majestic cathedral.

No sooner did Krupp hit the ground than Julian started receiving direct messages from all over the place, congratulating him for winning one for the team. A congratulatory message came on the monitor to the team from the Section Chief. Then, just as he expected, the call from Cassie came in on the headset. He closed the game and pressed the answer button.

"You do know he was luring you up there, right?" he said.

"Of course, I know. That doesn't make it a bad idea."

"You're lucky I was there."

"You always are," she said. "Except in person."

"Listen, about that, Cass. Something came up and I couldn't make it."

"If you don't want to meet in person, just say it. I just thought it would be nice. We've been playing for what, three years now?"

"It's not that, it's just I have so much going on."

"Your book? You've been working on the same book the whole time I've known you. A break for one night wouldn't hurt. Are you sure you aren't married?"

He laughed and leaned back in his gaming chair, looking around the spare bedroom that doubles as his office, where he'd spent most of his life.

"No," he said. "I'm not married."

"No girlfriend?"

"No girlfriend."

"Then why so mysterious?"

Just then, he thought he heard his mother calling him. He lifted the right earphone off his ear.

"Julian!" yelled his mother from the doorway. "Dinner's been ready for a half hour."

"Give me a minute," he replied.

"Okay," said Cassie. "Who's the girl?"

"It's… the maid," he said.

"The maid? She talks to you like she's your mother."

"No, definitely not my mother," he said. "And not my wife."

"But she makes you dinner."

"She's one of those maids that cook," he said. "Listen, Cass, can I call you in an hour?"

"Will you promise to meet me soon?"

"I promise," he said.

After he hung up and opened his door, his mother was still standing in the hallway.

"The maid?" she said. "Seriously?"

"I didn't want to tell her I'm thirty-five and live with my mother. What would she think?"

"She'd think you were a good catch."

He followed her downstairs to the kitchen. The big screen TV in the family room was playing Hitchcock's *To Catch a Thief*. He'd always loved that one. While *North by Northwest* was probably his favorite film overall, Cary Grant was never more debonair than in his role as retired jewel thief, John "The Cat" Robie. And the breathtaking vistas of the French Rivera were spectacular. Julian took a seat at the kitchen table, from which he still had a good view of the screen. On the TV at the moment was the scene where Grant, as Robie, meets Grace Kelly and her mother in the iconic Carlton Cannes hotel for the first time. They're having drinks in the casino, and Grace Kelly, as American oil heiress Frances Stevens, is giving him the cold shoulder.

"I love how she practically ignores him and then shocks him by kissing him in the hallway just after," he said.

"Completely unpredictable."

"I made spaghetti and turkey meatballs," said his mother, putting the plate down in front of him. "You may need to warm it up."

He stabbed a meatball with his fork and took a bite. "It's perfect," he said. He loved the way she included fresh basil and parsley.

"I think you should meet that girl."

He put down his fork as she meandered back to the counter and placed the dirty pots in the sink.

"You know I can't."

"You're in a prison of your own making," she said, scrubbing the spaghetti pot. "You'll never be like Cary Grant if you don't leave the house."

"I'll never be like Cary Grant anyway, so I'm already ahead of the game."

"Don't say that," she said. "You're thin. You have a full head of brown hair. A nice, friendly face."

"I'm afraid that doesn't qualify me."

"Either way, you should find your own Grace Kelly."

"Well, I can't go woo Grace Kelly, can I? Because all I have to do is accidentally touch her hand and I'll see some horrifying memory of hers. Maybe some trauma at the convent she grew up in, or some casting couch nightmare. It's like a potluck of humiliation."

"Julian, not everyone has traumatic memories." She grabbed her plate of spaghetti off the counter and took a seat opposite him.

"So, I should play Russian Roulette?" he said.

"Wear gloves. You do anyway when you go to the store."

"Oh, that'll look real nice on a date. I'll look like a serial killer. I may as well bring duct tape and a shovel."

"Funny. I'm just saying, this isn't a life."

"Mother, I'm perfectly fine staying here, watching old

movies with you. I can work on my book. When I'm bored, I play Stealth Invaders with Cassie."

"And you get less sun than a potato. Look at the TV." She pointed toward the screen.

He turned his head and watched as Cary Grant and Grace Kelly greeted each other in the lobby, both quite the fashion icons—he in a gray blazer with a crisp, white shirt, black cravat, and tan slacks, and she in a black swimsuit, wide-brim white hat, and a white coverup that could double as a fancy dress.

"That's quite a hat," he said.

"I mean Cary Grant. He has a nice tan. He lives a life. He goes out."

Julian twirled spaghetti onto his fork. "Okay, I'll buy some tanning spray."

Just then, a break for donation pledges interrupted the broadcast.

"Is this on public television?" he said.

"Looks like it. I'll change the channel during the break. The six o'clock news is on. Besides, I donated last month."

She got up to grab the remote and switched the TV to the local news.

"… road rage killing," said the blonde-haired anchorwoman. A photo of a pretty, young black woman was overlayed on the screen.

"Monica Hilson," she continued, "age thirty-five, a social worker at Sunny Ridge Nursing Home in Yardley, was shot and killed in a road rage incident on Roosevelt Boulevard this afternoon in Northeast Philadelphia. Police have not yet tracked down the shooter. Hilson's daughters, ages sixteen and seven, were in the car when it happened. Eric Hilson, the victim's husband, is asking the public's help to find the shooter."

A clearly distraught, thin black man with glasses and a gray turtleneck appeared on the screen. The reporter's hand and microphone could be seen below his face, capturing his every word. Two young girls clung to his side in tears, a teenager and a younger child.

"Monica didn't deserve this," the man said, his voice cracking. "She loved her children so much. She never said a bad word about anyone, never raised her voice. All she did her entire life was care for people. Please, if you have any information that could lead to catching this man, please help us. No child should ever have to witness something like this."

Julian heard his words, but the whole time, he was focused on the little girl's face. The poor kid was in a daze, but he could see the inner pain in her watery eyes. Even without seeing her memories, he felt an incredibly strong connection with this child. He envisioned himself at her age and could feel the emotions of seeing something so terrifying and unexplainable, as if he were experiencing it himself. It felt like a bad memory. For a moment, he envisioned someone shooting his mother, and the hairs on his arms stood up.

The man finished talking. Julian was zoned out, so he didn't hear the rest of it. Then the anchorwoman flashed up a phone number on the screen for people to call with any information.

Julian started scribbling down the number, just as his mother switched the channel back to the movie.

"Wait, leave i—"

"You know, they shouldn't call it the news," said his mother. "They should call it the bad news."

"I was going to call," he said. The pledge drive was still in progress on the TV.

"And tell them what? You never even leave the house."

He could feel his blood boiling at the thought of those two young girls suffering because some probably drunk or stoned rage-monster couldn't hold his temper.

"I may be able to help," he said.

His mother had a confused look on her face.

"How?"

"The girls are young. They're easier for me to read. One of them may have seen something. If they did, it'll be fresh in their minds."

"Are you sure you're willing to do that?"

He looked down at their two plates of spaghetti, both barely touched.

"Of course I'm not sure."

"I'm just saying, it means letting people know about your gift. Once it's out, it's out."

He thought about the consequences. His life would surely change if more people knew about his abilities. But if he stayed silent, this pond scum of a man would get away scot-free, possibly to attack someone else. And that poor family would never find justice. Nor peace.

He nodded his head to acknowledge he heard his mother's warning.

Just then, the film came back on. Cary Grant, John Robie the "Cat," picked up a note left for him in the lobby. The camera zoomed in on the note, which said, '*Robie, you've already used up 8 of your 9 lives. Don't gamble your last one.*' Julian felt goosebumps at the timing. An omen perhaps?

No, he knew in the pit of his gut what he needed to do.

He stood up from the table.

"I'm going," he said.

"Where?" His mother looked dumbfounded.

"The police station."

"Take my car," she said.

"I have my bike. It's not far, and you know how I am about driving."

He went to the hall closet and grabbed a pair of white, full-fingered cycling gloves and put them on. At least they looked somewhat sporty and would meet his needs. He grabbed a light hoodie and headed to the garage to get his bike, a white 7-speed Schwinn Wayfarer.

He rode about a block down the street and then started thinking about what he'd say when he got there. Then he began thinking of what would happen if he were even able to convince the police his talent was real. Of course, to him, it wasn't a talent at all, but a curse—a ball and chain he wore like Marley's ghost from *A Christmas Carol*. He learned to live with it, but it was far easier without seeing people regularly—people who'd have a million questions and wonder why he wasn't able to touch anyone. Typically, he had a ready-made excuse—that he had a skin disorder—but in this case, he'd be disclosing everything. He could end up becoming some big phenomenon, news at 11—a real freak show.

Suddenly, he found it hard to breathe. His legs were aching, too, and he felt like he was peddling through water. He could feel his heart beating through his chest, as the trees and sidewalk started shifting and spinning. He stopped the bike and held his head down, closing his eyes. He remembered a trick his therapist taught him. He breathed in for four seconds, held his breath for four seconds, breathed out for four seconds, and then held his breath for four seconds. Then he repeated the exercise.

He was beginning to calm down. But he came to a decision. He couldn't do this.

He rode back home, put the bike back in the garage, and entered the front door.

"That was quick," said his mother. "Did you forget something?"

He peeled the gloves off and plopped down on the white L-shaped sofa in the family room, feeling defeated.

"You were right," he said. "I couldn't do it."

"I never said you couldn't do it," she said, sitting next to him. "And I'd never say that to you. What I said was… 'Are you willing to do it?' That's something you have to think about."

On the TV, Cary Grant was swimming away from a jetty toward the Carlton Cannes hotel. Then he was back in the hotel, planning his next move. It seemed pretty clear he wasn't obeying the warning note.

Julian lowered his head and shook it in frustration. Or maybe it was shame. The more he thought about it, perhaps the time had come to take a gamble. Two young girls and their broken-hearted father were depending on it, though they didn't know it yet. Somehow, he had to try to help, whatever the cost. And if it meant an inconvenience to him, or a little bit of ridicule, well… he'd have to figure that out, too. The bigger trick would be getting the police to believe him.

CHAPTER 2

THE SARA JOB

Sebastian Blaine floated on his back in the warm, blue Mediterranean Sea—as relaxed as he'd been in a while. Martine grabbed him playfully from behind as he took her hand for leverage, flipping her over. She had no idea he was wearing silicone prosthetic gloves. Nobody could tell. Originally designed to conceal burns and scars, in his case it served a more fundamental purpose. Plus, they were waterproof.

He'd met Martine two days ago. She'd been sitting next to him outside at Café Brun and her blonde hair and golden tan had caught his eye. She looked to be about twenty-two. After some light conversation, she'd joined him at his table. Turned out she was a thirty-two-year-old race car driver from Marseille, trying to qualify for the Grand Prix.

He gazed toward the shore at the striped sunbeds at the chic Carlton Beach Club, where he'd placed their lunch order thirty minutes ago. Situated right on the beach, the seaside restaurant and lounging area was a perennial favorite of his. The magnificent Carlton Cannes hotel itself could be seen further back, just across the palm tree lined Promenade de la

Croisette.

The historic luxury hotel, known for its celebrity guests, was now part of the InterContinental chain, but it fortunately retained its classic Belle Epoque elegance. The famous domes on both sides of the ornate building were said to have been patterned after the breasts of Spanish actress and World War I-era courtesan, Caroline Otero. *La Belle Otero* they called her, and in the early 1900s, she was the most sought-after woman in Europe.

He had done his research on this particular locale. Nine years ago, just five months after the Brussels diamond heist, he'd orchestrated an even bigger robbery using a member of the same team—a solo gig that brought in $136 million worth of gems from an exhibition at this very hotel. A week prior, Blaine had stayed at the hotel to scout it out.

This time, however—just as every time since then—he had come here for pure leisure. In fact, it had become his home away from home.

"Sebastian, I'm hungry," said Martine in her delightful French accent.

"Here comes the waiter now," he said as he watched a tall, thin server in a white shirt approaching their sunbeds carrying a large tray.

He helped her get to her feet as they trudged across the hot sand to the sunbeds. He liked that the sunbeds had a button for placing food and drink orders; it was a perfect example of creative efficiency.

"Voila," said the waiter as they approached, placing their order on the small table by their umbrella. "Deux Salades Niçoises et une bouteille de Château d'Esclans Garrus Rosé." Sebastian couldn't wait to partake. The barrel-fermented Garrus made from 100 year-old Grenache vines was the cream of the crop when it came to rosé, and the berry notes of the 2017 vintage would pair perfectly with the rich Salade Niçoise.

After the two Negroni Sbagliato aperitifs from earlier and his morning tryst with Martine, this would amount to a perfect afternoon of libations, lust, and luxury.

Another white-shirted beach attendant approached from behind and stood beside them.

"Monsieur Blaine?" said the young attendant.

"Oui, c'est moi," he said.

"There is a lady in the lobby to see you."

"Now?" he said. "She's an hour early."

"S'il vous plait, what shall I tell her?" said the man.

"Tell her she'll have to wait."

"Yes, of course. As you wish."

As the attendant made his way back to the hotel, Blaine turned to see Martine looking at him with inquisitive eyes.

"So, it appears I have competition from another woman," she said, with a slight smile.

"Not this woman," he said.

♦

After a splendid lunch by the sea, Blaine sent Martine off shopping along the Croisette with 1,000 euros and then went upstairs to change. He loved the airiness of his suite; the retro furniture with light creams and beiges looked right out of the 1950s Hollywood era—spacious, stylish, and inviting. He went to the closet and threw on a navy, long-sleeved polo shirt and natural linen trousers, along with a pair of cognac suede loafers. Ready to go, he took one last look at the sparkling Mediterranean from his balcony, contemplating whether he was ready for yet another job. After all, he had enough money to last a thousand lifetimes. Maybe part of him was addicted to the thrill. Damn VIPER. He needed them as much as they needed him—and it had nothing to do with the money.

He took a breath, straightened his cuffs, and then headed

out the door. He made his way to the grand spiral staircase and headed down to the elegant lobby—its beige and white marble floors, classic white columns, and elegant chandeliers looking much the same as in its heyday in the fifties and sixties.

As soon as he descended the staircase, he saw her. She was standing straight ahead near a small seating area to the right, arms crossed like a mean schoolteacher waiting for an unruly student who's late to class.

"Olga," he said, headed toward her, smiling. She was probably seventy by now, her silver hair, impeccable dress, and stern features making her look more like Cruella de Vil by the day. She wasn't one to be reckoned with. She must've loved getting the message she'd have to wait an hour for him.

He reached out his hand. "So, what do I—"

"Not here," she said. She ignored his outstretched hand and turned and walked briskly toward an alcove to the right. Proceeding down the hall, she led him through the wood-lined glass doors into the Salon la Côte ballroom, which was empty. The ocean-facing side of the blue-carpeted, sun-washed salon consisted of three sets of floor-to-ceiling glass doors that led out onto a beautiful seaside terrace. She led him through the center doors. As soon as he stepped outside, he let the sunshine and salty, pine-tinged breeze wash over his face. It was like an elixir to his soul, at least the part he hadn't sold to the devil.

Olga stepped toward the terrace's white fence and looked out at the sea toward an enormous yacht that was anchored. It had to be at least 100 meters, which he estimated was worth about 250 million euros, or 300 million US dollars.

"They're here?" he said. He knew the yacht likely belonged to Viktor Volkov, head of VIPER.

"This will be your most important job to date," she said, in her half-Russian, half-Swedish accent. "It is vitally critical that you not fail."

He resented her tone. "God forbid some rich real estate developer or movie producer doesn't get his precious stones."

"This is different," she said.

"Either way, I don't fail. You know that. What's the job this time?"

"Interested parties have received word that the Americans and the British have developed a prototype communications mechanism called SARA."

"That's an awfully lovely name for a device."

"It is an acronym. It stands for Satellite Aerial Repulsion Adaptor. If this device is completed without intervention, it will enable the West to defend their satellites from missile attacks with ease. Without such a deterrent from the East, the balance of power would be... disrupted. These—"

"Wait a minute," said Blaine, interrupting. "You must be mistaking me for James Bond. I like my drinks and women, but the similarities end there."

"These interested parties," she continued, ignoring him, "have offered significant funding for us to retrieve these plans from an English scientist of German lineage, a Dr. Max Baumann. You are to retrieve Dr. Baumann from his home in Monkton Combe in Somerset and extract the location of the SARA plans by whatever means necessary. We will take care of the rest. Need I say, the funding for this operation is considerable."

"Well, it better be. I have no problem separating fools from their money, but this? Who are these interested parties anyway? Russia? China?"

"People who wish to oppose the West. It is not relevant to the operation."

"It's relevant to my health if I'm caught."

"You said you do not fail, and so far this has been our experience with you. You are not developing a conscience, are you, Blaine? That would be unfortunate."

"Not in the slightest. But I *am* developing a sudden intense passion for more money. Call it hazard pay. A little bonus of fifty million ought to do it."

"They are already offering one hundred million in British pounds."

"Then one-fifty shouldn't be a problem."

"Consider it done."

"Done? I should've asked for more if I'm going to start World War Three." He didn't need the money, but it was the principle of the thing.

"You will be maintaining the balance of power. Nothing more. Nothing less."

"Well, it feels like something more. I'll need the usual assistance. And I want Hans on this job."

"You will have Hans and the others."

She handed him a large envelope.

"Your tickets," she said. "You will leave for England in the morning."

As he grabbed the envelope, he was already thinking about how to best carry out the mission. He was accustomed to stealing from drug lords, the ultra-rich, corrupt politicians, and even vast corporations, but this was a different animal entirely. The implications were huge, not that he had any great love for governments of any ilk.

The bigger issue was that extracting information didn't exactly fit in with his skill set. He'd done his share of violence, more than he cared to admit, but his unique talent—his specialty—was making people forget. That might help with the kidnapping, but once he had the good doctor in hand, getting him to reveal what he knows could be a different story, especially if the man was well-trained. There was only one man he knew who could get in someone's head and actually see what was inside—but that was a door he didn't dare re-open.

CHAPTER 3

DETECTIVE MARS

I t took Julian two more tries to leave the house and finally head to the police station. As he approached the building on his bike, he rehearsed in his best Cary Grant voice, "Hello. My name is Julian and I do believe I can help you." No, that was silly. He tried again in his own voice this time. "About that road rage case, I have a certain set of skills, and…" No, that wouldn't work either. He gave it one more shot. "Okay, I can read people's minds, but before you judge…" Ugh, too millennial.

He was at the station and decided to just wing it. He left the bike out front, not bothering with the lock. "It's a police station," he said out loud to himself. "Who's gonna steal a bike from a police station?"

He opened the glass door and stepped inside. A young, blond man in a police uniform was behind the counter at the computer.

"Can I help you?" said the officer.

"I'd like to talk to someone about that road rage murder," said Julian. "The one on the Boulevard. It was a young woman. I have… um… some information that may be able to help."

"You want to see Detective Mars, then. The name?"

"I think her name was Monica Hilson."

"No, *your* name."

"Oh, sorry. It's Julian. Julian Black. I'm kind of new at this." Julian could feel his hands sweating inside the gloves.

The cop picked up the phone and pressed a button on the switchboard. "Hey, someone's here to see you," he said. "A Julian Black. Says he can help with the Hilson case." After a few seconds, he said, "Yeah, I'm serious. Okay, I'll tell him."

The officer looked up at him. "Detective Mars will be out to see you. You can take your gloves off if you want."

He looked down at his white bicycle gloves. "I... um... I have a hand condition."

"Suit yourself." The man seemed unphased by his decidedly silly response.

Julian paced around in front of the counter, wondering what he was going to say and how they'd react. Would they laugh at him? Throw him out angrily? Or would they humor him while they called in the CIA and their scientists? He'd probably seen ET one too many times. He kept an eye on the offices to the left rear of the building for signs of the detective. Just then, one of the office doors burst open and middle-aged, Latino cop with a crew cut in a white uniform shirt and black tie came storming out.

"Hey Shaw," he yelled at nobody in particular. "Where the hell's Shaw? He keeps doin' this and he's out on his ass. I'm in no mood for crap today."

Julian looked at the man's name tag. It said *Mars*. He knew at once; this was definitely a mistake.

Julian approached the blond cop at the front desk and leaned in. "I think maybe I'll come back another day," he said. "I just remembered I forgot something."

"Are you sure?" said the cop.

"Yeah, I'm sure."

"Oh Lela," said the cop, looking past Julian. "Sorry, this guy's just leaving." Julian turned to see to a beautiful young Latina woman approaching from behind, wearing a gray cashmere pullover and jeans.

"Julian Black?" said the woman, extending her hand to him. He was frozen for a second, captivated by her radiant smile and perfect teeth, not to mention her long cascades of dark brown hair and almond-shaped brown eyes that seemed to convey enthusiasm and intensity at the same time. "I'm Detective Mars."

"*You're* Detective Mars?" he said, shaking her hand. "But I thought…" he pointed to the white-shirted, gruff cop in the back, now standing at one of the empty desks and sifting through papers looking for something.

"That's Captain Mars. My father. So, I hear you have information about the Hilson case. Can you talk now? Or did I hear you say you forgot something at home?"

"No, no, I remembered it," he said, realizing that made no sense. "Now is great," he added, a little too enthusiastically.

"Good, follow me." She briskly headed back around the counter toward the side offices on the right. He scurried to catch up to her.

"His bark is worse than his bite," she said as he caught up beside her. "That *is* why you were about to run out on me." She glanced at him and smirked.

"I would've come back," he said, feeling his face turning red.

"No, you wouldn't. But I'm glad I caught you in time. I'm hoping you have something good. We've had no leads on this case, and the social media's been killing us."

"I hope so too," he said, as she opened a door on the right for him to enter.

He stepped into a room that looked like an interrogation room, though it could've been a small meeting room. A rectangular table was in the center with two folding chairs on either side. Behind it was a white counter with a coffee maker and a mini fridge.

"Coffee?" she said, directing him to sit at the table while she grabbed a water bottle.

"No thanks," he said as he took a seat.

"You're lucky," she said. "I'm usually over at Harbison at Divisional Headquarters, but I was here talking to Captain Mars about the case."

"I picked the right day then."

She approached the table with her water bottle and sat opposite him. He studied her face while she pulled out a small notebook and pen out of a purse that must've been attached to her belt. Her olive skin was perfect, without a single blemish, though he noticed for the first time that there was a certain sadness in her expression. Or maybe she hadn't slept much.

"Let's start with your contact information. Address and phone number?"

He gave her the information and watched as she jotted it down quickly.

"So, what do you have for me?" she said.

"Well, it's… um… not so much what I have, but what I can do."

"I'm not following."

"I almost don't know where to start, and you probably won't believe me."

"Try me." She stared directly at him, which made him even more nervous.

"Well, I can kind of get inside people's minds. Read them, and—"

"Wait, you're telling me you're a psychic? That's your big information?" She didn't seem happy, and she was still staring at him.

"No, I'm definitely not a psychic." He smiled to hopefully put her at ease. "I can't tell the future and I don't see dead people or anything. I mean I can literally get inside people's minds. I can see their memories, especially anything strong or recent. And not just see them. I experience them. I feel them like it's happening to me. I know it sounds crazy. It's not something I'm proud of or even like. In fact, I hate it. But I think it can help in this case."

Her expression was blank. He had no clue what she was thinking.

"You're not believing any of this, are you?" he said.

She folded her arms and leaned back.

"When I was about twelve," she said, "my aunt took me to a psychic. I wanted to try to reach my mother. The fact was, I didn't know if she was alive or dead, and I'm not sure I cared. She left me and my dad high and dry when I was two. Ran off with a drug addict boyfriend, leaving me alone in the house I might add. Until my dad got home from work, exhausted, only to find two-year old me sitting in the living room. Alone. I personally didn't care what happened to her, but I wanted closure. Well, this psychic gave me the closure I needed. She said my mom was dead. She talked to her right there. Had a whole conversation. I couldn't hear it of course; it was just the psychic talking. She said my mom apologized over and over. I didn't say anything at the time. I wasn't ready to hear it."

"So, she was able to help you?"

"At the time. At least until two years later, when my dad got a letter from my mom asking for money. She didn't even ask how I was doing. The psychic made the whole thing up." She took a deep breath. "So, no, I don't believe in psychics or mind-readers or whatever you want to call yourself, and I don't want to spend one second going down a wild goose chase. Do you have any idea how devastated this family is? What do you think Mr. Hilson would say if I told him I have a guy who can read his young daughters' horrible memories? How could they ever forget what they saw?"

"Excuse me," said Julian. "They saw. They didn't necessarily observe."

"Are you seriously quoting Sherlock Holmes to me?"

"You read Sherlock Holmes? I've read every book."

"You know what?" she said, slapping her hand on the table. "I think we're done here. The door is to the left when you step out."

"Wait, hear me out," said Julian. "I really can read memories. Especially younger people. Their brains are more malleable. With these girls, I might spot something their conscious minds didn't pick up. A face or a small detail. They won't experience it again, I promise. *I* will. They won't even know what I'm seeing. What do you have to lose?"

Her mouth crinkled. "Everything," she said. "This is a really high-profile case and I'm not banking my career on psycho-magic, and I'm definitely not opening fresh wounds for that family. If only it were that easy, but I'm not taking any chances here, and especially not on that. So, thank you for coming, but please go."

He was about to stand up but decided to try one last approach.

"Okay," he said, peeling off the glove from his right hand. "I understand."

She was looking at him inquisitively, clearly wondering what he was up to. Her arms were on the table in front of her, hands clasped together. Quickly, he reached across the table and wrapped his bare right hand around her folded hands. The look of shock on her face was immediate. But she didn't move. She stared at him as if frozen in time. He knew she would; he'd seen that look before. He closed his eyes.

In his mind's eye, he was now Lela Mars, and he had just entered a small living room from a hallway. He could sense she was furious in the memory; he could always feel their emotions. A thirty-something guy with a crew cut, white polo shirt, and muscular build was sitting on the couch. The man sprung to his feet the minute she entered.

"You told me you'd be there," she said.

"You knew I had a golfing trip."

"Yeah, and you said you'd be back yesterday."

"You got your dates wrong," he said.

She held up the white sock. "I put this around your golf balls before you left," she said. "I just checked, and it was still there."

He hesitated for a second like a deer in the headlights. He was caught and he knew it. "Yeah, I saw it," he said. "What are you saying? You think I'm cheating? Are you accusing me again? You know what I said about that."

"I'm not saying that. It's just that this meeting was important. You knew that."

"What, so your dumb-ass friend can take your side every time?" He returned to the couch, leaned back, and stretched out his arms like he didn't have a care in the world. "Babe, you're an idiot if you think some neurotic bitch is gonna figure things out that we can't."

"Brian, she's a family therapist, and she doesn't always take my side."

"Sure as shit seems like it."

"She's trying to help us communicate."

He jumped up again and puffed out his chest. "What, we need her to communicate? You can't talk to me yourself? You're the one who started all this in the first place. I'm tired of defending myself."

"That's not what I meant, and you know it. You know I want us to have a family. But I need to know I can trust you."

"That sounds like a 'you' problem."

"Damn you," she said, pushing him back. Julian could feel his own adrenaline pumping as the blood rushed to her face.

Just then, Brian threw a hard punch to the gut. Julian could feel it;

Lela's desperate gasps for air, the pain rippling through her stomach; the sheer terror of not being able to breathe. She was doubled up in pain.

Brian hovered over her. "How do you expect me to feel when you say you can't trust me? I do everything for you. You keep creating problems where there ain't none. Maybe I should move out. It's obvious you don't want me here. Ever since you became a cop. What is it? I embarrass you? It's your dad turning you against me, isn't it?"

"I...di—" She paused to catch her breath. "I didn't... mean ... it like that."

"Answer me this. Is it over? Because if it is, just say the word and I'll walk out that door right now. And you can say goodbye to our future kids."

"No, I don't want that," she said, standing up slowly.

Brian started pacing. "You Latinas are all hotheads. Jesus Christ, that's what it's come to?"

"I shouldn't have pushed you, I'm sorry."

He continued pacing around like a lion in a cage. "It just triggered me is all," he said. "You got me on the defensive, always accusing me of everything. It's gotta stop. Cause I can't deal with this every time I go on a business trip. If I didn't want to be here, I'd leave you. But I'm here, right?"

"I'm sorry," she said. "I should've worded it differently. That was my fault."

"No," said Julian, snapping out of the vision. "It was *not* your fault." Lela was just coming out of her trance; to her, barely any time would've gone by.

"What are you talking about?" she said. "That doesn't make any sense."

"Brian," he said. "You said it was your fault when he hit you. I mean, you were well within your right to push him. He's gaslighting you, but you can't see it. I would get rid of him before... you know. Before he hurts you."

He watched as her face turned to stone. He couldn't tell if

she was angry, shocked or both; she appeared to still be trying to comprehend what he just told her. Then her mouth opened as a look of sudden realization hit her face.

"Dammit," she said. "He sent you."

"No, he didn't send me. It's not like that."

"How else would you know about that?"

"Detective Mars, with all due respect, think about it. If he sent me, why would I try to convince you to leave him? I just told you I could see people's memories."

She started breathing rapidly as she shook her head in disbelief. He could see she was getting worked up, as if her whole world was turning upside down. Then she took one deep breath and exhaled slowly. "I don't know who you are or who sent you," she said through gritted teeth, "but you grabbed my hand, and unless you want to be booked with assaulting a police officer, I suggest you get up and get out of here now before I change my mind."

"I'm sorry," he said. "It was the only way to show you. I shouldn't have interfered." He stood up and made his way to the door.

"That was an invasion of privacy," she yelled. "And I'm going to have my apartment checked for bugs."

He turned briefly to see her eyes watering. What was before a calm and confident face was filled with fury. He went to the door and turned the knob.

"Well, that went well," he muttered to himself.

As soon as he opened the door, she said, "Wait."

He turned around and waited respectfully for her to speak.

"What color is my couch?" she said.

"Beige. With white pillows."

"What's on the table next to the couch?"

"Let's see. A photo of you and Brian, and one of your dad. At least I think it's your dad. Oh, and a little dog statue."

She looked surprised but then squinted. "And you saw all

that just from a two-second memory."

"Well, it was two seconds for you, but—"

"I wasn't even thinking about that memory. How do I know you didn't put a camera in my apartment? I'm gonna check, you know. So, if it's there, you're toast."

Julian returned to his seat opposite her. "Listen," he said, trying to sound as sincere as possible. "When he punched you, a lot of things crossed your mind. You thought about how you'd fight back. You wanted to hurt him, and you knew you could've—easily—with that elbow maneuver you learned, but you were afraid he'd leave you. You thought about all the money and hopes you put into the *in vitro* and you felt you had to bite the bullet and take the good with the bad if you wanted a family. You figured so what if he was cheating. You thought you could change him, even after the fourth time he disappeared for a few days, and you could smell the Versace Yellow Diamond on him from a mile away—the perfume Lauren wore, whoever that is."

He studied her face. He watched it go from doubt to fury to sorrow, and ultimately to passive acceptance. She wiped a tear from her eye with her trembling hand.

"I've had no leads on this case at all," she said, composing herself. "You probably saw all the posts on social media. They think we're just sitting on our asses. I'll look like a laughingstock if this doesn't work. And I know there are no guarantees. But I believe you. And if it can help this poor family, who am I to deny them their justice? So, if the offer stands, I'd be grateful your help."

"It does," he said.

"And after this is done," she said, "no matter how it turns out, I have about five hundred questions for you."

He smiled. "I was afraid of that."

She started writing on a sheet of notebook paper. Then she tore off the sheet and handed it to him.

"Meet me there at six," she said. "Wait outside. I'll introduce you to the family."

"I'll do that," he said.

When he finally left the room, he couldn't help but smile. Someone actually believed him and didn't treat him like a science project. At least not yet. And not just someone, but someone he felt like he could trust. Someone he wouldn't mind getting to know.

He opened the police station door to head outside into the fresh air. It would be a much less nerve-wracking ride home than on the way here, that's for sure.

"Dammit, he said, as he looked up and down the parking lot.

His bike was gone.

CHAPTER 4

KILLER ON THE ROAD

J ulian fidgeted with his gloves in the back seat of the dark blue Lincoln Navigator as the driver headed up Pine Road and into Huntingdon Valley, one of the more upscale suburbs of Philadelphia. He had walked home from the police station earlier, so he didn't feel like doing more walking. As it was, this was twenty minutes by car and the rideshare didn't cost much.

After a few turns, they made their way into the Shady Woods development where the Hilson family lived. Judging by the large, contemporary-style homes that were placed high up from the street—each with steep, terraced walkways—the Hilsons must've had some money. Monica Hilson couldn't have made too much as a social worker, so Eric must've had a fairly well-paying job.

The driver pulled in front of a modest home on the right with a white stucco exterior and charcoal gray roof—modest at least compared with some of the other homes in the development. It was a few minutes before six and Lela was already standing outside her black SUV. A police car was parked in front of her. Julian slipped his white cycling gloves on in preparation.

Just as he stepped out of the vehicle and approached her, a middle-aged Italian looking cop with obviously dyed dark hair and a white uniform shirt got out of the police car to join them.

"This is Lieutenant De Luca," said Lela. "He's the lead officer on the case."

"Nice to meet you," said Julian. "I'm—"

"I know who you are," said De Luca. "Your little magic trick better work. You don't wanna make us look bad, right?"

"I'm just trying to help," said Julian. He turned to catch up with Lela, who was already headed up the terraced walkway.

"I'm guessing you don't have any real serious crimes around here," he said.

"And you'd be guessing wrong," said Lela. "I'm dealing with four new armed robberies just this week."

"Try South Philly," said De Luca from behind them. "Back in the day, that woulda been a quiet Tuesday. And don't get me started on North Philly. Makes Iraq look like Sesame Place. But it don't affect me. I could eat a sandwich while I watch some guy bleed out on the street."

"That's an enviable talent," said Julian. He turned to see De Luca puff out his chest and smile. The guy clearly didn't even realize he was being mocked.

They were at the front door, which was white with an oval, frosted glass window in the center. The second Lela rang the bell, the door opened and Eric Hilson invited them in. He'd apparently already met Lela and De Luca. Julian recognized him from the TV interview. He was a soft-spoken man and, as could be expected, was in a somber mood.

The foyer had a vaulted ceiling and led into a spacious family room with modern gray and white decor. Julian felt queasy as an awkward silence filled the room, punctuated only by their footsteps echoing on the hardwood floors.

He took a seat next to Lela on the couch. Hilson and De Luca sat opposite them on two armchairs.

"Mr. Hilson," said Lela, "I'd like to introduce you to Julian Black. He's the one I spoke to you about. He's going to try to help."

"I'm sorry for your loss, sir," said Julian.

"Thank you," said Hilson. He looked at Julian's gloved hands and shook his head, as if he felt it was a folly to even try. "So where do we begin?"

"To start with," said Julian, "can I assume your older daughter was in the front passenger seat?"

"She was driving," said Hilson. "Monica was in the passenger seat."

"Your daughter was driving?"

Hilson sighed. "She's sixteen. Just got her permit. I don't think she'll ever drive again after this. Excuse me, do I have to rehash all this stuff all over again? I thought you were able to *see* things."

"No, I'm sorry," said Julian. "I was trying to get a sense of who might have had the better viewing angle. I know that sounds—"

"You won't be asking my daughters any questions, will you? Because they've been through enough."

Julian leaned forward for emphasis. "I swear to you, Mr. Hilson. I won't need to ask them a thing. I'm thinking we should start with your youngest, who was in the back seat."

"You want to talk to Tina?"

"Not talk. All I'll need to do is hold her hand for a few minutes. To her, no time will have gone by. You can just tell her I want to shake her hand. She'll only experience this as a handshake, nothing more."

"I can vouch for that, Mr. Hilson," said Lela. "I've seen it. I wouldn't have believed it either, trust me."

"Okay," he said, not sounding like he fully believed it. "I'll go get her."

Julian watched as Eric Hilson went upstairs to get his daughter. Slowly, he peeled off his gloves.

"You handled that well," said Lela. "Now let's hope she saw something."

De Luca was sitting with his arms crossed and a sour expression on his face.

"Anything wrong?" said Lela.

"Yeah, a lot's wrong. But I ain't saying nothin' right now. I'm just watchin' the process." He smiled as if he knew something they didn't.

Hilson descended the stairs holding hands with an adorable young girl with two pink bows in her hair. She was shy and moved hesitatingly, but he encouraged her to continue.

"You must be Tina," said Julian, smiling as Hilson brought her forward.

"This man is a special man with the police," said Hilson, nudging her forward. "He just wants to shake your hand for being so brave."

Julian could see a solitary tear run down Hilson's cheek. He nodded at the grieving man to indicate all would be well—she was in good hands. Hilson offered a soft smile and patted her back.

"Who did your bows?" said Julian. "They're beautiful."

"Janelle did them," she said quietly.

"That's her older sister," said Hilson.

Julian held out his hand, and Tina hesitated, as if she knew something unusual was about to happen.

"I just have to shake the hand of such an amazing girl," said Julian.

"Go ahead, Tina," said Hilson. "It's okay."

As soon as Julian's hand made contact with her tiny fingers, he closed his eyes. Nothing else in the room existed. He was in the back seat of a car that was driving on Roosevelt

Boulevard. The Boulevard, as it was known, was a twelve-lane, divided, tree-lined roadway that ran through Northeast Philadelphia and toward the Schuylkill Expressway that led downtown. From what he could see, they were headed south toward the city and the car was in the rightmost lane. He had an American Girl doll on his lap and was brushing her hair with a toy brush.

A broken-down truck blocked the lane up ahead.

"Janelle, move to the center lane when you can," said Monica from the front passenger seat.

The car shifted abruptly to the left, and, immediately, a horn from behind them blasted—and kept blasting.

"Careful, you have to look in both mirrors, honey," said Monica.

"I didn't see him, Mom."

The horn continued to honk. Julian felt a hard push as the car behind them tapped the rear bumper. He couldn't get a look because Tina didn't turn around. But he could feel her panic.

"What's happening, Mommy?" said Tina.

"Mom," said Janelle, "I think he's hitting us on purpose."

"Oh my God," said Monica. "Get in the right lane. Get away from him."

"I can't. There's cars there."

The car rammed them again, this time harder.

Janelle screamed.

Just then Julian heard a screech behind them and a rusty, red pickup truck sped dangerously beside them to the right. A guy with blond hair and a scruffy beard was behind the wheel, ranting and raving to himself and banging the steering wheel.

"He's beside us," said Janelle. "What do I do?"

Monica lowered her window.

"Mom, don't do that!"

It was then that Tina covered her eyes with her hands and leaned down in the back seat. Julian couldn't see a thing. He could only hear.

And he needed to see a license plate.

"I'm taking his picture," said Monica. "I'm taking your picture!" she yelled out the window.

"Mom, don't!"

Just then Julian heard the gunshot, following by a bunch of screaming from Janelle, which got Tina screaming. From there, all he could hear was Janelle repeating, "I have to pull over… I have to pull over…" She repeated it over and over again like a mantra as the car moved to the right and slowed down.

"Mom?" said Janelle.

Julian took himself out of the vision immediately. He looked around at everyone. They were all staring at him like they'd seen a ghost. Except for Tina.

"It's nice to meet you," said Tina, who seemed perfectly fine, as he knew she would. To the others, it would have looked like he and Tina were in a trance for several minutes.

"It's nice to meet you too," said Julian. "I'm honored to meet someone so brave."

She smiled for the first time.

"Come on, Tina," said Hilson. He took her hand and led her back upstairs.

"Okay, what the hell just happened?" said De Luca.

"What did you see?" said Lela.

"She covered her eyes," said Julian.

"I knew it," said De Luca. "I knew this was too good to be true. I could've t—"

"But I did see his face," interrupted Julian. "He had blond hair and a scruffy beard, like he hadn't shaved in days. He was driving a beat-up red pickup, probably a Ford or Chevy. The older daughter, Janelle, tried to move into the center lane and apparently cut him off and he went nuts. He pulled beside them on the right, and the mom tried to take his picture. That's when he shot her."

Lela's eyes were wide. "That matches the police report."

"Which means," said De Luca, "we don't know anything more than we already knew. He probably just parroted what was on the report."

"He didn't see the report," said Lela.

"As far as you know," said De Luca.

"I need to get the license plate," said Julian. "I need to see Janelle."

"Janelle," called Hilson from the bottom of the stairs. "We need you."

Julian didn't even see him standing there. "How long were you—"

"I heard it all," said Hilson. "And if you can get that damn license plate, do it."

Janelle came down the steps. She was tall and thin and was dressed in black jeans and a black pullover with an open denim shirt over it. She had no makeup on, and her eyes were red, but otherwise looked like the spitting image of her mother— at least from the picture he saw on the news. She certainly looked older than sixteen.

She walked right up to Julian.

"Are you the guy that's going to read my mind?"

Julian was shocked. "Well…um… I can't read your mind, but I can see certain memories. Strong ones. Especially recent ones."

"And that's *all* you'll see?"

"Yes, of course. I promise."

"And you'll only talk about this incident, right?"

"Yes, of course."

"Will I feel anything?" He was surprised at the way she rattled off her rapid-fire questions.

"No, to you it'll be just a handshake."

She held out her hand. "Then shake," she said, still all business. He got the impression she was trying to stay brave

46

to mask the trauma she'd been through.

"You would be an amazing lawyer one day," he said, as he reached out to take her hand.

As soon as he took her hand, he was plunged back into the car, except this time he was behind the wheel. He could feel her apprehension about driving as her sweaty hands firmly gripped the leather-covered wheel. The broken-down truck was up ahead. When she shifted lanes and the horn behind them blared, he could feel his own heart pounding with hers—and, as she glanced to see who was honking, he could see the man's scruffy face in the rear-view mirror as he pounded his horn, ranting and raving. Julian felt Janelle's breathless panic as she wondered what to do—panic that quickly turned to extreme fear when the raging lunatic rammed them from behind, and again when he pulled beside them. It didn't help that her mom was lowering her window. That's when Julian felt the hairs on his arms stand up along with Janelle's.

Then came the gunshot.

Monica Hilson's head lay forward. He could tell she died immediately, though Janelle didn't even seem to notice right away. She was too focused on escaping the madman beside them—a madman that was now pulling ahead of them as she tried to make her way over to the right. She saw the man pull ahead of them but didn't process it. The poor girl didn't think to get the license plate. But Julian did.

He brought himself out of the vision.

"Write this down," he said.

Lela scurried to get out her notebook and pen, while Janelle looked dumbfounded.

"Pennsylvania plate, two G..."

"Ok, two golf," said Lela.

"... Alpha tango..." He knew the NATO codes from years of gaming. "Then one, two, three. By the way, it was a red Ford pickup. Not sure of the model."

"Got it," she said. "Two golf alpha tango one two three. Pennsylvania plate. De Luca, can you run it?"

"Yeah, I'm on it," he said, getting up to head outside, though he still sounded skeptical.

"I don't know how you did it," said Hilson, "but I hope this is our man." He reached out to shake Julian's hand, but Julian paused to put his gloves back on. "Oh yes," said Hilson. "I almost forgot."

"I don't get it," said Janelle. "How did you do that in a split second?"

Julian smiled. "The secret is… it wasn't a split second for the rest of us. But I want you to know. First, I'm sorry for your mom. That man was a monster and we're going to catch him. But I saw, and felt, everything that happened, and none of this was your fault, or your mom's. I know you don't want to drive just yet, and I don't blame you. The truth is, I'm afraid to drive too. I have been for some time for a different reason. But one day I will. And one day you will again, too. When you're ready."

"I'm done with it," she said. "But thanks."

Lela stood and approached Hilson. "We'll be in touch when we know more," she said. "Fingers crossed."

"Thank you," said Hilson. He held up his right hand with crossed fingers.

After Lela hugged him and then Janelle, Julian followed her outside.

De Luca was standing by his patrol car as they approached.

"We got a male Caucasian," said De Luca. "Blond hair, blue eyes, five-eleven. Name's James Woodburn. Lives in Folcroft. I got the address. Two priors for domestic assault and one DUI, all served. Drives a 2015 Ford F-150. Red."

"Let's go pay him a visit," said Lela.

"Not so fast. We know this guy's a scumbag. But we got nothin' that links him to this murder."

"You just saw yourself what happened," said Lela.

"I don't know what I saw. Maybe this is our guy. Maybe he ain't. But I can tell you, I been doin' this a long time. You won't get a search warrant or probable cause based on mind readers or witch doctors or the Amazing Kreskin."

"I have some pretty exact descriptions that may help," said Julian.

"I bet you do."

"What's that supposed to mean?"

"How do we know you don't know that guy?" said De Luca. "Maybe you got a grudge against him."

"That's crazy. I don't know this guy."

"Man, if you're what you say you are, that's great. It'd be a first. But hey, I'm modern. I watched the Long Island Madam."

"I think it's Medium," said Julian.

"Whatever. The truth is, we don't know shit about you. We gotta investigate every angle. Every possibility."

"Gentlemen," said Lela. "Let's calm down and think about this for a minute."

Julian started fidgeting with his gloves again, which he did when he was uncomfortable.

"Okay, Michael Jackson," said De Luca. "Time to beat it. Detective Mars and I will sort this out. Thank you for your assistance. We'll be in touch."

"De Luca, shut up," said Lela. She turned to Julian. "I'm paying a visit to that address in the morning. I want to take a look at that truck. I'd like you to be there. Can you make yourself available?"

"Of course," said Julian.

"Good," she said. "I'll pick you up at nine."

CHAPTER 5

TWO WOLVES AND A SHEEP

The tiny English countryside village of Monkton Combe—a stone's throw from Bath—was home to only about five hundred people. Situated in Somerset near the ancient Roman road from Bath to London, it probably had more sheep than people. One of those people was Max Baumann, who'd apparently developed a device that would one day defend the Western world against satellite attacks, presumably from the East. Little did Baumann know, but he was about to be the most important man in the world.

Sebastian Blaine had visited the West Country, as the area was called, a few times before. He'd always enjoyed afternoon tea at the Pump Room in Bath, not to mention strolling the medieval streets and squares, marveling at the Roman ruins, and, on one occasion, taking in a mesmerizing organ recital at the seventh century Bath Abbey with a lovely young brunette whose name he'd since forgotten. But while Bath was a hub of activity, the surrounding countryside was mostly rolling hills, grazing sheep, and quiet hamlets. This is where Blaine now found himself, driving his alpine-green Bentley Flying

Spur sedan through Church Lane in Monkton Combe, with Hans at his side.

"This is the boarding school," said Blaine, as they passed through the nineteenth century, ivy-covered, limestone buildings of the picturesque Monkton Combe School campus. It looked right out of a Dickens novel. As they cruised past, he spotted a boarding house on the left and an old chapel on the right, followed by a larger building that must've been one of the school centers. It was a Saturday, so no children were about, though he did see two teen girls playing tennis on one of the two courts on the left. Once they passed the school, it was all wide-open green valley as the road wound to the right.

"Brassknocker Hill should be just up ahead," he said.

Hans was silent as usual. He was a man of few words and, from his indifferent expression as he stared out the window, appeared to either be enjoying the scenery or contemplating his next murder. Blaine never could quite get a handle on what made him tick.

As they made their way through the scenic valley, a smattering of sheep dotted the lush, sloping meadows on both sides. After about five minutes, a lone Tudor-style, thatched-roof cottage appeared ahead on the right, set back off the road at the end of a long gravel driveway. From the encrypted photos in the file Olga had sent him, there was no missing it. This was Baumann's house.

"Try not to kill anyone, Hans," he said as he pulled into the driveway and headed toward the cottage. "Unless you have to, of course."

Hans smiled for the first time.

Blaine pulled beside the small house, which looked like it could've belonged to Snow White. No sooner did he get out of the car, than he was rammed from behind by a body with the strength of a freight train. He hit the ground and instinctively rolled over to see who'd attacked him. Could they have known he was coming? Once his vision cleared, he finally saw his attacker.

"Well, that was damn rude," he said. A solitary sheep was staring him down.

"She's protecting her lamb," said a voice from the front of the cottage. "Take a look." The fit, young man of about thirty pointed to a small lamb that was chewing grass by the cottage on the other side of the car. Blaine glanced back toward the man just in time to see him casually pull out a pistol and shoot it into the air. The two animals went running toward a flock of sheep that were grazing further past the cottage. Blaine recognized the gun. It was a Glock 17, standard issue for MI6.

"That'll keep her away," said the apparent operative, who was wearing a wool fisherman's sweater and navy pants.

"That's okay," said Blaine. "It'll make a good story at the pub."

Blaine discretely slipped off his right glove as the increasingly curious man stepped toward the Bentley.

"That's a nice car. To what do we owe the pleasure of your visit?"

"Isn't this Tucking Mill Lane?" said Blaine. "They said it was just past the school. We're here to see Mr. Sharp about his will. But you don't look like Mr. Sharp. He's an older gentleman. White hair and bad teeth. Come to think of it, you don't look much like his caretaker either."

"I'm afraid you're all turned around. It's back behind the school. If you head back to the school, you'll see it."

Blaine threw up his arms in mock surprise. "Take me out of the city and I'm lost, but I stubbornly reject the idea of a GPS, so I suppose that's on me. I appreciate your help. And so will Mr. Sharp if he's still alive." Blaine extended his right hand. "By the way, thanks for the sheep rescue."

Blaine could see Hans standing behind the operative with his hand on the silencer just in case. The operative hesitated for a few seconds, but then reached out and accepted the handshake. That's when Blaine saw it and felt the hairs on his arms stand up.

The man had an artificial hand.

Blaine nodded to Hans, but the operative noticed the shocked look on his face and turned around.

Hans grabbed the man's neck while his right hand quickly brought out the silencer. The man reached for his pistol with his left hand, but Hans was quicker and shot him twice in rapid succession—once in the stomach, and again in the head.

As the operative fell to the ground, Hans looked up at Blaine and said, "I had to."

"I certainly won't argue that point," said Blaine. "I should've noticed he shot with his left hand. Now help me drag him around to the side of the house."

Blaine moved to pick up the man's legs, but Hans just bent down and picked the whole body up, throwing the dead operative over his shoulder like a rag doll.

When Hans returned from around the corner, Blaine approached the old, weather-beaten front door and tapped the wrought iron door knocker. He heard footsteps and braced himself in case there was another operative inside.

The door opened slowly and a slightly stocky, middle-aged, man with a salt and pepper hair appeared. It was Baumann.

"Can I help you?" he said, in a slight British-German accent. "Where's Stubbins?" Baumann glanced at the blank expression on Hans's face and seemed concerned.

"You're probably looking at the scar," said Blaine. "Yes, it makes him look a bit like a henchman, doesn't it?" He smiled. "Stubbins is in the car. Don't worry, he's okay, he's just filling out some paperwork. Meanwhile, you're the one we're here to see. Something important came up. May we come in?"

"Yes, yes, of course," said Baumann, opening the door wider to invite them in.

Blaine slipped his glove back on and followed the revered scientist into the room, with Hans tagging close behind. The room was adorned with wooden beams, stacked bookshelves, and was otherwise sparsely decorated. Baumann took a seat in an upholstered mahogany armchair and motioned for them to sit as well. Blaine remained standing, as did Hans.

"It looks like you're the man of the hour," said Blaine. "Some pretty important people would like you to come with us."

Baumann raised an eyebrow. "What's this about? Who are you people? Stubbins isn't in that car, is he?"

"As a matter of fact, you're right," said Blaine. "He's dead."

Hans pulled out the silencer and aimed it at Baumann.

"Stand up," said Hans.

"You're going to shoot me?"

"Shoot you?" said Blaine, casually taking the gun from Hans but keeping it aimed at Baumann. "No, we want you alive, Dr. Baumann. Like I said, you're the man of the hour. You're going to come with us, answer some very easy questions, and then we'll bring you back here, safe and sound. Then we can all go our merry ways. No harm, no foul. Except to Stubbins, of course."

"Stand up," repeated Hans.

Baumann slowly rose as Hans pulled out a syringe.

"Sodium thiopental, I suppose," said Baumann. "It doesn't work, except in movies."

"Your height," said Hans.

Baumann rolled his eyes. "A hundred and eighty centimeters."

Hans squinted. "Ninety kilos?"

"Eighty-six. What's this all about?"

"Have you ever heard of the Moscow Theater siege, Doctor?" said Blaine.

"Of course," said Baumann. "The hostage crisis. Chechen

terrorists if I recall. A lot of deaths. What's this have to do with me?"

"A hundred and seventy people died to be exact. Funny thing was, it wasn't the terrorists who killed them. Soviet special forces pumped a certain knockout toxin into the theater in a rescue attempt. A fentanyl derivative. Seems they didn't take into account the height and weight of the people in that theater. Or what they had to eat that day. Needless to say, that wasn't the best of rescues."

"I had fish and chips for lunch," said Baumann, starting to sweat. "Malt vinegar and mushy peas on the side. This morning I just had some plain yogurt and two slices of dry wheat toast with honey. Oh, and an apple. You're not giving me that toxin, are you?"

"As it turns out, Hans here is a trained anesthesiologist, so you're in good hands. And oddly enough, he really is a henchman." He glanced over at Hans, who was pulling a vial out of his pocket. "Hans, you have to do something about that scar, it's a dead giveaway. How did you get that, anyway?"

"No," said Hans firmly, as he readied the syringe.

Blaine shrugged his shoulders. "He doesn't want to talk about it," he said to Baumann.

"You know, they'll be looking for Stubbins if he doesn't check in," said Baumann.

"They won't have to go far to find him. He's right beside the house. Luckily, we'll all be in London."

"London? I won't be telling you anything there. Or anywhere for that matter. You're wasting your time."

"Oh, I hardly think so," said Blaine, as Hans applied the needle. "Now hold still. We have a three-hour ride, and as long as you didn't miss an extra apple, you should be waking up in about four."

CHAPTER 6

A RIDICULOUSLY STUPID BAD DAY

L ela Mars didn't know what to make of the curiosity sitting beside her in the passenger seat. Julian was an enigma for sure. But there was no doubt in her mind his talent was authentic, or that the man whose house she was driving to was indeed the perpetrator. Proving it would be another story. De Luca was right; she'd never get a search warrant. A *mind* witness wasn't the same as an eyewitness, but unless someone else came forward, that's all she had at her disposal. Unfortunately, calls for witnesses on TV and social media had gone unanswered. But if she could inspect the truck and perhaps see some evidence, it would be a start.

"Explain this to me," she said, glancing at Julian. "If you were able to see this guy's face through their eyes, why couldn't those girls remember seeing him?"

"You have to understand," he said, "memories are only about fifty percent accurate, depending on whether they're implicit or explicit."

"You lost me there."

"Think of implicit memories as riding a bike or brushing

your teeth. Things we inherently remember how to do because we've done them countless times. We recall them unconsciously. Explicit memories are trickier, remembering facts and dates and words."

"And faces," she said.

"And faces," he echoed. "As for events, it's tough without a narrative. It's why an actor can memorize Shakespeare, or why you can remember a bunch of random words by turning them into a story—a narrative."

"Makes sense. But what about trauma? That has to play into it." She thought about her own experiences fighting with Brian. Some of those memories will be etched in her mind forever.

"It does more than play into it. It takes over. The strongest memories are the ones you feel, the ones that hit your senses. If you're in a car accident, you may not remember whether the guy behind you hit you before or after you hit the car in front of you. But you'll remember the fear you had looking in the rear-view mirror and seeing that big truck barreling toward you. If you're attacked on the street, you may not remember what the mugger was wearing, or even what he looked like, but you'll sure remember feeling that cold, hard gun pressing against your face, or the rotten smell of his breath."

"But it's different for you, isn't it, going into people heads?"

"Only if I'm looking for something in particular. Otherwise, I feel the same emotions they do, which I can tell you isn't fun. With most people, they remember the emotion, but they're so focused on it that it warps their memory of other things, so they forget peripheral details. It's not like a tape recording; we have to mentally piece all these random bits together in our mind. And sometimes we piece together something that's completely wrong. Because it's contaminated."

She pulled onto Route 476 headed toward Chester as she thought about what he said about contaminated memories. Instinctively, she knew all of it; she'd been living it for years, seeing it firsthand in investigation after investigation. She could think of at least five cases where having Julian could've made all the difference, especially when it came to unreliable witnesses. And he still might.

"Where were you for the last five years?" she said.

"Avoiding hell."

"Well, now you're in it with me." She couldn't help but smile. Julian just might be her new best friend. She glanced over and noticed he looked nervous. He was tugging at his gloves again.

They rode in silence for a few minutes and before long she was approaching the exit toward James Woodburn's house.

◆

When they arrived at the dilapidated single home with gray siding, Lela immediately spotted the red Ford pickup truck in the driveway. It seemed surreal seeing a physical manifestation of what was so far only in Julian's mind. Now it was real.

"Is that the truck you saw?" she said, as she pulled into a spot across the street from the house.

"It sure looks like it. Dented. Dirty."

"Technically, we can't go on the property without a warrant."

"But?" said Julian.

"There is no *but*. I'll be right back."

Julian looked dumbfounded as she got out of the SUV and headed toward the red pickup in the driveway.

As she approached the vehicle, she could see it had so many dents it was hard to tell what came from where. She walked around to the front of the pickup and noticed a slightly dented front fender. Unfortunately, no paint from Monica Hilson's car was visible.

"Dammit," she said.

Without clear evidence, she wouldn't be able to get a warrant. She turned and made her way to the driver-side door and pulled the handle. She was in luck. The door opened.

She pulled her flashlight from her belt holster and aimed it inside the vehicle, looking for any sign of spent bullet casings. Still no luck. All she could see on the floor was a crinkled beer can and an empty bag of potato chips. She went to reach for the glove compartment and immediately heard a horn honking repeatedly, coming from the street. It was *her* horn.

She quickly pulled herself out of the vehicle and noticed that Julian was honking her SUV's horn and frantically pointing behind her. As soon as she turned around, James Woodburn was standing by his front door, looking disheveled and angry.

"You mind telling me what the hell you're doing in my truck?" he said, stepping forward.

She flashed her badge.

"I'm Detective Mars with the Philadelphia Police Department. You're not in any trouble, but I'd like to ask you a few questions."

"What's this have to do with my truck?" he said, casually approaching her.

"Mind if I come in?" she said. "It's better if we talk inside. I'm sure you don't want your neighbors wondering what's going on. It should just take a few minutes."

"If it's just a few minutes, then you can just tell me right now what you're here for," he said. He was guilty all right. At least of something. An innocent man would've been eager to cooperate.

"Like I said, Mr. Woodburn, I'm just here to ask a few questions."

"So, you know my name. You investigatin' me or something?"

"You *are* Mr. Woodburn, right?"

"Yeah, that's me."

"Good. So you own this vehicle. Listen, a truck like yours was spotted on Roosevelt Boulevard Thursday afternoon where an incident occurred. I'm just ruling things out and I'm hoping you can help me."

"I can save you the time. It wasn't me. I don't drive in that area. Now if you don't mind, I'm pretty busy so I have to excuse myself. Have a nice day." He gave a mock wave and started to turn around.

"Okay, here's my problem with that," she said as he turned to look at her. She wasn't about to let him off the hook so easily. "I have three eyewitnesses that saw *your* truck with *your* license plate at the scene of the incident. Now if you'll let me come in, we can hopefully rule you out and then I'll be on my way." She was lying through her teeth, but she wanted to see his reaction.

"Well, if my truck was there, it sure as hell wasn't me in it."

"Mr. Woodburn, if I can come in, you can explain it all to me, or we can have our discussion out here."

He stayed poker-faced as he paused to think.

"Sure, you can come in," he said, after a few uncomfortable seconds, "but I'll only tell you the same thing I said out here."

She watched as he opened his door to invite her in. Carefully, she stepped past him inside and then he followed her in. She could smell alcohol on his breath as he closed the front door. The house itself smelled of cigarette smoke.

"Leave that open, please."

"Don't worry, it doesn't lock from the inside," he said, opening and shutting the door to demonstrate. "Besides, you're the one with the gun."

She didn't respond, but something told her she should've

pushed the issue.

"Have a seat," he said, as they entered the small living room.

"I'm fine standing."

"Okay, then *I'll* take a seat." He sauntered over to the torn, dark brown sofa by the wall and sat facing her, reclining in total comfort—the picture of faux confidence.

"Mr. Woodburn, where were you Thursday afternoon around three?"

"I was probably right here on this sofa. Hell, I can't remember what I ate for lunch yesterday."

"What do you do for a living?"

"I'm a landscaper, but I hurt my back so haven't been working."

"Any relatives live with you?"

"Nope."

"You married? Kids?"

"I have an ex-wife who's nuts. If anyone stole my truck, it'd be her just for spite. Damn near tried to run me over once."

"No kids?"

"Hell no."

"Does anyone else drive your vehicle?"

"Not usually," he said.

"What do you mean not usually? Does anyone ever drive it? Anyone have keys besides you?"

"No, not that I'm aware of."

"So, the answer is no, correct?"

"Yeah, I guess it is."

"Then how did your truck get to Roosevelt Boulevard on Thursday? It didn't drive itself."

"I told you," he said, getting impatient. "I wasn't there and my truck wasn't there. You're on a wild goose chase."

"So, you're telling me three eyewitnesses were wrong. They

had your license plate. They had a vehicle description that matches your truck. And their description of you, as it turns out, was pretty damn accurate, so I doubt it was your ex-wife."

"I can't speak to any of that. Must've been another truck with someone who looks like me. Listen, I think I'm done here. Why don't you spend your time tryin' to find the real killer."

"Who said anything about a killer?"

"You did."

"I said an incident. It could've been a car accident."

"You wouldn't be goin' to all this trouble for a car accident," he said. "It's common sense." He squinted his eyes and stared her up and down. "You look young," he added. "You must be new to this detective stuff."

She felt the blood rising to her face.

"Mr. Woodburn, you *do* know I can get access to the traffic cameras, right? Are you aware they have cameras all up and down the Boulevard? If your truck turns out to have been there and you're telling me it wasn't, then that would discredit pretty much anything else you say. Now I'm trying to help you here. Is there anything else you want to tell me about what really happened. And don't tell me you weren't there, because I know you were."

He stood up. "Like I said, I'm done here. This is a setup job. Anything else, you can talk to my lawyer. I understand you lady cops wanna make a name for yourself, but it ain't gonna be at my expense."

She glanced around the room, wondering what her next move was. Then she spotted it. Partially illuminated by a tall, dusty table lamp on a wooden side table by the sofa, lay a stack of mail with a green porcelain ash tray on top overflowing with cigarette butts. Behind it lay a 9mm handgun.

"Take a seat Mr. Woodburn," she said as she texted for backup.

Out of the corner of her eye she could see him glance over at the pistol.

"That's my gun," he said, "and last I checked, I got a right to own it."

"I said take a seat."

He didn't budge as she continued to type the address.

"Who you textin'?" he said.

"Nobody you know."

"Listen, you get a warrant or get out." He puffed out his chest and stood defiantly.

She pulled out a pair of plastic gloves she always kept in her pocket.

"Are you familiar with the Plain View doctrine?" she said.

"What, you just make that up?"

"It's in the Constitution. Fourth Amendment. It gives me the right to examine any evidence found in plain view during a lawful observation."

"This ain't a lawful observation," he said. "You're in my house without a warrant."

"Don't need one," she said. "You invited me in." Most suspects were woefully unaware of their rights. She counted on it, and it nearly always paid off.

She looked him square in the eyes. "Are the ballistics going to match the bullet found in Monica Hilson's skull?" She knew she couldn't take the weapon with her without solid evidence, but she wanted to make him squirm. Maybe he'd get scared and say a little more than he should. People do stupid things when they're backed into a corner.

As if on cue, his face began to turn crimson and he pursed his lips. She could see he was contemplating making a move. He was getting angrier, more desperate. Just then, he lunged for the pistol, and she immediately tackled him against the table. She could feel her adrenaline pumping as the lamp went crashing against the wall, the bulb shattering with a pop.

"Bad move," she said, as she tried to restrain him while reaching to push the pistol further away. He grabbed her around the neck from behind, but she reacted instinctively, lifting her right arm and pivoting to crash her elbow down over his arms and break his grip. In one move, she brought the heel of her palm up against his jaw.

She heard a bang on the front door as she maneuvered to get Woodburn into a headlock. Just then, he rammed his head back against her, knocking her off balance as she fell back against the coffee table.

"Police! Open up!" said the familiar voice. It was De Luca. She cursed her carelessness at having let Woodburn close the door earlier. It must've locked from the outside.

Woodburn used the distraction to make another attempt to get to his gun, but she jumped up and grabbed his legs just as his hands hit the side table. He tumbled over as De Luca kept pounding on the door. As Woodburn gripped the legs of the table from the floor, the pistol fell onto the carpet in front of him, just out of reach.

Lela climbed over him and put her knee on his back and reached for her cuffs, but he was squirming too much. She stretched to grab his right arm before he could get the gun. Just then, De Luca smashed the front window open and jumped into the room. Woodburn started to get up, but De Luca pounced onto his left arm with his knees, fracturing it by the sound of the crunch. Lela quickly grabbed ahold of the other arm, while Woodburn continued to try to wiggle free. Even with the two of them on him, he was still squirming like a trapped animal, but she finally managed to cuff him and read him his Miranda Rights.

"What the hell happened?" said De Luca.

"Came to talk to him," she said as she rose. "Then I saw the weapon and he freaked. How'd you get here so fast?"

"I followed you," he said, pulling Woodburn up. "You

know. Just in case."

She smiled. "So, you did believe me." She pulled an evidence bag out of her hip compartment, slipped the gloves on, and picked the pistol up off the floor, dropping it into the bag.

"I wouldn't go *that* far."

"You guys have no right coming in here without a warrant," said Woodburn as they led him toward the door. "You can't just take my gun. I got rights."

"Correction," said Lela. "You *had* rights. And you know what's really funny? I wasn't even going to take your gun. I couldn't have. But since you decided to assault an officer— which by the way I'm glad you did—now that weapon is property. And when we run ballistics… well, I think we both know what we'll find. Looks like you've had a bad day, Mr. Woodburn."

"A ridiculously stupid bad day," added De Luca. "Dumbass."

◆

Julian was beside himself. Last he saw, Lela had gone into the house with Woodburn. Then, after what seemed like forever, De Luca had come speeding up in his patrol car, practically flew to the house, smashed the window, and leaped inside. If anything happened to Lela, he couldn't forgive himself. After all, it was he who'd led her here. His gloves were in his lap and his palms were as sweaty as could be.

Finally, the front door opened and Woodburn came out in handcuffs with De Luca behind him. Julian's heart dropped until he saw Lela come walking out a few seconds after. De Luca led Woodburn to his patrol car while Lela said a few words to him and then headed toward her SUV.

"I take it that didn't go well," he said as she entered the

driver side.

"It went great, actually. We have a murder weapon. Once they run ballistics, he's toast. Thanks to you, we have our man. Wait, please tell me that's our guy."

"Oh, that's him all right. Did he attack you?"

"More or less. It happens." He stared at her as she started the engine and drove off. She seemed awfully calm considering.

"I don't get it," he said. "How did you do all that without a warrant?"

"Simple. I got him to invite me in. That's the trick, to make him feel comfortable. Just a few questions, sir, then I'll be on my way. Once I'm in, then anything can happen. Lucky for us, it did."

"What if it didn't?"

"That's always a risk. In my line of work, you have to create opportunity. The name of the game is to keep the ball in play. Lie to the guy. Tell him a zillion people saw him commit the crime. See how he reacts. See if he volunteers anything. In this case, he didn't offer up squat. Then I saw the gun. He knew I had him. I could see it in his eyes. People will do anything when they're backed against the wall. He made a play for the gun. If he didn't, I would've walked away empty-handed."

"Couldn't you have taken the gun?"

A red truck passed them on Lela's side that looked similar to Woodburn's.

"Nope. He had a right to own it. And I had no evidence that would've allowed me to take it. But I could inspect it. He didn't know that, though."

He shook his head. "I don't know how you do this day in and day out. For a girl like you to—"

"What's a girl like me?"

"I mean you're smart, young. You could do anything. Why risk your life?"

She glanced over at him. "How would you like to help me on another case?" That wasn't the answer he was looking for.

"Detective Mars," he said.

"Lela. You can call me Lela."

"Okay Lela. As much as I really want to help you—I mean if I was going to help anyone, it would be you—it's really hard for me to do… what I do. Whenever I touch someone, all I see is trauma. I know you see trauma on your job, too. But I don't have a choice. All I see are bad memories, fights, heated arguments, shocking deaths, pain, the most horrible abuse you could imagine, and if I see one more car accident…"

"Is that why you don't drive?"

"After being in five virtual accidents? Um… yeah. By the way, once I almost went over a cliff." They passed the same red truck. He didn't get a look at the driver.

"Do you ever see anything good?" she said.

"Sure. I see people's daughters getting married. I see teenagers falling in love for the first time. I see a child getting a new puppy, or a college student's first big job. Sometimes I seen random memories, mostly recent ones. But then some trauma from the past usually creeps in. I have no control over what I see. Sometimes I see things the people themselves barely remember, things they buried deep in their subconscious. So, as much as I want to help, I just can't keep subjecting myself to this. I think I was destined to be a struggling writer, playing video games in a quiet room without people, except for my mother. I hope you understand."

"You know, you were right," she said as they pulled onto Route 476. He spotted the red truck cutting over to pull behind them.

"About what?"

"About Brian. My soon-to-be-ex-boyfriend. It *wasn't* my fault he hit me. And you were right, he was gaslighting me. That's been the endless circle for as long as we've been together. At first, he showers me with love. Gifts galore, compliments. We talked about starting a family. Then the insults start, and the abuse, and he always twists it around to make it somehow my fault. After a while, you start to believe it. It's gaslighting 101. So, then you start trying to get on his good side. I'm not sure why. It's just that you get tired of wondering what you did wrong, and all the fights, and you just want to get some peace. So, you suck it up and try to change, and then the cycle begins again. Lovebomb, abuse, gaslighting, repeat. Well, I decided it ends now. I'm getting off that train."

"I'm really happy to hear that," he said. "For what it's worth, I think it's the right decision." He appreciated her opening up to him.

"It's worth a lot, Julian. Because it was you who helped me come to that decision. My dad told me the same thing about Brian. So did my friend, Tamika. But you actually saw it."

"I'm sorry. It wasn't something I intended to see." He looked around for the red truck and then he saw it on his side catching up to them. He felt a sudden chill as he let his imagination get the best of him. He kept thinking back to the vision with the Hilson sisters. Clearly, it couldn't have been Woodburn, but could someone else have taken his truck?

"Julian, you can help people. I know it's painful, but you have a gift. This guy would've walked free if it wasn't for you. Think how many others will go scot-free. You asked me why I do this. There's a whole lot more to it, but the bottom line is I want to help people. You see, I don't think you were meant to be a struggling writer or play video games. You were meant to help people, just like I am."

"I'd like to believe that," he said. Just then, the red truck passed them on the right. He got a look at the driver and breathed a sigh of relief. It was an old woman of at least ninety.

"There's a missing teen," she said. "His parents are frantic. He's been gone for a week. Nobody knows where he is. His parents are divorced, and he lives with his mom. He was with his dad last, but he never came home. The kid's not the type to run away or get into trouble. His mom doesn't believe her ex-husband and thinks he knows something. Can you help me? Or is this kid gonna remain missing?"

He thought about it. It didn't seem all that difficult, and either the dad knew something or he didn't. He just hoped the dad didn't kill the kid, because that's something he didn't have the stomach—or the heart—to experience.

He took a deep breath as she pulled onto I-95, now content that they weren't being followed by some mystery vehicle.

"I suppose one more case couldn't hurt," he said. "As long as I can stay in the background."

"One more case," she said, smiling. "And then I won't bother you again and you can go back to your quiet little rabbit hole. But you have to admit, we make a good team."

He couldn't help but grin. It was the first time he felt part of anything, at least in real life. And he enjoyed Lela's company. But still, something told him this life wasn't for him. With all the crazy situations Lela would likely need him for, it would be like a roulette wheel of trauma. He thought back to playing Stealth Invaders and it seemed like a lifetime ago. It wasn't purposeful, but at least it was safe. He wondered what Cassie would be thinking of him now. One day, maybe he'd tell her.

CHAPTER 7

CHANGE OF PLANS

S ituated on the south bank of the Thames in London, standing 310 meters high—or 1,016 feet—lies the modern, pointed, glass skyscraper known as The Shard, the tallest building in Western Europe. A vertical 95-story city, it houses twenty-six floors of sleek office space; three floors of award-winning restaurants; the nineteen-floor, five-star Shangri-La Hotel; thirteen floors of luxury apartments; and five floors of viewing areas, including an open-air observatory spanning the seventy-first and seventy-second floor—the highest floors open to the public.

One of the businesses on the eleventh floor is an unlisted organization, Worldwide Research, Ltd. (WRL), Sebastian Blaine's biotech research company, to which he's invested considerable funding toward exploring novel neurotechnologies. With revenue coming from government contracts, private investors, and Blaine's own finances, WRL is also one of London's largest charitable donors.

Currently, in the vast WRL office space with floor-to-ceiling windows—in an area sectioned off by a tan, wood-paneled wall—Max Baumann sat tied to a chair with zip-ties and duct tape. Blaine sat comfortably opposite him on a swivel chair, relaxing and staring as the scientist began to awaken. Hans paced around impatiently.

An hour before, they had brought Baumann into the building on the public lift in a tall, wheeled box marked *Fragile*. There was a touchy moment where an Asian family had entered the same lift, and their child of about five started banging on the box. Hans had given her a sharp nudge and a firm look, and from there she hid behind her mother and remained there. Fortunately, Baumann didn't awaken. But now, finally, he was beginning to stir.

"Sleeping beauty awakes," said Blaine. "But something tells me I'm not Prince Charming." He glanced over at Hans. "And you *definitely* aren't." Smiling, he returned his gaze to Baumann. "Good afternoon, Max."

Baumann was still groggy and was squinting his eyes from the sunlight glaring in from the massive windows. "Where am I?"

"You're in my office in London. The Shard if you must know."

"So, you're going to kill me after all."

Blaine smiled and patted Baumann's knee. "Relax. Once we let you go, you won't remember a thing about us or where you've been. Of course, whether we let you go or not depends on you. I'm hoping for the best."

Baumann grimaced. "Who are you people? How did you find me in a safehouse? Only MI6 and the CIA knew where it was."

"We're concerned citizens of the world. And you're a smart man, Max. I think you know the answer to your second question."

"You have a mole."

"No," said Blaine. "But somebody does. I'm just the guy you're going to tell about SARA."

"Keep dreaming," said Baumann.

"My friend Hans can be much more convincing. In fact, he has a bit of a mean streak. I was hoping to have you avoid that."

"I have a mean streak too."

Blaine smiled. "So do lions in a cage. And you've already met my lion tamer." He nodded to Hans.

The tall, blond, scar-faced brute approached Baumann, carrying a small cloth bag. The scientist, defiant as he was, was frightened. Blaine could tell. With any luck, this would all be over within the hour.

Hans walked around beside the scientist and held the bag near Baumann's tied-up hands. The blond henchman glanced at Blaine for the go-ahead.

"Max, do you know what's in that bag?" said Blaine.

"Bees?"

"Bees!? I wouldn't use bees. They'd be flying all over my office. It's a gel. Sort of like a shaving gel, but this one you'd really appreciate, being a scientist. Now I leave the science to the men and women who work for me, but they tell me this gel has nanoparticles that'll devour your hand. From the inside. Oh, don't worry, from the outside, your hand will look fine. Just don't try using it for much. I mean, seriously, your handshake will feel like a dead fish. On the good side, they say the pain only lasts about a month. Now, if I were you, I'd want to avoid all that."

He studied Baumann's face, which was turning red as he pursed his lips. The determined scientist turned toward Hans with fury and spat in his face. Hans immediately grabbed the bag and forced it around Baumann's hand. Baumann at first looked shocked, and then, as expected, the screaming began. After a few seconds of that, Blaine motioned to Hans to remove the bag.

Baumann continued yelling in pain.

"That was just a little taste," said Blaine. "Be glad we started with your left hand. You *are* right-handed, aren't you?"

Baumann was still groaning.

"I'll take that as a yes. It's a good thing those panels are soundproof." He pointed to the windows. "Nobody out there's going to hear you. We're pretty high up."

Baumann began hyperventilating, but then started taking deep breaths to calm down.

"There are a few other body parts to try," said Blaine. "Feeling any more cooperative?"

The scientist looked up with a stern, rebellious, face, not uttering a word.

Without warning, Hans reached behind Baumann and dipped the scientist's left hand back into the bag, and the bloodcurdling shrieks resumed.

"Hans, stop," said Blaine. Hans removed Baumann's hand from the bag as the weakened man's head fell forward. Hans slapped him in the face hard, and he stirred again.

"You're much more stubborn than I expected," said Blaine, as Baumann opened his eyes. "I give you credit. It seems to me you won't tell us anything no matter what we do."

Baumann stared daggers at Blaine. "You have no idea how stubborn I can be."

"I have a pretty good idea," said Blaine. "Which is why we're going to try something a little different."

Hans looked at him inquisitively.

"Good luck with that," said Baumann.

"Luck has nothing to do with it. This is a sure thing. There's a man I know who can get the information we need from you. Don't worry, it'll be quick and painless. I haven't seen him in quite a long time. He owes me. His name's Julian. I think you'll like him."

73

"I told you, I won't talk for anyone."

"Who said anything about talking?"

Baumann looked baffled, as did Hans.

"Hans," said Blaine. "I need you to retrieve someone from the States, by any means possible. But I need him alive. You'll need to wear gloves. He's like me… but different." He patted Hans on the shoulder. "Let's take a walk, I'll give you the information. You people have a branch on the East Coast if I remember, so you should have all the sweet comforts you need."

He looked at Baumann. "I'll be right back. Oh, and don't go anywhere."

CHAPTER 8

BAD NEWS

n a small living room in a townhouse on Algon Avenue, Julian sat opposite Ivan and Natalie Petrenko. Lela and De Luca were standing, along with a red-headed boy named Devon, who'd just arrived. The tension in the air was palpable, as evident by Natalie's clenched fists. It was almost noon. As Lela had explained when she'd picked him up bright and early, the couple been separated for five years, and their son typically stayed with Ivan on the weekends. He'd been missing for a week. The rest of the morning, Julian had spent experiencing the memories of both Ivan and Natalie—including their painful breakup—as well as the memories of several of their son's friends. So far, nothing had led to a clue of Andrew's whereabouts. Now it was Devon's turn.

"Devon," said Julian, "You're not in any trouble, but as you can imagine, Andrew's parents are very worried about him. Can you have a seat next to me?" He patted the seat cushion next to him on the couch. The boy looked at the Petrenkos, as if to gain their approval. Natalie, whose Eastern European accent and blonde hair reminded him of someone from a sixties film, nodded, and Lela waved him to the couch.

"Um, I don't really know anything," said Devon as he awkwardly took a seat next to Justin, though he shifted as far away as possible.

"But you may have information that can help. You see, I have a kind of special ability. I can see people's memories. It's how I knew to ask you to come here."

The kid crinkled his face like he didn't believe it.

Julian took a breath and explained. "I saw in Mr. Petrenko's memory that you were visiting with Andrew the day before he disappeared. Now try to remember, did he say anything that could give us an idea of where he might be? Did he talk about any distress he was under? Did he mention going anywhere?"

"No," said Devon. "What do you mean you can read people's memories? Like, for real?"

"The kid's lying," said De Luca. "I can tell."

Lela held up her hand to shush him.

"We just want to know what Andrew said to you last," said Julian.

Devon huffed, annoyed by De Luca's comment. "No offense," he said, "but if you can read minds, then you already know, right?"

"It don't work that way," said De Luca.

"Okay, listen, I don't remember," said Devon. "I think we just talked about some girls at school. Anyway, dude, you're freaking me out, and I don't want my fortune told, so if you don't mind, I really need to go." He started to get up. "I really hope you find him. I do. He's my friend."

"Just grab the damn peckerhead!" said De Luca.

"Do it," said Lela.

Without hesitating, Julian seized Devon's hand before he could leave, and immediately, the kid froze and plopped back onto the couch.

Julian now found himself in a small bedroom, facing Andrew. It wasn't the bedroom from Natalie Petrenko's house, so it was either a spare bedroom at Ivan's apartment or Devon's room. On the walnut bureau to the left, he spotted a wooden sign that said *Drew*, so it was clearly Ivan's place.

"Dev, you should come with us," said Andrew, sitting on the bed.

"I wish I could. My mom would kill me."

"She doesn't have to know. Dimitri's cool. He's gonna drive us. He won't say anything. Come on, it's just a week in Monmouth. It's the last chance to have some fun before school starts."

"What the hell's in Monmouth other than Jessica?"

"Look, I'm not just gonna spend time with Jess."

"Yeah right."

"Seriously, we can hit the beach. Dimitri can get us a case of beer. Listen, I'm goin' either way. I'm leaving tomorrow. If you wanna go, text me. But you better not say anything to anyone, I swear."

"Who would I tell? Listen, I gotta go. I told Kev I'd meet him to shoot some hoops. You wanna join us?"

"Hoops with Dev and Kev. Nah, I would but I gotta call Jess."

Julian let go of Devon's hand. He'd seen enough.

"Who's Jess?" he said to the Petrenkos.

They both looked at each other in confusion.

"I never heard of her," said Natalie.

"Me neither," said Ivan.

"Did anyone check his cell phone?" said Julian.

"He took his phone with him," said Lela. "Otherwise, it's the first thing we would've checked."

Ivan and Natalie both turned their attention to Devon, who seemed a bit dazed. "Who's Jess?" they said in unison.

Devon rubbed the back of his neck, clearly confused by the question. After all, from his perspective, it was only a few seconds ago that he'd decided to leave and now he found himself sitting back on the couch. He paused before responding. "It's some girl he likes," he said. "She lives somewhere in North Jersey. I think near Asbury Park. Listen, Drew told me not to say anything."

Then a sudden realization hit his face. "Hey, how did you—"

"Who's Dimitri?" said Julian.

Devon looked embarrassed by the question and glanced at Ivan.

Natalie had fury in her eyes. "I should have known," she said, turning to Ivan.

"I didn't know anything about it," said Ivan. "I swear."

"Who is he?" said Lela.

"It's Ivan's alcoholic friend," said Natalie through gritted teeth.

"I haven't seen him in a year," yelled Ivan.

"That's not exactly true," said Julian.

Ivan looked at him, baffled.

"There was that car accident on Christmas." Julian couldn't help but glance at Lela, who gave him a knowing look. Yes, another accident to add to his memory collection.

"Be that as it may," said De Luca, "I think we can say that the kid's alive."

"We don't know that," said Natalie.

"What do you mean we don't know?" said Ivan. "You just heard, he's with some girl in Jersey."

"When he's with me, this doesn't happen," she said, her face turning red.

"Oh, because you're perfect?"

"Because I know what he's up to."

"Well, you didn't exactly know about this Jess chick, did you?"

"Guys, guys," said Lela, trying to calm them down.

Just then, the doorknob jingled on the front door and the door swung open.

It was Andrew, looking dumbfounded.

"What's going on?" he said. "What'd I miss?"

♦

After the uncomfortable encounter, Julian was glad to have the tension behind him as he sat in Lela's SUV on the way back to his house.

"Well, that was awkward," he said, making sure his gloves were on tight.

"Ya think?" said Lela. "Maybe the kid'll think twice before he disappears days at a time not giving a crap about people who care about him." He sensed a bitterness in her tone.

"I doubt it," he said.

"Yeah, me too. Still, you were amazing as usual. You really have a gift. Sure you don't want to put it to use? You could help a lot of people."

"Yeah, while it slowly kills me from the inside," he said. He had to admit, it did make him feel good to make a difference. But he wasn't sure how much pain and suffering he could handle day in and day out. "I promise I'll give it some thought," he added, smiling.

The car receiver beeped, and Lela pressed a button on the dashboard to answer.

"Mars, what the hell's going on?" The voice came through the car speaker.

"It's the DA," she whispered to Julian. Then she redirected her attention to the caller. "Not sure what you mean, Brad."

"I mean Julian Black," said the voice over the speaker. "He's all over the news."

Julian felt the hair on his arms stand up.

"What are you talking about?" she said, motioning for Julian to stay quiet.

"The Hilson case. Eric Hilson's all over the news talking about the miracle man who found his wife's killer. Do you have any idea what kind of impact that'll have on a trial?"

Julian was horrified. He could feel the blood draining from his face.

"Shit," she said. "Hilson mentioned Julian by name?"

"No, some other reporter got the name from his daughter. So, talk to me. What the hell's going on?"

She glanced over at Julian and mouthed, "I'm sorry."

"I'll find out and get back to you," she said to the DA. "Gotta go." She hung up immediately and pounded the steering wheel. "Dammit!"

"Well, that's my worst nightmare," said Julian.

"We'll fix this," she said.

"How?"

"A little PR, and I'll pay a visit to the Hilsons. They meant well."

They rounded the corner to Julian's street, only to see a mob of press on the sidewalk outside his house.

"Are you going to fix that, too?"

He glanced over at her and she looked as horrified as he did.

"Jesus, I'm sorry," she said. "This is just temporary."

He felt his whole life changing in this moment. The last thing he wanted to be was a celebrity. He should've kept everything to himself, just writing and playing video games with Cassie. This is what he got for trying to play Good Samaritan.

Time seemed to stand still as he looked out the window. They passed a few television vans and a number of other cars parked on the side of the street, including a red Maserati with no TV network markings.

"I guess they're paying reporters a lot these days," he said.

Several neighbors were standing outside their front doors, watching the media circus.

Lela pulled up to his house and, as expected, the reporters

rushed the car.

"Don't say a word to them," she said.

Julian stayed put as Lela got out of the car and made her way to his side, waving off the reporters. She opened his door and escorted him through the eager bunch. They reminded him of a bunch of dogs at feeding time, all worried some other mutt would be first to the kibble.

"Can you really read minds?" shouted a female reporter holding a microphone up toward his face. He couldn't read the label that said what network she was from.

"Don't believe everything you hear," said Lela.

Julian tried to ignore the din of the questions being fired from all directions. As he approached the front door, he turned to see the group of reporters. It looked like all the major networks were there. He really wanted to say something, but he knew Lela would be upset with him. He decided to trust her. With a million thoughts dancing in his head, he scanned the group one last time. Then he noticed something unusual. Standing in the back of the crowd was a tall blond man in a suit. He wasn't holding a microphone like the others and didn't seem all that eager to rush to the front. As Julian squinted, he could see that the man had an unusually pale complexion and a scar running down the side of his face.

CHAPTER 9

NO SECOND CHANCES

Blaine sat opposite Baumann and poured himself a glass of single malt scotch, even though it was technically still morning. He brought an extra tumbler for Baumann.

Blaine had an affinity for single malts, ever since he first visited Scotland in 1998. Made from water and malted barley, the single malts were distilled at a single distillery, whereas the blended Scotch whiskeys were made from malt and grain whiskeys sourced from various distilleries. While it didn't necessarily make the former better, he appreciated the purity of it. Aside from scotch, he stuck with French wines, Negronis, the occasional gin and tonic, and, when it came to cognacs, nothing beat Hennessy X.O. as far as he was concerned.

"Why don't you join me in a drink," he said, holding up the glass.

Baumann smirked defiantly. "I would think getting me drunk would be beyond you."

"I'm afraid you think too highly of me. Let me rephrase that. Why don't you join me in a glass of thirty-year-old Macallan? Think of it as a celebration."

"A celebration of what?"

"A celebration of me. Getting what I want." He poured the extra glass.

Baumann grimaced. "I think your celebration is premature."

"You're as stubborn as a mule's mother-in-law," said Blaine. "Do you know how much easier it would be for us both if you just tell me where those plans are? Maybe you don't understand who's coming here. He'll be able to read your mind in a second and get it anyway."

"I'm not going anywhere, apparently. We can wait."

Blaine tried to hide his frustration. He brought the tumbler toward Baumann's mouth, but the scientist turned his face to the side.

"Last chance," said Blaine. "I hate to drink alone, especially a four-thousand-pound scotch."

"I don't like scotch, so have at it."

"You're no fun." He took the glass away. "I thought scientists were supposed to be fun."

Just then, Blaine's phone buzzed. It was Olga on the secure line. He took the call and walked a few feet away.

"Do you have the information?" she said. She was never one for warm greetings.

"I have Baumann, so I'm halfway there." He turned and winked at Baumann.

"If you have the scientist, you should have the information, no?"

Blaine rolled his eyes.

"Tell Volkov I'll have it for him soon. Tell him I have a foolproof backup plan whether Baumann talks or not."

"You can tell him yourself. Be at the Hotel Napoleon in Paris this evening. Eight PM sharp."

"Good. I know a girl in Paris. She won't remember me, so we'll have to get acquainted. Again."

"Just be there. And Blaine…"

"Yes?"

"I hope your plan is a good one. No matter how talented you are, there are no second chances."

"Ye of little faith. I have to go. I have a train to catch."

He hung up the phone abruptly—partially to remind Olga who really holds the cards—and stepped toward Baumann.

"Looks like you get your wish," he said. "I'll just be gone a couple days. Enjoy the view." He motioned toward the enormous floor-to-ceiling windows, which overlooked all of London. "It's a clear day. You can almost see your future from here."

As Blaine turned and gazed out into the horizon, he could see the Thames leading up to the London Eye in the distance, spinning round and round like a small clock, teasing him, reminding him that time was running out. But he knew Hans would deliver. Hans always delivered. It was only yesterday he'd sent the impeccable operative on a plane and by now he'd be shadowing Julian somewhere in Philadelphia. That is, if he didn't have him already.

He was more concerned about how Julian would react when he got here. Not that he'd remember anything from the old days; Blaine had made sure of that. But if push came to shove, he'd have to force Julian to use his talents one way or another. If all went well, Julian would do it willingly. Then they could go their separate ways. But if Julian resisted, more desperate measures would be needed. And that wasn't something he wanted to think about.

He took a deep breath, then turned and left the room. After giving the guards instructions, he headed to the lift. He had to go up to his suite to pack a change of clothes, and then it was on to the St. Pancras station to catch the Eurostar. With any luck, he'd be in Paris by three.

CHAPTER 10

MOVING DAY

Lela was back at the apartment she'd shared with Brian for over five years, doing a last inspection of the bedroom closet. Nothing had gone as expected today, but she was used to that by now. More things to take care of— starting with Brian. She was finally finished packing her belongings, all of which she'd managed to squeeze into two large yellow suitcases, a tan canvas duffle bag, and a dark brown leather carry-on. The more she thought about it, she had probably subconsciously avoided accumulating too many things, knowing this day would eventually come. She thought about writing him a note, but that would've been too easy. She needed to face him head on. He had to know it was final.

She heard the latch on the door unlock. He knew she was there—he would've seen her car—but as usual, he didn't bother greeting her or calling for her. That's how it was these days, especially since he started again on the steroids. She heard the hall closet door open as he hung up his jacket.

Finally, he emerged in the bedroom door, holding his gym bag. He spotted the suitcases immediately.

"What the hell are you doing?" he said. "You takin' a trip?"

"Sort of," she said. "Except I'm not coming back, Brian."

"The hell you're not!" His face turned beet red.

"Listen, you had to know this was coming." She kept her voice calm and matter-of-fact to avoid riling him further. "I could've left before you got here, but I felt I owed it to you to tell you. Trust me, it's best for both of us. We weren't going anywhere and it was only getting worse."

"Oh, that's real nice of you, Lela! That's not for you to decide. Now unpack those damn bags so we can talk."

"There's no more talking, Brian. I'm leaving."

"You stay there a minute," He pointed at her like she was a dog and then ran out of the room. She knew exactly where he was going.

As expected, he stormed back in after about ten seconds.

"Where are they!" His temples were bulging.

"You really think I'm gonna leave guns with you raging on steroids? I hid them. They're safe."

"Where… are… they?"

"Get off the drugs. Maybe you'll get them back. But one thing you'll never get back, Bri… is me. I don't do narcissists anymore. Now please get out of my way."

"You ain't leaving this house until I get my goddamn guns." He started rushing toward her to grab her. In a flash, she drew her weapon and aimed it at his chest. He froze in his tracks as she backed up slightly with her weapon pointed. She needed to keep some distance between them.

He laughed. "What, you're gonna shoot me?" He took another bold step forward, obviously to see what she'd do.

"Why not? It'll be self-defense. Wanna do time for assaulting an officer? Keep coming. I'll try to hit your shoulder the first time. No guarantees."

He shook his head and smiled, mocking her. His face said it all. Clearly, she was being a silly little girl whose bark was worse than her bite.

"Come on, babe," he said. "I get it, you probably had a bad day. We can talk about this."

She stayed firm. This was the cycle that always happened—lovebomb, abuse, gaslighting. She wasn't falling for it this time.

"Just so we're clear," she said, "I don't want any phone calls, texts, or emails. If you try to make any trouble or harass me or my family in any way, I'll put a bullet in your chest, and I won't lose a minute of sleep. Do you hear me?"

He chuckled. "You know you can't do that."

"I said do you hear me?"

"Babe, you couldn't shoot me even if you wanted to. You'd lose your precious job. You can't do it and you know it, so let's just talk." He grinned.

"I can't?" she said. "You mean I can't set it up to look like you attacked me? Maybe scratch up my face a little with your fingernails once you're lying there losing pints of blood? I'm willing to go that far. Are you? *Babe*?"

The smile left his face.

"You're fuckin' crazy. You know that? In fact, I'm gonna get a restraining order against you, how's that?"

"You mean a PFA? Go ahead. Have fun with that. You'll need to file a petition. Somehow, I don't think the judge would like what I have to share."

For the first time since she'd known him, he was speechless, his face shifting between anger, fear, and the realization that he'd lost.

"Go sit on the couch," she said. "I'm leaving."

"Leaving for where?"

"I don't know."

"The hell you don't!"

"I don't, Brian. Now get out."

"Crazy bitch," he said. "You walk out on me, you'll be sorry." He banged on the door and stormed out of the room.

♦

The last thing Lela wanted was to move back in with her dad, her stepmom, and her sister, who was commuting to college, but that's where she now found herself, at least for the time being—back on Matthew Lane. She always thought it was silly that the builder named all the streets in the development after his relatives. Her dad and stepmom had bought the house when it was new, fully furnished. Since her dad was a cop, they had to live within the city limits, and this was as close to the edge of the city as they could get. In fact, it was more like a suburb, without the suburban taxes.

At least her dad helped her bring in her suitcases from the car, which is more than Brian did.

"I hate to say I told you so," he said, as he put down the last of the large, yellow suitcases.

"And I hate to hear it," she said, tossing the duffel bag onto the couch, "but I have to admit you were right."

"I'm always right. That's lesson number one. You know what lesson number two is?"

She smiled. "You're always right?"

"No, but that's a good one, I have to remember that. Lesson two is, never… look… back. You learn and move on."

Her cell phone buzzed. It was Brian texting. This was the sixth message in the last half hour, all either asking where she was, begging her to come back, or saying he was worried about her. She typed 'I'm Safe' but then she erased it and pressed *block*. Satisfied with her decision, she walked into the dining room to head toward the kitchen for a snack. She yelled back to her dad, "I'm getting a—"

Her thought was interrupted. Against the right dining room wall, a giant *Congratulations* sign hung from the ceiling over a long table filled with desserts.

"Oh my God, is that tonight?" she said, rushing back into the living room.

"Hell yeah, it's tonight. You forgot? Five years on the force is a pretty frickin' big deal. Shelly and your sister have been baking everything under the sun for a week. And they're out buying more."

"Crap, I better get unpacked," she said.

"Before you do that," he said, "I need to talk to you about something. You want a beer?"

"No thanks." She took a seat on the couch. She knew what this was about.

"Okay, we'll skip the beer." He sat on the canary yellow lounger on the other side of the mahogany coffee table. He called it his *Archie Bunker* chair, though she had no idea who that was.

"Listen, Dad," she said. "I know exactly what I'm doing. If you saw what this guy can do—"

"I know you know what you're doing or we wouldn't be throwin' you a party. Some people, they don't have five years' experience. They have one year's experience five times, you know what I mean? There's a difference. You made detective after two. What I'm tryin' to say is you're good at what you do. I know that. Which is why I want you to be careful."

"I don't know whether that was a compliment or an insult," she said. "Of course, I'm careful."

"Have you ruled everything out?" he said. "I mean you have to admit it's a helluva thing to be able to read people's minds—a helluva thing." He pulled a cigar out of his shirt pocket. He always liked wearing those Cuban-style camp-collar shirts at home because it hid his belly and he looked good in them.

"Could you not?" she said. She loved the smell of unlit cigars, but couldn't stand them once they were lit. Usually, he smoked his cigars in the basement den.

"Sorry," he said as he tapped the wrapped cigar back into his shirt pocket.

"Let me put it this way," she said. "I watched Julian Black ID James Woodburn, his license plate, and the exact make of his truck just by touching a girl's hand, and it turned out to be a hundred percent accurate."

"How do you know he didn't know the guy?"

"You've been talking to De Luca."

"It's a logical question."

She took a breath to calm down, as she was tired of being second-guessed everywhere. "Okay," she said. "I also saw him repeat a private conversation between two kids just by reading the one kid's mind. And there, too, he was right on the money about where the other kid disappeared to."

Her dad sat back in his chair and contemplated what she'd said. Finally, she had him stumped—the consummate skeptic.

"And you're sure he didn't talk to them first, or do a little digging on his own?"

"You're kidding, right?" she said. "He barely leaves the house. He's a total recluse."

"But he came to the station to volunteer his services."

"Out of the goodness of his heart," she said more firmly. "And I had to talk him into the second case. He wanted to quit after the first."

"How come?"

"He didn't want the fame. Or the trauma. Can't say I blame him."

He took the cigar out of his pocket, then remembered and put it back.

"All I'm saying," he said, "is that every damn psychic I see on TV is either blatantly fake or they get fifty things wrong and then they film the one thing they get right, and everyone says, 'Oh my, what an amazing frickin' psychic.'"

"This isn't like that," she said, "and Julian isn't a psychic."

"I get that. I do." He leaned in. "Here's what I want you to do," he said. "Invite him to the party tonight."

"Dad, no way."

"I just want to meet him, that's all."

"And by meet him, you mean interrogate him." She'd seen way too many times where her dad wanted to *just meet* a boyfriend of hers. And this wasn't even a boyfriend.

"I won't interrogate him, I swear. I just want to learn a little about him. A friendly party conversation, that's all."

"What if he won't come, which I'm telling you is pretty likely?"

"Lela, I promise you. I'll put this Hilson thing to bed. Give your guy some peace. I'll get on the news and do a quick press conference. And then you can tell him that we took care of him, and the only thing we want in return is for him to attend a party in your honor. Is that so much to ask?"

She thought about the offer. It was a good one if he actually did what he said. But she knew the chances of that were practically zero.

"This better not be an interrogation," she said. "Let me do my job and be the detective and you got a deal."

"Good," he said, getting up from the chair. He took the cigar out of his pocket and headed toward the downstairs den. "It'll be a nice party," he added as he walked away. "I'm looking forward to it."

CHAPTER 11

KNOCK KNOCK

Julian could hear the press outside on the sidewalk, jabbering amongst themselves. He sure wasn't about to leave the house any time soon, so from his perspective, they were wasting their time. He peeked through the front blinds, and immediately a couple brazen reporters who spotted him rushed onto the property and started firing questions, which he could barely hear.

"Hey, they're trespassing," he said. "They can't trespass!"

"Julian, don't drive yourself crazy," said his mother from the sofa. "Sooner or later, it'll die down." She seemed to be handling this better than he was.

He heard her turn on the TV, apparently trying to make everything seem normal. But as far as he was concerned, things would never be normal again—at least to whatever degree his life was normal before. He rushed upstairs to get a better view from a higher vantage point. Slowly, he went to his mother's front bedroom window and slid the delicate beige curtains aside just a fraction. Fortunately, nobody outside noticed him. He scanned the group slowly. A few had left, but most were still there, about ten or fifteen at least, roughly evenly mixed between men and women. Standing toward the back of the group was that strange guy with the scar, still with no camera. The man looked up toward the window briefly and Julian quickly closed the curtains. He fell back onto his mother's king-sized bed, lying there in a daze and contemplating possible versions of his future.

Within a minute or so, he heard a commotion outside and then heard three loud bangs on the front door. Someone was knocking. He rushed to the window. It appeared the reporters were still by the curb—except for the guy with the scar, who was no longer there.

"Don't answer it," he yelled down to his mother. He turned and ran toward the stairs.

As he scooted down the steps, nearly tripping, he heard three heavy bangs on the door, followed by the doorbell. He looked back at his mother, who shrugged her shoulders in confusion. He wasn't sure what to do.

Two more loud knocks and increasingly frantic doorbell rings gave him a sinking feeling in the pit of his stomach. He took a quick peek out the front window. The press was still by the curb, watching whomever it was at the door with great curiosity. He took a deep breath and quietly made his way toward the front door. Just then, his cell phone started ringing. He pulled out the phone and tapped the red X without even checking who it was and then put the phone back in his pocket.

A sudden bang on the door startled him, and then the doorbell rang again. As far as he knew, even the most annoying of reporters wouldn't actually knock on the door.

He decided to take a chance. He turned to his mother. "Just stay where you are," he said. "I'm gonna open the door."

"Are you sure you should do that?" she said.

"No."

Slowly, he turned the knob and then pulled the door open. As soon as he saw who it was, he exhaled a sigh of relief. It was Lela.

"I tried calling you," she said. "Turn on the news. Quick."

"Mother, turn on the news," said Julian.

Lela smiled and waved to his mother, who returned the favor before switching the TV to the local five o'clock news. A commercial for some drug with five thousand side effects was playing.

"I'm Laura Black," said his mother, who looked surprised to see a young woman visiting him. "It's nice to meet you."

"Lela Mars," said Lela, coming forward to shake his mother's hand. Your son has really helped us out."

"Oh, you're the detective," said his mother in a friendly tone.

"Wait, here it is," said Julian.

Julian directed his attention to the TV, where the same pretty blonde anchorwoman from the other day was reporting. The headline at the bottom of the screen said, *Breaking News: No Miracles in Hilson Case*.

"We have some breaking news," said the anchorwoman. "It turns out that the man responsible for identifying Monica Hilson's alleged murderer is just that—a regular man. Let's cut over to district police captain Angel Mars, who has an announcement."

Julian looked over at Lela. "Angel?" he mouthed. He thought it funny, considering the guy's disposition. She grinned and pointed at the TV.

On the screen was Captain Mars, with Eric Hilson standing next to him. It appeared they were outside the Hilson residence.

"This morning," said Mars, "it was reported that the prime suspect in the tragic murder of Monica Hilson, Mr. James

Woodburn, was identified by a Philadelphia resident named Julian Black. It was also reported that the lead was the result of a psychic reading by Mr. Black. We are here to clarify that this is *not* the case, and that Mr. Black was in fact, offering an opinion based on his knowledge of circumstances surrounding the case, which led us to investigate and find evidence implicating Mr. Woodburn. Please realize, we are not in the habit of using psychic phenomena as evidence. I want to be clear. Mr. Black did not misrepresent himself, and neither did Mr. Hilson, but this was, in fact, a misunderstanding. We ask that you respect the privacy of the Hilson family and the family of Mr. Black. This case will be tried in a court of law, and I have no further information at this time."

Mars and Hilson, who never said a word, walked off camera and the screen flipped back to the anchorwoman.

"In other news…" she said, as Julian turned down the volume.

"Wow, he's good," said Julian. "I'm not even sure what he said, but I liked it."

"Told you we'd handle it," said Lela.

"What about the reporters?" he said, motioning to the window.

"Take a look," she said.

Julian went to the window and peered through the blinds. De Luca was outside updating the reporters as they scattered back to their vehicles. Finally, this brief nightmare was over.

He turned around and exhaled. "I think you and De Luca are my new best friends."

"Thank my dad," said Lela.

"Julian's a worry wart," said his mother.

Lela smiled. "It's understandable."

Julian glanced over at Lela. He was grateful for her help in giving him his life back. She stayed true to her promise. Part of him wanted to continue working with her, but he knew that the police life wasn't for him. If anything, he took this as a warning. Like Icarus, he'd flown too close to the sun and had nearly gotten burned.

"So, what's next for you?" he said, hoping Lela wouldn't take offense.

"That's kind of what I wanted to talk to you about. I uh…"

"I think I'll leave you two be," said his mother. "The laundry awaits." He knew she didn't have any laundry—she'd already finished it—but she was always diplomatic to a fault.

As his mother headed upstairs, Lela smiled at him.

"Your mother's amazing," she said.

"I think I'll keep her. I'm sure yours is too."

"Well, my biological mom left when I was two."

"Oh yes, you did tell me that. Sorry. She ran off with the drug-addict boyfriend." He felt horrible.

"It's okay. I consider my stepmom Shelly my real mom, so yes, she's pretty amazing. And I guess I'll be seeing more of her now that I left Brian. So that should be interesting."

"Ah, you finally left him. Well done. He wasn't good for you."

"It only took a mind reader to make me see it. Anyway, I'll be living back home for a bit. Believe me, it's the last thing I wanted to do. As much as I love my dad, I see him all the time at work and we drive each other crazy. I'm as headstrong as he is, which is saying something."

"Well, you both make things happen, I'll say that." A wave of emotion washed over him as he thought about all they'd done for him. He went to the L-shaped sofa and sunk into the white leather, trying not to show his feelings of both gratitude and relief. He motioned for her to take a seat as well.

"Do you have any siblings?" he said, as she sat diagonally across from him.

"Just Crystal. She's my younger sister—well, half-sister technically, but we're like two peas in a pod. She's twenty-two.

We're ten years apart. She goes to Temple University, so she still lives at home. You'll get to meet her tonight."

"I will?"

"It's what I wanted to talk to you about. My dad's throwing a party in my honor. Five years on the force. I'd like you to be there."

"Congratulations," he said, but… um… I'm not sure your dad would want me there after all the trouble I—"

"Julian, he's the one who insisted. And I'd like you there, too. We made a good team. And we still can if you want to keep working with me. I could sure use your help."

"Lela, I would love to help, but it's hard to describe how painful it is. I just can't imagine seeing people's trauma day in and day out." He studied her face for her reaction. She would've been a good poker player. He sensed she was disappointed, but she also had a slight smile.

"It's okay," she said. "You don't have to decide now. But come to the party anyway."

He nodded, even though he had chills down his spine at the thought of being in a room full of people. "When and where?" he said.

"If you're ready, I can take you now. You can go like that."

He was wearing a navy-blue quarter-zip sweater, gray chinos, and brown penny loafers. It was certainly adequate for a party. With no excuses, he nodded.

"One second," he said, as he got up and jogged halfway upstairs.

"Mother, I'll be out for the evening," he shouted. "Call if you need anything."

"Enjoy yourselves," she said, coming to the top of the stairs. She winked at Julian, which made him cringe. He couldn't say out loud that it wasn't like whatever she was thinking. Instead, he just shook his head discreetly.

Fighting a panic attack in the name of what was starting to

feel like a real-life friendship, he went back downstairs and headed out the door with Lela. He was relieved not to see anyone around—no reporters, and not that weird blond-haired guy with the scar.

He climbed into the passenger seat of the SUV and Lela got in the driver side.

"Now don't let my dad intimidate you," she said. "I'll give you some pointers."

"That's not making me feel a whole lot better," he said.

"Don't worry, it'll be fine."

She started the engine and pulled out of the spot.

As they drove off, Lela told him about her family and gave him the rundown on the other officers who would be there, including De Luca. She told him her father asks a lot of questions, but means well.

During the ride, she recounted how she'd made detective after being on the force for two years. At the time, she and her father would meet on Sundays and have dinner. As she told it, one evening her dad was lamenting about being unable to fill a vacant detective position. She didn't have to think twice to volunteer. She'd been a narcotics officer at the time, hoping to rid the streets of drugs, especially knowing her mom had run off with an addict. It hadn't taken her long to realize it was an exercise in frustration. Prior to that, she'd been a social worker for the same reason, but she quickly grew tired of fighting the system. At least as a detective, she felt like she was making a difference—or at any rate, a dent.

As she shared her story with him, he especially identified with her burning desire to make a difference—to find meaning in life. If there was one thing that touched his soul in these recent cases, it was that he could truly change people's lives for the better. But at what expense?

He stared out the window and contemplated his future as he gazed blankly at the passing neighborhood homes and some of its residents who happened to be out—an old Russian woman sweeping her walkway, a teen redhead in a school uniform walking her overweight golden retriever, and a guy with a bushy mustache and a thick head of gray hair pacing back and forth on the sidewalk and animatedly talking with his hands to someone on his Bluetooth, or so Julian assumed.

What Julian didn't know—or Lela for that matter—was that tagging behind them, nearly out of view, was a red Maserati—the same one that was parked outside his house for the last couple hours—a car registered to a shell corporation called VLQ Enterprises, and, for all intents and purposes, belonging to the strange man with the scar—a methodical, patient, and ruthless operative waiting for the right time to act.

CHAPTER 12

VIPER

The Hôtel Napoléon was Blaine's home away from home when he was in Paris, so he was delighted to be back, though not so delighted that the VIPER meeting should be in this very building. He made the mistake of recommending it once to Olga, who in turn must have passed the word up the chain of command. Knowing VIPER, the location for this little gathering was a not-so-subtle message: *Your territory is now our territory.*

The boutique, mansion-style, 5-star hotel—once the haunt of Ernest Hemingway, John Steinbeck, Salvador Dalí, Errol Flynn, Orson Welles, Miles Davis, Josephine Baker, Ella Fitzgerald, and other notables—was perfectly situated on Avenue de Friedland, just a block from the Champs-Elysées and the Arc de Triomphe. Blaine always asked for the Imperial Suite, which was designed as a prestigious private apartment on the top floor, with a wraparound private terrace overlooking the majestic Arc de Triomphe and, further in the distance, the Eiffel Tower. He liked to imagine the luminaries from the past who likely stayed in this very suite.

As he propped himself up on the red, white, and green striped Napoleonic-style pillow, Astrid rolled over and spread her arm across his bare chest—her long brown hair draping over her shoulder and arm, illuminated by the early evening sunlight coming in through the open terrace. He loved the intoxicating floral scent of her hair and the softness of her skin. She crossed her left leg over his and settled her warm body close to him.

He'd been here with her before, but she wouldn't have remembered it. It wasn't intentional; he'd accidentally touched her after his old gloves tore. But he knew from experience, chemistry spanned situations and lifetimes, and he could almost spot a recognizable *déjà vu* glimmer in her eye when he'd hired her for the Parisian tour earlier in the day. Of course, he also had the advantage of already knowing her likes and dislikes.

But making women forget wasn't his thing. In fact, it was after that first time with Astrid that he'd perfected his silicone prosthetic gloves—or rather, his research scientists did. Now they were virtually undetectable, like a second skin. He could feel every nuance of her body. Still, her sharp eyes noticed them when she'd studied his hands earlier. What was it about women and hands? He told her what he always told women who spotted the gloves: that a chemical accident had left his hands overly sensitive. To think there was a time when he avoided women for fear of touching them. That *50 First Dates* movie was cute, but not something he wanted as a lifestyle choice.

He glanced over at the wheeled silver tray table to his right, which still had the empty bottle of 1996 Dom Perignon Rose Gold champagne they'd shared earlier, along with the remnants of the Petrossian smoked salmon and baguette toasts. It had been a good day so far.

The room phone rang, disturbing the quiet moment. Astrid

barely stirred.

He delicately lifted Astrid's arm and slid out from beneath her leg, kissing the back of her hand before getting up. Trying not to disturb her, he climbed out of bed and made his way to the elegantly appointed marble and mahogany bathroom and grabbed a white robe off the hook. Then he headed to the suite's other bedroom to answer the phone, which was still ringing.

It was Olga, calling to inform him that the meeting had been moved to nine and would be in the Friedland room. She insisted on naming all the constituents who would be there, twenty-two rogue agents, former generals, and mobsters representing some fourteen countries, including Russia, China, North Korea, Yemen, Pakistan, and nine others. Viktor Volkov, head of VIPER, would be chairing the meeting, as expected. She cautioned him not to reference anyone by name in the meeting, only by the number in front of their seat. It was a strict rule, and breaking it could lead to unwanted consequences. The meeting was reserved under the name Global Distribution Council.

After the call, he meandered back into the other bedroom, only to see an empty bed.

Confused, he wandered into the living room and as he looked to the terrace doors, he could see Astrid was standing outside in the other white robe supplied by the hotel. He stepped onto the terrace and joined her. She was leaning against the black guardrail that ran along the wraparound white terrace wall, which was tastefully decorated with red flowers, gazing at the magnificent view of the Eiffel Tower.

"It's beautiful, isn't it?" she said, in her slight Scandinavian accent. "Did you know the four pillars were aligned with the compass?"

"How did I get so lucky to nab a tour guide?"

She looked at him and smiled, studying his face the way an

artist might examine her subject before crafting a sculpture. "I feel like I've known you for ages," she said.

"I have that face."

"Yes, your face. And your eyes are a mix of blue and green. It's rare."

"Let's talk about your face instead." He brushed her hair out of her face with his hand and admired her perfect features.

"You know, it wouldn't be the first time a rich man fell in love with a young girl at this hotel," she said. "Do you know the story?"

"Which one?" he said. "I'm sure there are lots of them."

"It was during the First World War. A wealthy Russian man moved here to Paris. He met a French student at a literature salon and fell in love with her and married her. He bought this hotel as a wedding gift. It's nice, no? His name was Alexander Pavlovich Kliaguine. Did you know his family still owns this hotel?"

"Good old Alexander," said Blaine.

"You know of him!?" Her eyes lit up.

"Never heard of him. But it's a lovely story."

"Would *you* buy me this hotel?" she said, smiling. "I would like it very much."

"Let's go big time," he said. "I'll buy you *that*." He pointed out in the distance.

Her eyes lit up in mock surprise. "The Eiffel Tower?"

"Why not?"

"It's too cold and open," she said, as she pouted teasingly. "You can't live in it. You can't love in it." She gazed longingly out toward the horizon. "Do you ever think about that?"

"Living in the Eiffel Tower?"

"No, silly. Love."

"Oh. I dabble. But right now, I'm thinking I should buy you dinner at Le Cinq. It's getting late." He playfully smacked her bottom and headed inside, as she chased him trying to smack his.

They headed into the stylish marble and mahogany bathroom and took a shower together under the English-style rain-shower heads, then got dressed, he in a gray wool Armani suit, and she in the navy and white striped dress she was wearing earlier, which he convinced her would be just fine for dinner. They were just about out the door when he realized he'd forgotten the room key. He held the door open while she went inside to grab it and then they were off.

Le Cinq was just as he'd remembered it, an exquisite, white marble, grand Rococo dining room with gilt moldings and plush carpets in the Four Seasons Hotel George V. They both started with the poached foie gras and a glass of Sauternes—the apricot, butterscotch flavors of the wine perfectly balancing the rich, creamy texture of the pâté—and then moved on to the succulent blue lobster with salted butter and avocado crepes, along with a bottle of Louis Latour Montrachet Grand Cru from 2018, which perfectly complemented the main course. Finally, for dessert, they both ordered the iced coffee mousse with infused blackberries. He'd had the same meal here before and took tremendous pleasure seeing Astrid's reaction to it.

After dinner, while he paid the bill, Astrid excused herself to go freshen up. When she returned, she lamented that she'd lost an earring. He tried to help her search under the table, as did the waiter, but it was nowhere to be found.

"No matter," she said, "What is an earring when you've had the most perfect day of your life?"

"It was quite a perfect day, wasn't it," he said.

"I will never forget it for the rest of my life, no matter what happens next."

He smiled at her. And, as he reached under the table to feel his gloves, he thought of how many people he'd made forget him, including Astrid in the past. But this time would be different.

"Well, let's not end it quite yet," he said. He glanced at the time on his silver Breitling watch, a rare chronograph he'd acquired at an auction a year ago. "The stores are open for another forty-five minutes and I haven't bought you anything yet. It seems to me you need new earrings."

◆

After taking her shopping at Hermès and Bulgari on the luxurious Avenue George V, Blaine had parted with Astrid on the Champs-Élysées before walking back to the hotel alone. He'd told her he had a business meeting to attend and would then be traveling. Sadly, he knew he was unlikely to see her again. He simply couldn't risk relationships in his situation. But at least he felt, in some small way, he was able to atone for making her forget him the first time, even if it *was* inadvertent.

Back in the room, glancing down at the ruffled sheets where she'd been only a few hours ago, he spotted her lost earring just below her pillow. He smiled and picked it up, tucking it into his jacket pocket. He might have to see her again one day after all, if only to surprise her. At the least, he'd mail it to her.

At precisely 8:50 PM, he headed downstairs and made his way to Napoléon level, where the meeting room was situated. After looking around, he approached the mahogany doors next to the electronic sign that said *Salon Friedland*, and under it, *Global Distribution Council – Privée*.

He took a breath, opened the double doors, and stepped inside.

Three luminous frescoes of Parisian landmarks brightened up the nearest section of the large hall, in which stood several round cocktail tables. To his left at the far end of the room, a U-shaped table was set up, with everyone already seated. It dawned on him that Olga was probably instructed to have him arrive after the cocktail hour to keep him from engaging in small talk with the members.

"Our guest has arrived," said a voice in the front of the room over the microphone. "Esteemed visitor, come take a seat at number one-one-six." He recognized the clear, articulate voice with just a hint of a Scandinavian-Russian accent as belonging to Viktor Volkov, who was seated at the head of the table.

He remembered what Olga had said about referring to people by their seat number. In front of each seat was a small name tent showing a random three-digit number and a country. The card in front of the sole open seat on the right said *116 – Visitor*. He casually made his way to the seat while everyone stared at him, some in mild curiosity, some in recognition, and some sneering at the new intruder to their private world. Olga was seated to his right. He recognized a few of the faces from a prior meeting, not to mention his own research. He made it his business to know the big money players.

"Our Sicilian contingent was just discussing a certain Wilhelm Hegler Diamond Company in Geneva," said Volkov. "Continue, number nine-six-two."

The dapper, salt-and-pepper haired man opposite Blaine, whom he recognized as Adolfo Drago, cleared his throat. "The industrial diamonds are en route to my contact in Catalina," said Drago. "The operation is going as planned." Drago was a 62-year-old former member of the Sicilian mafia, who'd started his own independent cell, which has since grown to vast proportions internationally. Blaine recognized his missing right pinky and ring fingers, one of Drago's trademarks along with wearing a Panama hat.

"And the weapon?" said Volkov.

"Secured."

"That is good news indeed," said Volkov. "But I understand that an American agent has caused some difficulty. Is this true?"

"It is of no consequence," said Drago. "It is being dealt with."

"I am glad to hear."

Blaine studied Volkov's face. For someone facing a room full of powerful international figures of the criminal underworld, he maintained an extraordinary sense of calm. Then again, he must've seen quite a bit in his seventy or so years.

Besides being a Russian tycoon worth some twenty billion dollars from his shares in the metals megafirm Zolomark, Alexei "Victor" Volkov was a former KGB agent and believed to be the money behind the long-running grand scheme to fund sales of U.S. secrets to Russia and to obtain American technology. His ties to the GRU have never been proven, but some say he operates behind the scenes with them on such matters, generally working through several levels of intermediaries. To the public, he's just another Russian billionaire with a huge yacht.

"Before we proceed to more sensitive matters," said Volkov, "let us hear from our visitor, number one-one-six, before he is dismissed." Volkov looked toward Blaine. "Please enlighten us as to your progress."

"I have the scientist," said Blaine. "He's resisted our charms so far, but not to worry. I have a foolproof plan in motion to retrieve the information we agreed on."

"In my experience, there is no such thing as foolproof, one-one-six," said Volkov. "Please continue."

"There's a man who can extract any information we need, let's say... more scientifically. My contact is retrieving him from the US as we speak."

"Truth serums are unreliable," said Volkov, matter-of-factly.

"This isn't a serum. It's a natural ability. When I say it's foolproof, I mean it. I know this man personally." Blaine heard a few chuckles around the room.

"Your work for this organization," said Volkov, holding up a hand to silence the others, "has been impressive. I think most of us can agree to that. Your success in the Brussels diamond heist and your many jobs along the Southern European region speak for themselves. Number one-three-zed was right to refer you to us. But I cannot stress enough the criticality of this assignment."

"I understand, sir."

"Nevertheless, I will explain it, so it is explicit. There are certain parties within our representative governments that would like to see the West suffer. We empathize with these parties and have the strength to realize what they have until now thought of as dreams. The governments are too afraid to act, despite their strong rhetoric. We are not. Are you familiar with the current state of anti-Satellite weapons in the world?"

"I know they exist. ASATs, I think they're called."

"These are weapons built with the purpose of incapacitating an enemy's satellites for strategic or tactical purposes. They can be fired from the ground, from the wings of an aircraft, or from an object in space. While it has yet to be used in warfare, several countries, including the United States, Russia, China, and India, have successfully demonstrated the ability to shoot down their own satellites as a deterrent to others. Now the United States is calling for a global ban on testing such weaponry, as they claim it creates dangerous shrapnel in space. Yet the ability to shoot down satellites is critical, not only in nuclear warfare, but in any future space-based warfare as well. Do you understand the importance of this?"

"I do."

"To be clear, whoever shoots down an enemy satellite can bring about the complete shutdown of communication and global positioning systems and incapacitate the enemy on the battlefield. The SARA device that has been secretly developed by the United States renders anti-satellite defense weapons useless, throwing off their trajectory into empty space. We must level the playing field by obtaining this technology, and as a deterrent. No one country can have this technology. I hope this is satisfactorily clear."

"Yes, it's quite clear," said Blaine. "But, if you don't mind me saying, something else is becoming clear, too. Who's funding this operation and for how much?"

The others in the room began chattering to one another, and Olga stared daggers at him.

"You will excuse one-one-six," said Olga, turning to Volkov. "He is unfamiliar with our protocols."

Volkov held up his hand again to silence the room. "We never reveal our sources," he said. "If you have a grievance, speak it."

"Well, it just seems you've offered me a fee of a hundred and fifty million pounds. For something so important that'll impact the balance of power in the world, it would seem the fee should be higher, commensurate with the risk."

Volkov paused before answering, still the picture of calm. Then he spoke, deliberately and serenely as usual. "The funding for this operation," said Volkov, "is budgeted at two and a half billion euros. Twenty percent goes to our organization to fund operations. Ten percent is my fee as chairman. After your fee, the rest is distributed among our twenty-two members. If the membership agrees, I am willing to advance your rate to ten percent, or two-hundred-and-fifty-million euros, payable in British pounds. This leaves sixty percent to be distributed among our members at a rate of approximately sixty-eight million euros per member, a negligible difference. Does this meet with your acceptance?"

"It seems reasonable." What he really wanted to say was that it seemed like he took all the risk and they took the lion's share of the money, but he figured he better quit while he was ahead.

"Are there any objections to this change in distribution," said Volkov, looking around the room.

Blaine glanced at the others. He recognized some of them. To the left of Adolfo Drago was Ibrahim Mohammed Al-Jaziri from Yemen. Also around the table, he noticed Diego Santos from Brazil, Ali Farook Barazani from Pakistan, Dr. Ellery Wu from China, and Augustin Zoomov from Russia. Of course, none of them claimed to be official representatives of their countries.

After about twenty seconds, which felt like forever, nobody objected.

"Let it be noted that there were no objections," said Volkov. "But, one-one-six, I would like to educate you, if it were, the chosen name of our collective—VIPER. In the reptile world, a viper has three traits. Do you know what they are?"

"They slither?"

"They have long, retractable fangs contained in a small head. Like our namesake, our leadership is small in number and our aggressive fangs are hidden, but we have the ability to strike far and wide. A second characteristic is that a viper's triangular head is distinct from the body. We retain anonymity through many layers of intermediaries, with triple redundancy for added security. The last thing to know about vipers is this. They are everywhere. We have placed our trust in you, one-one-six. Do not fail us."

"Thank you. You can rest—"

"You are dismissed," said Volkov.

"Sure thing," said Blaine, smiling. "It was a pleasure as

always."

He stood and left the room, his footsteps echoing in the silence as they all stared.

CHAPTER 13

THE DINNER PARTY

J ulian felt relieved when Captain Mars blew a whistle to get everyone's attention. He wasn't accustomed to parties, and he made a mental note not to attend another anytime soon. Something about awkwardly wandering around in a roomful of strangers while wearing white gloves and trying to avoid the stares was less than his idea of fun—though he did meet Lela's stepmom, Shelly, and her sister, Crystal, both of whom tried to make him feel as comfortable as possible. He could see why Lela loved them so much. Crystal tried introducing him to a few people, but he didn't have a whole lot to say, so he excused himself after a few initial pleasantries. At one point, De Luca patted him on the back and said, "If it isn't Michael Jackson." At least he meant it in a lighthearted way, which left a better impression than his initial meeting with De Luca. For now, Julian was glad to get a respite, as the captain was about to make a speech.

Julian looked over at Mars, who stood in the corner of the living room holding a framed document while everyone gathered around clutching their drinks. Mars was wearing a yellow V-neck sweater over a collared shirt, so he was pretty easy to spot.

"As you all know," said Mars, loudly enough for everyone to hear, "we're here to celebrate Lela's five years on the force."

Most of the attendees applauded, at least those not holding cocktails, and the rest just cheered. Julian recognized a few officers from the police station, including the young blond guy who'd been at the front desk.

"My daughter, in her very first case," said Mars, "intercepted four packages of meth mailed to this area, and identified the scumbags who were sending this stuff to our community. That was back when she was in Narcotics. These two guys had sixty-five grams of crystal meth in their possession when she found them. Turns out they were running a five-state distribution network, so her good work allowed the Feds to finally catch and prosecute these assholes."

The people in the room whooped and shouted, including De Luca, who made his way closer to the front.

"When she made detective," Mars continued, "her first investigation led to the prosecution of Marisa Jean Gonzalez for the death of a one-year-old kid she was babysitting—from fentanyl no less. That couldn't have been easy, but Lela handled it like a pro. She also cracked that ATM crime spree last year using sheer willpower and a helluva lot of legwork. And you probably heard just recently, she cracked the Monica Hilson murder when it seemed like a lost cause. So, in honor of her five years on the force—and I'm sure the best is yet to come—I'm presenting Detective Lela Mars with this service award."

Julian looked around as everyone resumed cheering. He was delighted to see her get the recognition. That's exactly what he wanted, to remain in the background. He observed from afar as Captain Mars gave Lela a framed certificate. He felt a strange sense of pride seeing the grin on her face as she accepted it, and, as uncomfortable as he was, he was glad she'd invited him to witness it. He didn't know about those other cases she'd worked on. In the short time he'd known her, she'd never talked about them. Then again, she wasn't the type to brag or tell war stories. She let her actions speak for themselves, and it was obvious to anyone who saw her how persistent and determined she was.

After Lela hugged her father, she was immediately bombarded by people looking to congratulate her. Meanwhile, Julian froze in place as Captain Mars came walking right toward him with an outstretched hand.

"You must be Julian," he said. "I can tell by the gloves." Julian shook his firm hand. "You'll excuse me for not mentioning your name up there. I figured you're trying to keep things on the down low."

"No, that's perfect," said Julian. "Captain, I—"

"Call me Angel, please."

"I just wanted to thank you for what you did for me."

"For you?" said Mars. "My daughter tells me you worked miracles, so it was the least I could do. I'm curious, though. How does it work?"

"Well, I'm not sure exactly. For as long as I can remember, if I touch someone with my hands, I get these visions. It took me a while to realize it was actually their memories I was seeing."

"You're a lucky man," said Mars.

"Oh, I wouldn't call it luck at all."

"Skill?" Mars looked confused. "Did you practice it?"

"More like a curse," said Julian.

"When do you first remember it happening?"

Mars would've made a good detective himself. He sure asked a lot of questions.

"That's the thing," said Julian. "Anything from my childhood is... well, I don't really remember much of it."

"So, you can see everyone else's memories, but not your own. Interesting. Does it work every time?"

"Pretty much."

"Can you demonstrate it for me?"

Julian started sweating. With all the rapid-fire questions, he got the feeling Mars was interrogating him. "Oh, I don't think that would be such a good idea," he said.

"Just for a few seconds," said Mars. "I'm curious. I want to see it firsthand."

"Captain, with all due respect, I may see things you don't want me to see."

Mars smiled. "Ah, but I'm an open book. I don't mind. Satisfy an old man's curiosity."

"You mean here? I'm not so sure—"

Mars put an arm on his shoulder in a fatherly manner. "Listen, Julian. I'm sure you can understand this. My daughter tells me about a guy who can solve cases by reading people's memories, which is a really cool thing. *Really* cool. I tell you, as a father, I want to see firsthand who she's working with, if you know what I mean. Just for a few seconds, and you can tell me what you see. What do you say?"

Julian looked around. Everyone seemed engrossed in conversation. Perhaps he could do it quickly here without causing a scene. He didn't see Lela anywhere or he would've tried to excuse himself or call her over. He took a deep breath and slid off his right glove. Slowly, he held his bare hand forward.

Just as Mars reached out to take his hand, Lela yelled, "Stop!"

Julian put his hand down as she rushed forward. Everyone was staring at them.

"What were you thinking?" she said. He couldn't tell who she was talking to, him or her father. Maybe both.

"Um... he insisted," said Julian, as he slid his glove back

on.

"Lela," said the elder Mars, "It's okay, I just wanted a little demonstration, that's all."

"Do you know the damage that could've caused?" she said.

"What are you talking about, damage?" said Mars.

Lela took Julian's arm and pulled him away. "Come with me," she said.

She led him through the crowd as most people went back to their conversations, though a few were still staring. He followed her downstairs and out a sliding door that led to the back yard.

"I figured you could use a break from my father," she said, as they made their way to a white gazebo with a wooden porch swing in the center.

"It's okay," he said, walking beside her.

"It's not okay. Do you have any idea of the horrors you would've been exposed to if you saw my dad's memories? The stuff he's been through on the force?"

She sat on the swing, and he took a seat to her left.

"I guess I forgot about that part," he said. "It wasn't like he gave me much of a choice." He looked up at a crow cawing away on the branch of a huge oak tree. "It feels good to get some fresh air though. I'm not used to all those people."

"What was he saying to you, anyway?"

"He was asking when I first remembered seeing these visions. Funny thing is, I don't really remember. I hardly remember anything before I was about nine or ten."

"I can relate," she said. "I don't remember my biological mom at all. You know, when you first touched my hand, I was kind of hoping you might have seen something from back then."

"I only saw Brian," he said.

"Just as well," she said. "And now here we are, both living with our parents."

He smiled as the crow cawed again and flew off.

"So, what do you do when you're not reading people's minds?" she said.

"I'm a writer." He never really knew how to answer that question.

"See, I didn't know that. Would I know any of your books?"

"Not unless you can read minds too," he said. "I haven't published any yet. But I will."

"I know you will," she said. "What kind of books?"

"I'm working on a mystery about a psychic who's helping a detective track down a serial killer."

"You're kidding."

He laughed. "No, I'm not. And believe it or not, I started this before we met. Except in this one, the psychic turns out to be the killer and isn't really psychic. He predicts his own murders. He commits them right under the detective's nose. That's his modus operandi. He gets them just close enough, but not enough to catch him."

"That sounds really good. I'd read it."

"I also play a lot of video games. Ever hear of Stealth Invaders?"

"Can't say I have."

"It's fun. You're part of a team and you have assignments to catch targets in different parts of the world."

"So, you play with others."

"Well, yeah, and we can talk through our headsets. That's how I met Cassie."

"Oh, Cassie," she said teasingly. "Do tell."

"We haven't met in person or anything. She wants to, but I keep making excuses." He looked down at his gloves and then held up his right hand to illustrate his point. "I doubt she'd understand, you know?"

"You should give her a chance," said Lela. "Let her decide.

She might surprise you."

"I suppose so," he said. "Maybe one day."

"You have to. Promise me. Anyway, I'm glad you have people you see, even if it's not in person."

Just then, Lela's cell phone rang.

"One sec, it's the DA" she said, before picking it up.

"Yes, Brad," she said into the phone. She pressed the speakerphone button.

"I have good news and bad news," said the voice over the phone. "The ballistics match, so Woodburn's our guy."

"That's great," said Lela. "What's the bad news?"

"His lawyer's claiming self-defense. Woodburn says the Hilson daughter tried to run him off the road, whether on purpose or not. He says Monica Hilson was in the passenger side and rolled down her window and started yelling at him. Says she pointed a weapon and he panicked."

Julian felt his blood boiling and shook his head to indicate that wasn't what happened.

"It was a cell phone," said Lela. "There were no weapons at the scene other than his."

"Sure, everyone knows that," said the DA, "but things happen fast, so who knows what he thought at the time. He owned the weapon legally. Says he has it because he carries a lot of cash for his landscaping business."

"There's no way that girl tried to run him off the road," said Lela. "I think that'll be obvious in court."

"Teens don't make the best witnesses, and the other kid's too young," said the DA. "My take? It could go either way."

"My guy knows exactly what happened," she said.

"Your guy? You mean the psychic your dad said was fake on the local news?"

"That was PR."

"What are you saying?"

Lela took a deep breath. "I'm saying he does have skills

that helped me track down Woodburn in the first place."

"Lela, even if this guy was the second coming of Christ, the evidence wouldn't be admissible. We couldn't bring him into a courtroom. They'd laugh me out of the room."

"I'm not saying that," she said. "I'm saying it gives us the advantage of knowing what actually happened. Maybe we can use that to make Woodburn crack."

There was silence on the other end. Julian breathed a sigh of relief. He was trying to picture having to prove his skills in a courtroom.

"If you can get an original medical diagnosis with definitive proof of your guy's abilities," said the DA, "then *maybe* I'll get you some time with Woodburn. No guarantees."

"Then that's exactly what I'll do. Thanks, Brad. I'll owe you one."

"I said no guarant—"

She hung up before he could finish.

Julian looked at her. "Lela, I think that's going to be a problem."

"What is?"

"Getting a medical diagnosis."

"You have to have a doctor, right?" she said. "Who do you go to when you're sick?"

"Well, I can't go to a regular doctor. That would… not be a good idea. But my mother used to be a nurse, so she can help with most things. And if there's something she can't handle, I see Dr. Schaffler. He's a neurologist. He's the only one I trust. But even he doesn't understand why I can do what I do."

"Then it looks like we're gonna have a chat with Dr. Schaffler tomorrow," she said. "I'm not giving up on this. Besides, you might learn something about yourself."

CHAPTER 14

GODS, UNICORNS, AND DRAGONS

J ulian sat in the waiting room of Dr. Leon Schaffler as Lela spoke to the young receptionist, who must've been new. Julian hadn't seen her before. Then again, it was quite some time since he needed the doctor—a side benefit of never leaving the house. He and Lela had to wait until noon to arrive, as the doctor didn't have morning hours today. One other person was in the waiting room, a woman who looked to be in her seventies who was typing on her cellphone like a teenager. He wasn't sure what Lela was saying exactly, but he saw her flash her badge, and then the receptionist excused herself to go in the back. After about five minutes, a mousy-looking nurse opened the door to the patient rooms and called Julian's name. The woman in the waiting room shook her head, clearly annoyed that Julian was called first.

Dr. Schaffler greeted them in the hallway and led them to his office. He was probably nearing retirement by now. He had to be in his late sixties at least. Julian dreaded the day he'd retire, as he was one of the few people in the world he truly trusted and who seemed to understand his situation.

"Have a seat," said the doctor, pointing to the two wooden

armchairs opposite his mahogany desk. The desk was meticulously organized, with one short stack of manilla folders to the right, a desk calendar, and a white *World's Best Grandpa* mug full of pens. "It's good to see you again, Julian. How's your mother?"

"She's doing well, thanks," said Julian, as he and Lela took their seats.

"Good to hear. I picked up Detective Mars's voice message, and it sounds like you've been doing some great work."

"Well, I did some work for the police, yes."

"Good for you. That's great. Maybe a new career?"

Julian smiled. "I'm not sure about a career just yet." He glanced over at Lela and then directed his gaze toward the countless awards hanging on the wall.

"Doctor, the problem is," said Lela, "in order for me to use the information Julian gave us, the DA needs some kind of medical verification of his condition."

"Yes, yes, I got that from your message," said Schaffler. "The detailed records aren't in our new computer system. They're stored in the archives offsite. But I've pulled some records from Julian's chart. Maybe they'll help." He opened the topmost folder on his desk and pulled out a sheet of paper.

"Julian first came to me when he was nine," said the doctor. "The most remarkable case I'd ever seen, if you don't mind me saying. The kind of case you just want to study, but in the interest of Julian's privacy, we all thought the better of it. Besides, it was getting into some areas that went beyond classic neuroscience."

"In what way?" said Lela.

"Are you familiar with what a neurologist does, Detective? I'm not being facetious. I just want to give some context."

"A little. You study the nervous system and the brain."

"Correct, or more specifically, we address disorders of the

brain, the peripheral nerves and muscles, and the spinal cord. We treat conditions like MS, Parkinson's, strokes, and epilepsy, you get the idea. Depending on the disorder, we might collect spinal fluid or perform an EMG to assess muscle response. To record electrical activity in the brain, we do an EEG to convert electrical signals into patterns we can read and diagnose. And, of course, we do other imaging and bloodwork. The EEG is what I used to test Julian."

"But you'd have to do it while he was reading someone's memories, right?" said Lela.

"And that's exactly what I did."

"Whose memories?"

"Mine." He smiled.

"That had to be when I was younger," said Julian. "Because I don't remember that at all." It made him wonder what he might have seen in the doctor's memory. "I hope I didn't say anything insensitive."

"On no, it's quite alright," said Dr. Schaffler. "You saw my daughter's wedding, that was it. And you described every little detail in the room as if you were there. Remarkable! You even described my conversation with the groom's father about our mutual love of tennis. Do you play?"

"No, but I'm glad it was a good memory at least," said Julian.

"You said you did an EEG during that?" said Lela.

"Yeah, and it was pretty interesting. During the episode, Julian experienced extremely low levels of activity in the frontal lobe in the areas that are definitely linked with reasoning and problem solving. Don't worry, it just means he wasn't consciously manipulating anything. If you measured a virtuoso violinist's brain functions as she played, you'd see the same response—an almost complete loss of self-awareness. With a novice, it would be a whole different story. You see, when you're in a state of flow—that is, if you're doing something that comes so naturally to you that you don't need to think about it—you'll have exceptionally low activity in these neurons. It's amazing when you think about it."

"So, it's something that comes naturally," said Lela.

"It comes naturally to Julian. I would phrase it like that. Several years ago, a study was led by the University of Pennsylvania to assess brain activity in ten Brazilian psychographers."

"Psychographers?" said Julian.

"Mediums who let a spirit take control of their body as they write texts in the physical world. Sounds like a lot of woo-woo stuff, doesn't it? But they had similar results, with one exception. In addition to the low frontal lobe activity, they also had low activity in the hippocampus, which controls emotion. This actually supports their claim. It shows that their conscious minds were almost completely removed from the equation. Julian's activity, on the other hand, was high in that region, so his sense of emotion was still intact. There's something else that the hippocampus controls, though, that makes this even more interesting."

"What's that?" said Lela.

"Memory."

"So that proves it," said Julian. Lela looked at him with a broad grin.

"It's a start," said the doctor as he looked at Julian. "It proves that during these episodes, you're not consciously trying to do anything. This is a mostly subconscious activity for you, and it specifically activates the parts of the brain that influence memory and allows you to feel the emotions of your experience."

"Amazing," said Julian.

"The mystery, of course, is how you're able to read the memories of others, and that's where we leave the field of classic neuroscience and enter a whole new world."

"Any clues what that world might be?" said Lela.

The doctor smiled. "I have a theory. I said neurologists treat disorders of the brain. In my humble opinion, this is not a disorder at all, but something completely different. And it may be more in the realm of quantum neurobiology, a field a lot of my colleagues view as quackery."

"Does that have to do with quantum physics?" said Lela.

"It's the intersection of quantum physics and neuroscience. The idea is that quantum mechanics plays a significant role in higher cognitive functions, like consciousness and decision-making."

"And memory?" said Julian.

"Yes, and memory. Quantum neurobiology proposes that our true processing units are far below the cellular level and are governed by the rules of quantum physics, which science is still trying to get a grasp on. But one area of quantum physics seems to apply here in particular—quantum entanglement. To put it in layman's terms, that's when two particles are connected in a way where they share the same state, no matter how far apart they are. They're linked, just like you link with whoever you touch."

"That actually makes sense," said Lela.

"It's not a new concept. Eugene Wigner proposed it back in '61, but most of my contemporary colleagues think the whole thing's a myth. They quote Victor Stenger, who said the idea should take its place alongside gods, unicorns, and dragons. The trouble is, it's difficult to prove one way or another. In this case, if Julian's issue does involve quantum anything, the question in my mind is where did it come from? Why him?"

"So, where does that leave us?" said Lela.

"Well, at the very least, I can write up the results of my test that shows not only the phenomena I personally witnessed, but the medical proof these are not conscious activities on

Julian's part. I can also add that the neurons involved in memory are, in fact, active during these episodes. That should be good enough for your purposes. But if you want to explore the possibility that quantum physics may be at play, I'd suggest we find a neurophysicist willing to entertain the idea."

"I would appreciate that," said Julian. "For now, the letter would be really helpful."

"Good, then I'll have it for you in the waiting room. My noon appointment is probably having fits by now. I'm also going to dig up the old records in the archive and I'll let you know if I find anything else of interest."

"That would be great," said Lela, handing him her card. "I really appreciate you taking the time."

"Happy to help," said Dr. Schaffler. "Julian's good people."

Julian and Lela both stood and shook the doctor's hand.

"Oh Julian, one more thing," said the doctor. "If you want the detective to have access to your records, you'll need to fill out an authorization form at the front desk. HIPAA rules and all that."

"I'll do that," said Julian. "Thanks, Doc."

♦

After signing the patient information release form and obtaining Dr. Schaffler's medical letter from the receptionist, Julian nodded to Lela that all was taken care of and it was time to go. The woman in the waiting room shot them a nasty look when the nurse finally called her name—Alison Tardy.

"I'd say Mrs. Tardy's a bit tardy," he whispered to Lela, who tried to keep from laughing.

They stepped outside the doctor's neighborhood office on Pine Road and made their way toward Lela's SUV.

"How are you feeling?" she said.

"I think it went as well as it could have, considering."

She stopped and turned toward him. "I mean you, personally. That was a lot of stuff to dump on you at once. How are you handling it?"

"It's okay. I mean, I'd love to know more, but what can we do, right?"

Just then, a red car screeched out of a parking space and zoomed past them down the street.

"Where's that idiot off to in such a hurry?" he said. For a minute, he thought it might've been the red Maserati he saw back near his house, but he didn't get a good look at it. Ever since laying eyes on that strange man with the blond hair, he couldn't shake the feeling he was being followed by someone.

"Forget him," said Lela. "I'm more concerned about you."

"I'm fine, really. I honestly don't remember a thing before I was nine and I don't think I ever will." He didn't want to get into a whole sob story of how much pain it's caused him over the years having an entire chunk of his childhood mysteriously missing.

"How about your mom? Wouldn't she remember?"

"Not really. She just says I had a regular childhood before that. She says I was always a bit of a loner. She doesn't seem to remember much herself. Maybe I had a head injury and she didn't know it. Who knows, really?"

They continued walking.

"Something's not adding up," she said.

"How do you mean?"

"I'm not sure. It's just a gut feeling. I can't help it, I'm a detective."

He smiled. "That you are."

They climbed into Lela's vehicle and continued discussing the doctor's assessment on the way to drop him off. He found the whole quantum idea fascinating, though he couldn't imagine how or why he was singled out by the universe.

Before long, they were at his house. He headed to his door as Lela turned around to drive off. That's when he spotted the red Maserati parked a short distance from his house, and a black van parked behind it. Confused, he turned the key and opened the door. As soon as he walked in, the hairs on his arms stood up. His mother was lying on her stomach in the middle of the living room floor.

"She'll live," said a male voice from the sofa.

As he looked toward the sofa, the blond-haired man with the scar was sitting there with gloves on and an aerosol can in his right hand.

"What do you want?" said Julian. "Who are you?"

"Time to sleep," said the man, who, in a single motion, sprayed the can toward Julian while pressing a wet rag against his own face with his other hand.

Within seconds, the room started to spin. A minty scent permeated his nostrils. He could feel himself falling as everything went black.

CHAPTER 15

VALUABLE CARGO

Lela was halfway down the street when she glanced in her rear-view mirror and noticed a black van backing out of a parking spot and stopping in front of Julian's house. She slowed down to a stop and continued to watch. A stocky bald man came out of the driver side of the vehicle, leaving the driver door open. At the same time, she spotted a tall blond-haired man walking from the house to greet him, carrying what looked like a large, black canvas sack over his shoulder. They both walked quickly to the van and carefully loaded the oversized sack into the van's rear door. Then the bald guy climbed into the back and shut the rear door, while the blond man got into the driver side. Suddenly, a horrible thought came to her mind.

She put the car in reverse and sped backward, just as the van took off. She screeched to a halt in front of Julian's house and dashed out of the car and ran to the front door.

She banged on the door and rang the bell, but nobody answered. Then she tried the knob. The door was unlocked. She turned the knob and opened the door, calling Julian's name and then Mrs. Black's. She heard a groan and ran inside.

As soon as she entered, she saw Laura Black sitting in the middle of the living room floor in a daze.

"Oh my God, are you okay?" said Lela, rushing up to her. "What happened? Where's Julian?"

"Julian?" said Laura, half asleep. "I don't know... I..." She looked up at Lela. "Was he here? The carpet man was looking for him."

"The carpet man? What did he look like?"

Laura tried to get up. "He had blond hair. A tall fellow."

"No, stay there. Don't try to get up yet."

Lela grabbed her cell phone and called De Luca. Her heart was pounding as she thought of Julian being taken God knows where. He answered immediately.

"Listen, she said. Some guys in a black van took Julian and drugged his mother. Ninety-eight-fifty-nine Gifford Street."

"You're kidding me."

"I wish I was. If you could send an ambulance to have her checked out, I'd appreciate it. I'm in pursuit now. Put out an APB. Be on the lookout for a black van, make unknown. Driver is a male Caucasian with blond hair, extremely tall, six-foot-four to six-seven in height, thirty to forty-five years of age. At least one accomplice is in the rear of the van, a heavy-set, bald male Caucasian. Five-nine to five-eleven in height, age unknown. This just happened, so they couldn't have gotten far."

After she hung up with De Luca, she instructed Laura to remain where she was until the paramedics got there. Then she darted out of the house and tried calling Julian's cell phone. Almost immediately, she heard his ringtone in the grass just behind her.

"Damn it," she said. She grabbed the phone and put it in her pocket, then ran to her SUV and took off in the direction of the van. She figured they may be trying to get to a major highway, so she headed toward Welsh Road, the quickest route to I-95.

♦

The first thing Julian realized when he started to drift in and out of consciousness was that his hands were tied behind his back. Zip ties. That's what it felt like. They were sharp and cutting into his wrists. His eyes were still closed. He was seated and being tossed back and forth, as if his chair was atop an unruly washing machine. What was holding him in place? He opened his eyes partially, but he still felt groggy. He glanced at the floor and to his sides. He was in some kind of van, on a long bench seat that ran along the side. A seat belt kept him in place as the vehicle shifted and rocked. He looked to his right. A driver. Someone was driving, but he couldn't see who. The vehicle hit a pothole. It reminded him of the airport shuttle he was in once when his mother took him to Florida, with every bump in the road rattling his bones. He closed his eyes again. He was half asleep, and for a minute he thought he might be headed on vacation somewhere. But where? Then he remembered the zip ties. This was no vacation.

His pulse quickening, he opened his eyes fully and realized there was a bald man sitting opposite him, smiling. He appeared to be in his sixties or seventies. Julian looked down and saw that the man had a gun aimed at his chest.

"Oh good, you're awake," said the man, with a heavy Russian accent. The Russian's happy demeanor seemed at odds with the pistol he was holding. He reminded Julian of the pizza delivery guy who delivers to their house once a week, a chatty man from Siberia with a wonderfully jovial personality. Except, *that* man never pointed guns at him.

Then he remembered the blond guy sitting in his living room. It started coming back to him. His mother. Last he saw her, she was lying on the floor in their living room.

"My mother," he said. "Where is she?"

"She's f-i-i-n-e," said the Russian. "Don't worry."

"Why did you take me? Where are we going?"

"You're going to save the world," said the man.

Save the world? These people must be fanatics.

"Listen," he said, "whatever you saw on TV, that was all wrong. I can't really—"

"I see nothing on TV," said the Russian. You're going to visit old friend. This is what I know. You'll be fine."

"If it's a friend, then why the gun?" He couldn't imagine who the guy was talking about. He didn't recall any old friends, at least none who would have him kidnapped.

"It's for your good," said the Russian. "To make sure you sit still."

Julian looked at his seatbelt and thought of the zip ties holding his hands together. "How could I *not*?"

The man just smiled at him.

The van swerved sharply to the right, sending intense pain through Julian's arms.

"I'm more likely to get hurt from bad driving," he said.

Just then, the van pulled to the right and then backed up until it slowed down to a stop.

"Time to get out," said the Russian.

The van's rear door opened, and the Russian man undid his seatbelt and escorted him out of the van. As soon as Julian stepped out of the van, he was face to face with the tall blond man with the scar. He must've been the one driving.

"Hurry," said the blond man. He pointed to another vehicle parked behind theirs, a red van that had a "Percy's Catering" sign on the side.

The Russian led Julian toward the back of the red van. Just as Julian was about to climb into the back of the vehicle, he thought he spotted Lela's SUV approaching in the distance. He turned and noticed a green highway entrance sign ahead of them that said I-95 Philadelphia.

Just then, the blond man pushed him into the van and jumped in behind him, shutting the door. "Go!" he yelled to the Russian, who had now climbed in the driver seat.

The van took off with a jerk as Julian tumbled off the seat. The blond man dragged him back up like a rag doll and strapped him into the seat. The interior was like the other van, with two long bench seats on opposing sides. There were no windows, aside from the front widows, which were visible from the back.

"We're being followed," said the Russian. "It's the woman."

"Lose her," said the blond man.

"What woman?" said Julian.

He tensed up as the van picked up speed. It had to be going a hundred miles an hour. The van shifted sharply to the left, and then to the right, each time causing Julian's wrists to throb with pain from the zip ties. At one point it felt like it was going to tip over.

"You know what woman," said the blond man.

The high-speed hell continued, and Julian was beginning to wonder if they'd get wherever they were going alive. He was too tense to even ask questions. The vehicle shifted again to the right, and then a loud bang coming from the rear of the van startled him. Then another, like the sound of a shovel banging against the van.

"She's shooting at us," yelled the Russian.

"Just the tires," said the blond man, calmly. "She won't risk hitting him."

The van swerved to the left sharply, throwing Julian against the seat belt straps. He winced as they dug into his shoulders.

"Careful," said the blond man. "He's valuable."

Valuable cargo. Julian started thinking about one of his stories he never published; about a kidnapped politician who was so aware of his value that he used it as leverage to get his kidnappers to do pretty much anything he wanted. If only it were that easy.

Just then, he heard another loud bang and the van started shifting erratically from side to side.

"She got one of the tires," said the Russian.

"Keep going," said the blond man.

The van sped up again.

Julian felt like he was in a rodeo as the van weaved in and out of traffic on a blown tire.

"She's a few cars back," said the Russian.

"Get off at Callowhill," said the blond man. "We'll make the next switch. If she gets too close, kill her."

"Listen, this isn't worth it," said Julian, as the van continued its high-speed evasion.

"It's well worth it," said the blond man.

"If I'm worth so much, then you can't afford to get me killed," he said, thinking of his story. "You don't know her. She doesn't give up."

The van shifted again, throwing him back against the seat.

"Neither do we."

"Let me go," he said. "I promise, I'll go voluntarily wherever you want me to. Nobody has to die."

The blond man peered at him for about ten uncomfortable seconds. "You are close," he said. "You and Detective Lela Mars. She will do anything for you."

"Yes," said Julian, as the van shifted again. "That's right."

"Would you do anything for her?"

He was surprised the man knew her name. He nodded. "Don't hurt her. I'll go wherever you want me to go."

Just then, the van pulled off the highway to the right. The blond man turned to the driver. "Stop here," he said.

"But we're not at—"

"Do as I say."

As the van stopped, the blond man quickly removed Julian's seat belt.

"You have a strong sense of duty," said the man, as he pulled a knife out of his holster.

Julian tensed up as the blond man brought the knife toward him and then reached around him to cut the zip ties.

"Let's see how strong."

In one motion, the man kicked open the rear doors and threw Julian out of the van. Julian tumbled onto the street. Pain ran through his arms and legs as he rolled on the hard asphalt. He stood up gingerly just as a car screeched its brakes to avoid hitting him. He froze.

It was Lela's SUV.

He practically jumped into the passenger side as quickly as he could.

"My mother?" he said, winded.

"She's fine. Are you okay?" He realized they were on the exit ramp, with several impatient drivers honking their horns behind them.

"I think so," he said, as cars started squeezing around them.

"Good. Buckle up."

She hit the gas as he rushed to put his seatbelt on.

"I put out an ABP on the red van," she said, as they drove straight ahead onto 2nd Street in the Old City historic district of Philadelphia, which Julian recognized, having reluctantly visited once with his mother.

"It won't do any good," he said. "They're making another switch."

"We can still catch them. Why'd they let you go, anyway?"

"I don't know, I think—"

"You've got to be kidding me," said Lela, hitting the brakes as an old Chrysler sedan ahead of them was stopped in the middle of the right lane, with construction blocking the left lane. She honked her horn.

The driver-side door opened slowly, and an elderly man got out. He looked to be in his eighties, at least, and made his way toward their car. Lela rolled down her window.

"Sir, you need to move your car," she said.

"I'm looking for Bookbinders," said the old man.

"I have no idea what that is," said Lela. "Now please, you have to move your car."

Just then, the man's wife got out of the passenger's side and starting meandering toward them with a cane.

"Harry," she yelled. "I told you. That hasn't been here in twenty years."

"It's straight ahead, Harry," yelled Lela. "Just go!"

The man turned around and yelled to his wife, "I told you it was here."

Julian turned to Lela. "Is it really straight ahead?"

"I have no idea," she said.

After the elderly couple got back in their car, Lela and Julian were finally able to get moving, but it was clear the van had quite a head start. They continued straight ahead and then Julian spotted the red van up a side street to the right—a narrow cobblestone alley called Quarry Street.

"There," he said.

Lela skidded to the right and stopped the SUV. She ran out of the car holding her gun and darted toward the Percy's Catering van, which was stopped.

Julian got out of the car and watched. He was kicking himself for not insisting Lela let them go for now. But she wouldn't have listened anyway. He observed helplessly as Lela ran toward the red vehicle with her weapon pointed. He wanted to yell to her to come back and wait for backup, but he didn't want to distract her. He made that mistake once in his game and it cost Cassie—or at least her avatar Natalya—her life. But this wasn't a game. There were no do-overs. He could feel the sweat on his palms as Lela opened the driver door, keeping her gun aimed inside the vehicle. He prayed nothing would go wrong.

After a few seconds, she put the weapon down and looked back at him, shaking her head. She slammed the van door shut and trotted back to Julian.

"They're gone," she said, before grabbing a few photos of the license plate.

After they got back in her SUV, she handed Julian his cell phone.

"Thought you might want this," she said, smiling.

"Oh my God, thank you."

He immediately called his mother, and, after a few rings, she answered.

"Julian, thank God, are you okay?"

"I'm fine. I'm with Lela. How are you feeling?"

"I'm okay. I'm at Holy Redeemer. They're sending me home. Listen, I don't know who these men were, but I spoke with Officer De Luca. They're bad people, Julian. After your TV report, I don't think we're safe at all."

"We'll take care of it, don't worry. They were after me and it's being taken care of. For now, you're in good hands."

"I sure hope so. Please be careful. I'm so worried."

"I'm okay. I'll talk to you when I get back. And mother?"

"Yes?"

"You did say you wanted me to get out more."

"Very funny."

As soon as he disconnected, Lela backed the SUV out of the alley and onto 2nd Street.

"By the way," she said, as she merged into the traffic, "you never answered my question. Why did they let you go?"

Julian tried to think of a non-awkward way to put it. "I told them I didn't want anyone to get hurt," he said. "I said if they let me go, I'd come voluntarily."

"And they just let you go?" she said. "Just like that?"

"Pretty much."

"Something doesn't sound right," she said. "It's too easy."

"Well, you *were* shooting at their tires," he said, as they passed a lively Cuban restaurant called Cuba Libre on the right. "They probably realized I was right."

"And what arrangements did you make?"

"Arrangements?"

"You said you told them you'd come voluntarily. Where did you arrange to meet them?"

"I didn't." That hadn't even dawned on him. "I guess they'll contact me."

"Did they say anything else? Think. What exactly did they say before they let you go?"

He tried to remember what they said as they passed Chestnut Street. It was hard to recall the details, as everything happened so fast and he was focused on staying alive, not to mention keeping her alive.

For now, he decided to share the awkward part, in case it was relevant.

"He asked if you and I were close," he said. "The blond guy. He knew your name. He was the same guy I saw back at my house with all the press."

"They did their homework. Anything else?"

"I told him you wouldn't give up until I was safe. Because I didn't want them to think they were home free, right? But then the guy said something weird. He asked if I'd do anything for you, too."

"And what did you tell him?"

"I said yes. Of course." He looked at her as if she had to ask.

"Is that when he cut you loose?"

"Yeah."

Lela's face went pale. "Shit."

"He said I had a strong sense of duty. Then he said, 'Let's

see how strong,' and he pushed me out."

"Dammit, we have to get back to my house," she said. Frantically, she pulled onto the sidewalk to get around the other cars and then skidded right onto Walnut Street.

After a couple of wild turns and a near-miss incident with a taxi, they were back onto I-95 North. It occurred to him he might have been better off in the van.

"What's wrong?" he said, once he could loosen his grip on the door handle and breathe. "What are you thinking?"

"It's just a hunch," she said. "I hope I'm wrong. Otherwise, they have a hell of a collateral in case you don't cooperate."

"What?"

"My family."

CHAPTER 16

LONDON CALLING

Lela couldn't wait to get home. She had called De Luca on the way to check on her family, but he hadn't called back yet. She prayed she was wrong, but she had a sinking feeling she wasn't. She never felt more helpless in her life. Finally, after about a half hour, the call came in through the car speaker.

"Any news?" she said.

"Looks like nobody's home," said De Luca. "The door's locked. No sign of foul play. It's your dad's day off, maybe they're out."

She breathed a sigh of relief. "Can you wait there till I get back?"

"Sure thing. By the way, I just noticed. His car's here. Could they have taken someone else's car. Your mom's maybe?"

"I doubt it. She drives a Mini Cooper."

"Bright blue?"

"That's the one. Is it there?"

"Yeah."

Now she was starting to worry again. Their door was

locked, but nobody was answering and their cars were home. It was highly unlikely they'd been picked up by any friends. He dad was such a control freak, he always insisted on driving. Just the thought of him being a passenger in someone's car was ludicrous. And it wasn't like them to not answer the door, which made her even more nervous. All these guys had to do was knock on the door and someone would've answered. The more she thought about it, either someone was in the house with them waiting for her, or her family was already taken.

"Do you want me to call a locksmith?" said De Luca. "Your dad might not like me breakin' the window."

"No, I'll be home soon," she said.

"I'll wait here."

Lela wasn't sure what to think as she disconnected.

"These guys couldn't have gotten there yet, right?" said Julian. "And now De Luca's there."

She thought about it. On one hand, Julian was right. The door was locked and De Luca was there, and it's unlikely the men would've gotten there already. But what if they had other contacts working with them—men who could've gotten there sooner?

"No, it's not right," she said. "They should be home."

"Do you think maybe someone picked them up?" said Julian.

"I can't imagine who." She picked up speed and raced home as quickly as she could. Her mind was all over the place. She hoped her fears were unwarranted, but she sensed something was wrong. And usually, her instincts were correct. She thought again about everything Julian had told her. He said they had let him go just after asking if he'd do anything for her. Then they said they were going to test his strong sense of duty. It *had* to involve her somehow. They had already done the research. They knew her name. What else did they know? The more she thought about it, the more she was convinced they were going to go after her family—and probably have already.

Finally, she pulled onto her street. She saw De Luca standing outside by his car. She was almost afraid to get out.

She pulled behind De Luca and stepped out of the car. Her legs felt like jelly, as if she were in a dream, trying to step though four feet of water. She heard Julian leave the car too, but she was barely processing anything. She just wanted to get to the door.

De Luca approached her. "Don't panic," he said. "I'm sure they're okay."

Half-dazed, she went to the door and put her key in the lock. She hesitated. It felt like she was frozen in time. As long as she stayed out here, things would remain as they were. Nothing in her life will have changed. But as soon as she crossed that doorway, all bets were off. Then again, she wasn't raised to avoid problems. She steeled herself, took a breath, and then quickly turned the key and pushed the door open. She took her pistol out of her holster just in case.

All was quiet as she walked in the house. There were no signs of a struggle. Everything was in its place. She looked up the stairs and called out for her father and Shelly. Then Crystal. They couldn't have all been sleeping.

"Hey Lela," said De Luca from the dining room. "You better see this."

Her heart sunk as she ran to the dining room. Julian was standing there with De Luca. Both made way for her as she spotted a yellow sheet of paper taped to the dining room chandelier. She was hoping it was a note from her dad saying where they were, but from the look on De Luca's and Julian's faces, she knew it wasn't. Then she realized it was typewritten. She placed her pistol back in its holster, then pulled the note down and read it aloud.

"To Detective Lela Mars," she said. "We have your family.

If you wish to see them again, these instructions must be followed explicitly."

She looked up at Julian and De Luca, who were visibly shocked. She continued reading.

"Julian Black," she said, "is to proceed directly to the Grand Concourse at 30th Street Station in Philadelphia, where at precisely five-thirty PM he will be given further instructions to be taken by car to a private plane. He will be delivered to London tomorrow morning to meet with an old friend, where he will perform a simple task."

"What the hell!" said De Luca.

"London?" said Julian. She could see the panic and confusion on his face. "What old friend?"

She resumed reading the note. "He must arrive alone on the R3 Regional Rail. If there are any signs of police interference, he will be collected at a future time and your family will be disposed of. We see everything."

She paused for a moment to digest what she'd just read. Then she continued.

"If instructions are followed, your family and Mr. Black will be returned unharmed within three to five days. Warm Regards, Friends of SB."

"Who's SB?" said Julian.

"I was hoping *you'd* know," said Lela.

"No clue. But it's obvious I have to go."

Lela held up her hand. "Wait a minute," she said. "I got you into this. I have to figure a way out."

"You didn't get me into anything," said Julian. "I came to you, remember? Besides, they said they'll return everyone unharmed."

"And you believe them?" said De Luca. "Believe me, I've dealt with ransom notes. You have to negotiate, and then when you make the transfer, you track the bastards."

"This isn't a ransom note," said Lela. "They're not after

money. And we have no way to contact them if we wanted to."

De Luca threw up his hands. "Then I don't know. Who the hell are these guys anyway?"

"Whoever they are," said Lela, "they must have a pretty big network. These are pros. And these couldn't have been the guys I was chasing. They had to be somewhere close to get here this fast."

"Well, that's pretty clear," said De Luca.

"The only thing clear right now," said Julian, "is that one of you has to take me to the train station."

"I can't let you do that," she said. "Let's think."

"Lela, think about it. If I never came to you in the first place, this never would've happened. They wouldn't have even known about me."

"You don't know that," she said. "The note said it was an old friend. Are you sure you don't know anyone with the initials SB?"

Julian shook his head. "I can't think of anyone. You'd be surprised how few people I know."

She tried to think about options, but nothing was coming to mind.

"So, who's taking me to the train?" said Julian. "Or do I have to call a taxi?"

"I hate to say it, but he's right," said De Luca. "I don't see any other choice here."

Lela looked at Julian. "Are you sure you're okay doing this?" she said.

"Of course not," he said. "But I'm doing it, and that's that. Like the note said, it's a simple task. How bad can it be?"

"One thing I learned from years on the force," said De Luca. "Never say 'How bad can it be?'"

"Not really helpful," said Julian.

Lela turned to De Luca. "Listen, I'll take him to the train.

But the word on the street has to be that my dad took the family to visit a sick relative, you got it? I don't want any eyes on this."

"Sick relative it is," he said. "Now *you* listen." He put a hand on her right shoulder and squeezed. "This is gonna work out, you got it? Julian's gonna do his thing and come back, and in a few days' time we'll be havin' some beers with your dad and figurin' out how to track down these assholes."

She nodded. She thought she could see a small teardrop forming in his eye and she remembered something her dad said. De Luca was like a good piece of Italian bread. Rough and crusty on the outside, and soft as a pillow on the inside. Now she could see what he meant.

She hoped De Luca was right. She was counting on it. More than anything, she would owe Julian big-time. He may have spent his life clinging to the shadows, but this was the most selfless, courageous thing she'd ever seen anyone do. The least she could do was keep the faith that it would work.

♦

After dropping Julian off at the Philmont train station, giving him a heartfelt hug for his noble sacrifice and wishing him luck, Lela headed back to what was now home for her. It felt weird walking into an empty house. It seemed like a lifetime ago that they'd had the party for her five-years' service. Now, her whole life and everyone in it was in the hands of complete strangers.

After about an hour of sitting at her laptop and searching license plates and multiple variations of Percy's Catering—including words like *deli* or *food services*—she wasn't having any luck. She sat for a few moments to contemplate what else she could do without drawing too much attention to her situation. She decided to head out to a place she'd always visited to clear her mind—the immaculate, sprawling grounds of the old cathedral in nearby Bryn Athyn. Luckily, it was only a ten-minute ride, as it was getting dark.

When she got there, she parked in a small, empty lot on the grounds. The signs said the grounds closed at dusk, but she'd wandered there before at night without incident.

She'd always marveled at the Bryn Athyn Cathedral itself, an Early Gothic-style building she once heard was modeled after the seventh century Gloucester Cathedral in England. The acres of rolling hills and old stone castle-like mansions and courtyards made her feel like she was back in the times of King Arthur. Her father used to tell her there was a wise old lion way up in the main tower of the cathedral, and if she listened closely, the great king always gave good advice. She could really use it now.

As she stood at the foot of the floodlit cathedral, dusk had set in and the moon was rising, giving an eerie, Van Gogh-like luminescence to the cloudy evening skies above. She gazed up at the imposing main tower and noticed a plane going by. It was headed east. Somewhere up in those same skies, a private plane would soon be taking Julian to London in that very direction—if it wasn't in the air already.

A wave of inspiration came to her. She wouldn't let her search be a dead end and she wasn't about to give up. She was a detective and she needed to get back to what she did best. She would do some private groundwork and try to find out what she could about the organization and where they might've taken Julian—with or without license plates. She'd see if she could dig up who this mysterious SB was. At the least, she'd be prepared to strike back when Julian and her family finally returned. And if they didn't return in a couple days, she'd go after them herself and try to bring them back. She'd start with Dr. Schaffler in the morning and see if he found the old records. She'd talk to Julian's mother to see what she remembered. Somehow, she needed to learn more about Julian's past, because that's where the answers had to be. She was sure of it.

Maybe there was something to that wise old lion story after all.

CHAPTER 17

A FOGGY DAY

J ulian stood in the cavernous main concourse of 30th Street Station, marveling at the towering limestone columns and the ornate, coffered ceiling that had to be at least a hundred feet above his head. At Lela's suggestion, he'd gone to the currency exchange and purchased some cash for London in case he needed it. He had a small carry-on bag of toiletries and a change of clothes. Now, he could hear people's voices echoing as they scurried to and from their respective trains. He glanced around for any sign of someone coming toward him, the mysterious person who would be meeting him. The uncertainty of it all was disorienting. He realized he probably wouldn't be too difficult to spot with his white gloves on. Just then, his cell phone buzzed with a text. He pulled it out of his pocket to see who it was. It looked like it was from a foreign phone number. He brought up the message.

Exit the glass doors to your left.

At once, his thoughts ran rampant as to the levels of personal intrusion this violated. How did they know his cell phone number? And how did they know where he was standing? He scanned the area around him, but there was nobody in the vicinity who looked particularly suspicious. It was hard to tell with so many people scampering in different directions. A father and his two kids were sitting on one of the benches behind him. Six feet from them sat a man who looked practically homeless, rooting through his bags and pulling out a sandwich. Two teenage girls on another bench were horsing around and pushing each other, giggling nonstop.

He gathered up his courage and headed toward the glass doors that led outside. As soon as he stepped into the open air, he saw a black sedan with tinted windows. The rear door was open. He glanced around and saw no other cars, aside from a taxi that was picking up a man in a navy suit. He wasn't sure if he was supposed to wait for someone, or if the black sedan was for him. He assumed the latter. He waited for about a minute, and then received another text. He looked at it. The message consisted of two simple words.

Get in.

He stepped inside the car and the door automatically shut and locked. A solid metal barrier separated the two rows of seats, so he couldn't see who was up front or driving.

"Hi," said Julian.

There was no response.

"I thought the note said I was going to see an old friend," he said, "It feels more like an old enemy."

"Pass your phone through the slot," said a metallic-sounding male voice through a speaker.

He noticed a small unopened slot at the bottom of the metal barrier. He pushed his phone through the little swing door and could feel someone grasp it from the other side. He tried leaning down and pushing on the slot to see if he could see through it, but it was apparently locked. It occurred to him they must've done this a lot.

"Do I get it back?" he said.

"Yes," said the robot-ish voice, after a slight delay.

As soon as the car began to move, the side windows automatically frosted up so he couldn't even see where they were going. He put on his seat belt and began to wonder if this was such a good idea.

"Where are we going?" he said.

They didn't answer. He realized it was a stupid question, considering the trouble they took to keep him in the dark, but he figured it couldn't hurt to ask. He closed his eyes and told himself that all would be well. He was just there to do a simple task, like they said. Most likely they'd need him to read someone's mind, and then he'd be sent home, back to his mundane life. At least until they needed him again for something else, a thought that suddenly disturbed him the more he thought about it. He couldn't help but feel Pandora's box had been opened.

His mind wandered to the events of the day. Lela was right. These people were well organized. He racked his brain trying to think of who from his past might want to use him and for what purpose. Eventually, he gave up, too exhausted to think. He'd find out soon enough. At least he wasn't in a crazy van ride this time with a gun pointed at him.

He was startled when someone up front tapped on the barrier and his phone appeared through the slot. He took it and examined the display. There was no mobile signal. The phone wasn't in airplane mode, so somehow they must've disabled the ability to call or text—and more importantly, to be tracked. He put it back in his pocket and closed his eyes again.

After about half an hour, the car came to a stop.

"Proceed to the plane and board," said the voice from the

front. "Leave your bag."

"But it has—"

"Leave your bag."

His door opened automatically. As soon as he stepped out of the car, he saw that he was in the middle of a private airfield, with some kind of hangar off to the left. It was nearly dark outside, but a couple of floodlights on tall poles illuminated the area. A small white jet was parked up ahead with no markings on it, aside from a sleek, maroon stripe running across the side. A set of steps led up to the aircraft door. There wasn't a soul around. He made his way to the boarding steps and climbed up. His feet felt like dead weights.

As he stepped into the main cabin, he could see that nobody was inside either. No passengers. No flight attendants. He assumed there was a pilot. Three white leather seats with tables ran along either side.

He noticed the table by the middle seat on the left had a glass of red wine and a small plate of assorted cheeses and crackers on it, along with a couple of miniature jars of jam. Next to the plate was a place card that said *Mr. Julian Black*. As far as treatment went, this was starting to seem a little friendlier—at least in terms of kidnappers and international criminals. He took a seat and buckled himself in.

He wasn't much of a wine drinker, but he didn't want to upset his hosts, so he tried a sip. It was much too dry and tart for his taste and he felt his cheeks pucker. He picked up one of the small multigrain crackers with brie and spread some of the fig jam onto it and took a bite. It felt good to eat something, as he realized he hadn't had a thing to eat since an early lunch before Dr. Schaffler's. They probably knew it, too. They seemed to know everything else about him. He devoured the rest of the plate in minutes. As he waited for the plane to take off, he began to feel dizzy. He heard a slight hissing sound and thought it might be in his head. Then he noticed what looked like gas or steam coming from the overhead vent. That was the last thing he remembered before dozing off.

He felt someone slapping his face softly.

"Mr. Black," said a voice with an English accent. "Mr. Black."

Groggy, he opened his eyes. "Did we take off yet?" he said to the man talking to him, a black-haired, Latino-looking man in a pilot uniform. Then he realized, the sun was shining on his face from the window through the clouds. It was daytime.

"Sir, we have landed. We are here in London. Please follow me."

That's when he realized. They drugged him! Fortunately, he felt no worse for wear, other than his head feeling like a bowling ball. He unbuckled his seat belt and carefully stood up from the chair, trying to get his bearings. Once firmly upright, he shook off the cobwebs and followed the pilot out the exit door and down the steps into the daylight.

As soon as he set foot on the ground, he could see it was quite foggy, which shouldn't have surprised him in London. The sun was peeking through the haze, looking like God's judgment coming down onto the empty airfield. He wasn't sure if that was a good sign or a bad sign. Since he was neither religious nor superstitious, he shrugged the thought aside.

He heard footsteps behind him. He turned to see the blond man with the scar descending the steps from the plane. He must've been in the cockpit with the pilot the whole time. The blond man nudged him forward as the pilot headed back toward the plane.

Ahead in the distance, he saw someone approaching through the fog. As a figured emerged, he could see it was a woman. As she got closer, her features came into view. She was a stunning, older woman with silver hair. She carried herself as if she owned the world. She nodded to the blond man and then reached out her gloved hand toward Julian.

"Welcome to London," she said with a slight smile as he shook her hand—glove against glove. "I hope your trip was sufficiently peaceful." He couldn't place her accent. It sounded Eastern European or Scandinavian; he wasn't sure.

"I hardly remember it," he said, looking over at the blond man, who was standing stoically, like a sentry at a castle.

"Come, we will drive you," she ordered, the forced smile leaving her face. That smile must've been quite the ordeal for her to muster. She turned like a soldier and strode in the opposite direction at a swift pace.

He followed the steadfast woman to another black sedan, similar to the one back in Philadelphia. The blond man kept pace beside him.

As they approached the car, the woman directed him toward the right side of the vehicle where the rear door was open, while she headed toward the left front passenger side. He remembered from his video games that the driver is on the right in England.

"Is Lela's family here in London?" he said.

"They are being taken care of," she said, without turning around.

"Who's SB?" he said.

She didn't respond.

The blond man grabbed his shoulder before he could get in the car.

"Wait," said the blond man.

Another man got out of the front right side of the car, a tall, well-built guy in a dark suit, with sunglasses and a tweed flat cap. He must've been the driver. He approached Julian and put a black blindfold on him, tying it tightly behind his head. The next thing Julian knew, his hands were being tied behind his back once more. The two men guided him into the back seat of the car.

"Watch yer foot, lad," said the man, as Julian leaned back

against the seat and brought his right foot into the car. He waited for the door to slam, but instead he heard something else.

It was another spray, like the one the blond man sprayed at him back at his house. Within seconds, he smelled the familiar minty scent. He tried to gasp for whatever outside air he could breathe in. Then everything went dark.

CHAPTER 18

DR. SCHAFFLER'S NEWS

Lela was dying of curiosity as she approached Dr. Schaffler's office. Oddly enough, she was about to call him this morning when he had called her. He'd sounded frantic on the phone. He said he'd dug up the archives and discovered something she had to see. He'd tell her what it was when she got there. He said he didn't believe it himself. Huge news, he called it. He was of course concerned and supportive when she'd told him what had happened to Julian and her family, but more than anything he seemed preoccupied with his news.

Half out of breath, she entered the waiting room and rushed to the receptionist, who told her the doctor would see her as soon as he was done with his current patient.

"He really wants to see you," said the receptionist, who recognized her from the last time.

Lela took a seat on one of the waiting room chairs. There were two other patients in the waiting room, an elderly man and a younger guy who looked to be in his twenties. She picked up a magazine that was lying on the table nearby and blindly leafed through it, scanning the photos of celebrities going to cocktail parties and lounging in the sun on their fancy vacations. She couldn't even process what she was looking at. All she could think about was whatever the 'huge news' was the doctor was talking about, and how it might help her get her family back.

Finally, the door to the patient rooms opened. Instead of a nurse, Dr. Schaffler himself appeared and hurriedly waved her in. He looked like he was sneaking her in the back room for a covert drug deal. She practically jumped out of her chair and walked briskly to him, though she wanted to run. She didn't even bother checking the reactions of the other patients. As she took notice of the doctor's face, he looked more concerned than excited, though, like something was making him anxious.

"Are you okay?" she said.

"Honestly? I'm not sure," he said. "For the first time in my life, I'm stumped. Good thing you're a detective."

She followed him into his office, where just a day ago she'd sat with Julian. It was hard to believe it was only yesterday; it felt more like a lifetime ago. Her whole world had changed after that last visit when Julian was kidnapped. She wondered how he was faring in London, and where her family was being held. For all she knew, they were in London as well. One way or another she was determined to find out, and maybe this news would help shed some light on the situation.

"Like I told you on the phone," said the doctor, "I found the old archives. But I'm absolutely stymied by what's in them."

"What did you find out?" she said.

"I have a damn good memory," he said, ignoring the question. "I may be getting up in years, but I'm not senile and I'm sharp as a tack. At least that's what I've told myself, but now I'm starting to wonder. I specifically remember Laura bringing Julian to see me when he was nine years old. As sure as I'm sitting here, that was the first time I saw him. I can tell you, you don't forget a case like that."

"Do the archives say something different?"

"Hell yes," he said. "Apparently, his mother brought him here to see me four years earlier. When he was five."

She could see sweat starting to form on his brow; hopefully that wasn't the big news.

"That doesn't seem that unusual," she said, trying to reassure him. "It was a while ago. Maybe you forgot the details."

"I haven't gotten to the strange part yet," he said.

This was more like it. She could already feel a rush of adrenaline course through her veins, the way she did on her favorite cases when she knew a breakthrough was imminent. She could almost smell it.

"It says here in my notes," said Schaffler, "Julian wasn't the only kid his mother brought in that day. Get this. There were *two* kids. Julian was five and his brother was ten."

"His brother?" Julian never mentioned a brother.

"Sebastian," he said. "And here's the thing. Julian could read people's memories just by touching them. But his brother had a whole different issue. He could make people forget. Any strong or recent memories, he'd just touch them with his hand and they'd totally forget."

"That doesn't make any sense," she said. Her face must've looked like he'd told her the Earth was rectangular. She didn't even know how to process all the implications of what she'd just heard. "How could there be two people like that? And with the opposite skills?"

"I'm as lost as you are," he said. "It seems pretty clear the kid must've touched me and I forgot about him completely. Maybe it was by accident or maybe I tried to test him, but it specifically says in the notes I did *not* test him. Which doesn't surprise me because, well, we can see the results. It's like the whole incident was zapped from my memory I don't recall any of it, not even his m——."

"SB!" she said.

"I'm not following," said the doctor.

"Sebastian Black. When those kidnappers left the note, they signed it 'Friends of SB.'"

"Well, it wouldn't have been Black," he said. "That's Laura's last name."

She was confused. "Wouldn't Laura have been Sebastian's mother, too?"

"Oh, I thought you knew," he said. "Laura Black isn't Julian's real mother."

"What!?" She wasn't sure how much more bizarre information she could digest.

"No, Laura used to work for me. She adopted Julian when he was nine. The state brought him in for evaluation. That's when we learned about his 'gift.'" He made quotation signs with his hands. "On top of that, the poor kid was practically catatonic. Couldn't remember anything except his name and a few irrelevant details. Now I'm starting to understand why."

"His brother made him forget," she said.

"Exactly."

"But what happened to his real mother?"

"The story at the time was his birth mother ran off with a boyfriend or something. Turns out that was all a load of bunk, too."

"What do you mean?"

"Take a look at this." He pushed an old newspaper clipping across the desk toward her. She turned it around and examined it.

It was dated from ten years ago. The headline read: "Two Bodies Discovered in Pennypack Woods."

As she read the article, she wasn't sure what she was

looking at.

"I'll save you the time," he said. "It says some family's dog was digging in the woods behind their house and it uncovered two dead bodies, identified as Eve Galloway and Jack Rimshaw. Eve was the prior owner of the family's house."

"What's this have to do with Julian?" she said.

"Eve Galloway was Julian's real mother. That's where Julian—and apparently his brother—grew up. Rimshaw must've been the boyfriend she allegedly ran off with. Except it turns out they didn't run off, they were murdered, though nobody knew it till sixteen years later when those bodies were found."

She did the math in her head. That would've made Julian twenty-five at the time the bodies were found. Sebastian would've been thirty.

Lela tried to process everything as she studied the article. "Let me get this straight," she said as she looked up at the doctor. "Julian and his brother, Sebastian, are nine and fourteen years old when their mother disappears with the boyfriend. According to the article, the house was foreclosed and sold to the new owners after the mother vanished. Then, Julian ends up in a state agency and can't remember a thing. Plus, he seems in shock. Nobody remembers Sebastian. Then sixteen years later, the boys' mother is found murdered with the boyfriend behind their old house."

"That's about the size of it," he said. "But explain to me why Eve Galloway brought both those boys to see me when Julian was five and I have no recollection of it. And then I save the newspaper clipping from all those years later, and don't remember that either. Even Sebastian couldn't remove specific memories, could he?"

"You're the neurologist," she said, "but I don't see how that's possible."

"It's *not* possible," he said. "Plus, he would've had to come back all those years later and make me forget it.”

Lela thought more about the situation. “If Julian was that much in shock when he was nine,” she said, “it doesn’t seem a stretch to say he knew his mother was murdered. That leaves me with one horrible thought.”

“Sebastian killed the mother and made Julian forget.”

“And he killed the boyfriend,” she added. “It’s the only thing that makes sense.”

Dr. Schaffler’s face was pale. “I hope you’re wrong,” he said, “but I’m afraid you’re probably right.”

“It’s a bad habit of mine,” she said.

“But how could he have come back later and make me forget that article? And Laura too, probably. That’s one scary kid. Well… he’s not a kid anymore.”

“Until I find out more, it’s the only explanation,” she said.

“I agree.” He seemed to be contemplating this new theory, and then he slapped his forehead. “Oh yes,” he said, “there’s something else I found.”

“I’m not sure I can handle any more,” she said. Her head was already swimming with questions.

“This is technical,” he said. “I’ll keep it simple.” He took a pair of black rim eyeglasses out of his pocket and put them on, then pulled out a sheet of paper from his files. He studied the paper for a moment and then looked up. “It says in my notes, the DNA tests for both boys showed a possible abnormality.”

“What kind of abnormality?”

“Just some specific gene sequences that looked like they were altered, according to the geneticist. The trouble is, unlike, say, eye color, which is determined by a handful of genes, the genes that influence cognitive function are all over the place. Individually, the genes only have a small impact, but together? They account for about half the differences between people like you and I, cognitively speaking.”

“And which genes are different in Julian?”

"That's the problem. Right now, genetic science has only identified a small number of the genes that control our thinking. There are some sequences that are different in Julian than would be expected, but nobody knows what they influence. The bigger question to me is how they could've been changed in the first place."

"Isn't that possible these days?"

"Today? CRISPR-based technology could theoretically be used to alter genes through medicine. But even now, the technology isn't quite there yet, and it sure wouldn't have been back then. It's in the early stages and there's all kinds of legal and ethical challenges going on. So, either someone altered these kids' genes using a technology that didn't exist yet, or it was a one in a gazillion freak of nature that struck twice. Take your choice."

Her head was about to explode. She started thinking about all the possibilities—all the implications. Then she realized she was getting off track. "Doctor, this... just... blows my mind. But before I can even think about what caused all this, I think I need to first find out where Sebastian is, and then we can go from there."

He nodded. "Fair enough. So, what's your plan?"

"Now I pay a visit to Laura Black and see what she knows. I'd bet anything that SB is Sebastian. What he needs Julian for, I'm not sure. If he's that devious and if he's working with the kind of guys who took Julian, it could be anything. Now the question is what the B stands for. Are you sure he wasn't also adopted by Laura?"

The doctor put his glasses back in his pocket. "Hell, I'm not sure of anything at the moment. I doubt it. I do know if Laura knew about those murders, there's no way she would have told Julian, for his own good. I don't think she even told him he was adopted."

That Julian was probably in the dark about all this made

Lela feel a little better. She didn't think he'd hide something so monumental from her. Then again, how much did she really know about him?

"If you don't mind," said the doctor, "I have to ask. What are you going to do about Sebastian?"

"I'm gonna find him," she said, as she took a photo of the newspaper article with her cell phone camera. "I have to. He has my family. That's my angle. I know his secret now. So, it's his freedom for my family. Then I'll hunt him down after I get them back."

The doctor crinkled his forehead. "That's good in theory," he said, "but if he's in London, there must be hundreds of Sebastians. You'll be looking for a needle in a haystack."

"I'll talk to their old neighbors," she said. "Someone's bound to remember him. I figured, he couldn't have made the whole neighborhood forget, right? I know he's about forty years old. Who knows what else I'll find out?"

"Smart," he said. "You oughtta be a detective." He smiled.

"I'll look into it," she said, tongue firmly in cheek. "One last question."

"Shoot."

"Julian and Sebastian. If they touch hands, who wins?"

"Well, Julian doesn't remember him," he said. "So, there's your answer."

"But would Julian remember Sebastian's memories?"

"If he did," said the doctor, "then he's fooled all of us. But it's a good thought. Julian might have some of the answers in his head and not even realize it. So, for everyone's sake, I hope you get him back."

"I will," she said. "I have to."

CHAPTER 19

JULIAN'S DILEMMA

Julian's eyes began to open. He could sense he was lying flat on his back. Was he in bed? A ceiling fan started to come into focus. It wasn't spinning and he was able to see his own reflection in a couple of the silver blades. He was still half asleep and wasn't quite clear where he was or what day it was. Then it started to come back to him. The plane. Last he remembered, he'd deboarded the plane in London and had been unceremoniously blindfolded and thrown in a car.

He lifted his head off the firm pillow and realized he'd been sleeping on a brown leather couch. He moved his hands, relieved to see he wasn't handcuffed. He still had his white gloves on. Between being drugged and the jetlag, he just wanted to put his head down and fall back to sleep.

"Morning, Julian," said a male voice with a slight British accent. Julian practically jumped to a sitting position and saw a man sitting at a desk—a well-dressed dark-haired guy in a black turtleneck and a gray tweed suit that looked expensive. The man got up and approached him with an outstretched hand.

"Excuse the gloves," said Julian, as he shook the man's

hand.

"Oh, I know all about your gloves, Julian. That's why you're here. I'm Sebastian Blaine."

So, this was SB. He seemed genial enough. Julian stared at the man's face. He looked vaguely familiar, but he didn't know where from.

"Do I know you?" he said.

"Of course you know me," said Blaine. "You just don't remember."

"Why not?" Julian was beginning to think this guy might be able to explain why he couldn't remember his childhood.

"We'll get to all that," said Blaine. "I wouldn't want to put dessert before the main course."

Julian gazed at the floor-to-ceiling window that overlooked London. He recognized this view from his Stealth Invaders game, particularly the time he and Cassie were hunting down the mastermind, Gunnar Hawkes.

"We're in the Shard," he said, getting up and walking toward the window. He'd never seen a view like it, at least not in real life, and this didn't even seem to be one of the higher floors.

"Two points for Julian," said Blaine. "For a man that doesn't get around much, I'm impressed."

Julian turned to face Blaine. "But if we're in the Shard, why'd they bother blindfolding me?"

"They blindfolded you?" said Blaine, leaning against his espresso-colored desk. "How rude."

"I thought they worked for you."

"It's more of a partnership of necessity. They need me. And I need *you*."

"I don't get it."

"You will. Have you eaten? I can call for something." Blaine reached toward a panel on his desk.

"I had a little on the plane. Where's Lela's family?" Part of him was starving, but between being drugged, the exhaustion, and the anxiety about what was next, he couldn't stomach the thought of eating.

Blaine moved his hand away from the panel and smiled. "Happy thoughts, Julian. They're here in London enjoying the hospitality. Once you help me, then you'll all be on a plane back to Philadelphia, and all this will have been forgotten."

"I doubt any of us will forget this."

"I'm willing to bet you will," he said. "Now if you don't mind, I think we're both anxious to get this over with, so what do you say we get started?"

"Doing what, exactly?"

Blaine pointed to his office door.

"Once we go out that door," he said, "we're going to pass some very pleasant fellows and ladies working at their desks. Well, they're not *all* pleasant, but they don't know a thing about the business you and I have. And if you do want to return to the City of Brotherly Love, I suggest you keep it that way."

"You have my word."

"Good. We'll be heading to a separate part of the office that's a little more private. We're hosting a scientist named Max Baumann there. And by hosting, I mean we have him tied up."

"Tied up!?" Julian was wondering what he'd gotten himself into.

"Don't worry, he's a bit annoying anyway, but we do need some information from him. And it just so happens, you're tailor-made to get it."

"And what happens to him after?"

"He goes home."

"Seriously. You've kidnapped a tied-up scientist in the Shard and you're just going to let him go? You'll have to excuse me if I find that hard to believe."

Blaine patted him on the shoulder. "Trust is a virtue, Julian. Besides, your job is simple. I only need you to touch his hand and tell me everything you see. Compared to your usual fare, it should be a walk in the park on a cheery afternoon."

Julian wondered how Blaine would know what his 'usual fare' was.

"What am I looking for?" he said.

"The less you know, the better. Plus, I know how it works. You can't control what you see. You just see whatever floats to the top—random emotional memories, anything notable that's more recent. Weddings. Accidents. Big secrets. I'm counting on that last one."

"How do you know all that?" He kept getting the feeling Blaine knew exactly what it felt like, but he couldn't have.

"Ah, that's the big question, isn't it? I told you, Julian. We know each other better than you think."

"How?" He was dying to know, but he knew Blaine wasn't about to tell him. Not yet, anyway.

Blaine smiled. "Work first, then answers."

"Then I have one question I do need answered."

"What's that?"

"What if I fail? What if I don't see what you're expecting?"

"Then we go to Plan B."

"What's Plan B?"

"Happy thoughts, Julian. Happy thoughts."

◆

Julian followed Blaine out the door and down a corridor that ran through a bright, open office area, with white desks, light hardwood floors, and glass-enclosed offices and conference rooms on either side. Everything was sleek and modern. Floor-to-ceiling windows, just like in Blaine's office, offered spectacular views of London along the entire left side of the building. People were busy doing their work, having hallway conversations, or sitting in meetings. Most were dressed in casual business attire—sweaters, polo shirts, chinos, and so on. In one of the conference rooms, he noticed a few men and women in lab coats. He couldn't tell what kind of company this was, but it all looked legitimate. Not that he'd know, as he'd never worked in an office. In any case, he could absolutely believe what Blaine had said about none of them knowing anything about a kidnapped scientist in their midst.

He and Blaine approached a light wood-paneled wall straight ahead, which separated one part of the office from the other. Blaine led him to an obscured door built into the wall straight ahead toward the right, tapped a few numbers on a hidden keypad, and held the door open for him. Julian proceeded into an empty office area that looked to be under construction.

"Next room," said Blaine, before leading him to a similar door on the next wall and tapped a code again.

As soon as Julian entered the next room, he could see a stocky, middle-aged man with graying hair sitting on an armchair facing him—the scientist, no doubt. There was nothing much else in the large space other than a few other chairs placed randomly, and a small table. It looked like the poor scientist had duct tape around his legs and torso, and his hands must've been tied behind the chair.

Julian heard footsteps coming from the right and turned to see who was entering the room. He wished he hadn't looked. It was the blond man with the scar.

"Julian," said Blaine. "I'm sure you've met Hans."

"Yes, he's a real gas," he said.

"See, Hans," said Blaine. "He's funny."

Blaine turned to Julian. "Don't mind Hans," he said. "He doesn't laugh much. And neither does this guy." He pointed to the scientist.

"I have nothing to laugh about," said the scientist. He had a slight hint of a German accent. Or was it some British dialect?

Blaine looked over at Hans. "Hans, would you do the honors?"

Julian watched nervously as Hans pulled a large knife out of the black leather sheath on his belt holster and approached the scientist. The tall, blond behemoth, without a hint of emotion on his face, stepped behind the scientist and made what looked like an upward stabbing motion. A pained expression came upon the scientist's face as he brought his hands around to his lap and stretched his fingers in relief—no doubt glad to have had the uncomfortable restraints cut loose.

Julian knew exactly what that felt like. It wasn't too long ago when he'd had his hands tied in the van, and then later in the car when he'd been blindfolded. Whoever Blaine and his cronies were, they had to own stock in zip ties.

"Julian," said Blaine. "Meet Max Baumann. I think you two should shake hands. Without the gloves of course. You don't want to be uncivilized."

Julian slipped off his gloves and stuffed them into his pockets. He wasn't sure what he'd see in the scientist's memories, but he gave Baumann an apologetic look and extended his shaky arm toward him as a friendly gesture. Baumann didn't return the favor and instead kept his hand firmly where it was—on his lap.

Julian glanced at Blaine, who in turn nodded to Hans. Hans came around in front of Baumann and grabbed his right arm with an iron grip, forcibly raising it toward Julian.

"I don't mean you any harm," said Julian, as he grasped Baumann's hand. The scientist glared at him silently.

Julian closed his eyes, and immediately, he found himself sitting at a U-shaped conference table in some kind of government office. Photographs of space satellites and missiles adorned the ivory-colored walls. A highly decorated military man with silver hair sat opposite him, next to a middle-aged, fit black man in a navy-blue suit. At the head of the table to the right sat a large-framed man in his sixties or seventies with thinning gray hair and an intimidating stare. Next to him was a fortyish woman with auburn hair, wearing a navy-blue blazer and a white blouse. Judging by the two small flags standing on the table in front of them, they represented Britain and the US, respectively. Then Julian noticed the place cards in front of them—UK Permanent Secretary for Defense Ian Whitmore and US Deputy Secretary of Defense Allison Marx.

The US Deputy Secretary spoke first.

"Dr. Baumann," she said, "we're all grateful you could join us here today at the Pentagon. Secretary Whitmore is my UK counterpart, and across from you is United States General William Branson and Bernard Townsend, who represents MI6. We're here to present some good news, and I'm afraid some not so good news. First, I'll let General Branson share his update on the testing. General?"

Julian could already sense Baumann's anxiety level was high. He could feel the scientist's muscles tense up as he waited for the news.

"In a word, Doctor," said the general, "promising. Highly promising. We directed an ASAT vertical missile launch from an F-15 Eagle that was flying at thirty-two thousand feet. The goal was to hit a simulated target satellite orbiting at three-hundred miles. Same scenario as a similar launch that successfully destroyed its target. This time, your SARA device redirected the missile harmlessly into space. By all accounts, it would've been a direct hit otherwise. We also tested a ship-fired missile, with similar results."

"That's excellent news, General," said Baumann, relieved.

"The most encouraging test was the co-orbital one," said Branson. "That's where we launch a shrapnel warhead from an orbital satellite toward a target satellite. Then, as soon as the missile and the target are

orbiting in proximity to one another... boom! We detonate the warhead."

"But wasn't that what we were accusing the Russians of? Causing all that debris? I thought we were calling for a ban."

The general smiled. "This was quite a limited test. And again, the difference is, we're using simulated targets. No actual satellites were destroyed... or, I should say, would have been destroyed had SARA failed. Even the shrapnel was controlled. We didn't really detonate anything. The good news was, not a single piece of shrapnel hit its simulated target."

"I would expect nothing less," said Baumann. "What about energy weapons? Lasers."

"Well, that's why I say promising, Doctor. "We're in a pretty hot race with the Russians and the Chinese to get orbital laser platforms up and running. Luckily, the Russians' Polyus program failed. We're close to an orbital solution, but not quite ready to test yet. But with ground-based laser simulations in a controlled environment, SARA performed well, so, like I said—very promising."

"So, was that the bad news?" said Baumann.

"No, not quite, Doctor," said the deputy secretary, interrupting. "If the general is finished, I'll let Secretary Whitmore explain."

"The floor is yours, Secretary," said the general.

"Good evening, Doctor," said Whitmore, whose deep, resonant British voice made him sound like a butler from an old castle. "As you've heard, Beijing and Moscow already have ground-based weaponry that could disable our satellites. Our collective sources also tell us—and this is no surprise—that other parties are feverishly making strides at procuring the same capability. Need I remind you that in addition to your American satellites, the seven satellites in our Skynet program provide crucial services to nearly the entire planet. If they fail, Doctor Baumann, it's not just that Mr. and Mrs. McGillicuddy won't be able to watch the telly while they eat their porridge. Planes and ships will be isolated from communication. Soldiers will be separated from their command. Civil infrastructure, transportation, and food and medical supply chains will grind to a halt. So will the Internet and people's precious phones. Shall I go on?"

"Not necessary, Mr. Secretary," said Baumann. "I am well aware of the impacts."

"Good. I'll put it simply then. The risk of catastrophic loss due to hostile actions by an unfriendly nation—with the West unable to defend itself—is significant and growing by the minute. It is not a matter of 'if' someone will plunge us all into the dark ages. It's 'when.'"

The permanent secretary cleared his throat, and a waiter standing unobtrusively in the far corner of the room immediately rushed up to refill his glass of water. Whitmore took a sip and continued.

"Doctor," he said, "let me be clear. The SARA device changes everything. It neutralizes a significant global threat, and I might go so far as to say it makes the space war irrelevant. It is perhaps the single most important strategic asset on Earth, and I do not say that lightly. None of what I described will play out because of your device."

He stared at Baumann as if expecting a response.

"Pardon me," said Baumann, "but that is good news, is it not?"

"Allow me to finish, Doctor. Our men at MI6 have uncovered credible evidence that certain unsavory parties are aware of your achievements. How they came to this information is another matter, and I'm assuming you've followed security protocols."

"To the letter," said Baumann, surprised. Julian could feel Baumann's heart begin to pound with the fear that he was being stalked. He knew that fear all too well.

"Who are these individuals?" said Baumann. "Do you know?"

"We do not."

Townsend, the MI6 man opposite Baumann, interjected. "We've intercepted some communications, but we're still trying to trace them."

"What this means," said Deputy Secretary Marx, "is that we're securing your labs and transferring all existing plans and prototypes to Dugway."

"Dugway? said Baumann. "That's bioweapons."

"And more," she said. "We'll make the space. But I'm afraid for you the problem goes beyond that."

"How so?"

"If people are aware of what you're working on—and we don't know how much they know at this point—there's a good chance you'll be a target when you're not at the base."

"They would kill me? Surely, they must know there are other scientists who could continue my work."

"I think kidnapping is more likely," she said. "They want information."

"Let, them," he said, defiantly. "I won't tell them a thing."

"We don't doubt your integrity, Doctor. Still, we have to minimize the risk."

"By doing what?" said Baumann.

The deputy secretary nodded to Townsend.

"We've taken the liberty of building an underground facility at a safehouse in the English countryside," said Townsend. "Monkton Combe, to be exact. To everyone else, it's an unassuming old cottage in a tiny village. We think it's best that you officially retire there."

"Our joint agencies will put out the word internally that you've retired," said the deputy secretary. "And, of course, that your work has been moved to a secure area in Utah."

"That should muddy the scent a bit," added Townsend. "Meanwhile, you can access all your files from the underground facility—through an encrypted network, of course. I realize there'll be some inconveniences, but it's unavoidable I'm afraid."

"Is it safe?" said Baumann.

"Extremely," assured Townsend. "We'll have one of our best men stay with you to keep watch. He'll go by the name of Stubbins. It's an alias of course. The less you move around, the less chance there is of someone spotting you. All they need is a photo and they can follow you. How many people do you stay in contact with?"

"I'm afraid they're all dead, sadly."

"I'd like to say I'm sorry," said Townsend, "but in this case it's for the best. The only ones who'll know your whereabouts are in this room. And of course, select members of our mutual intelligence communities so they can keep an eye on things. But don't worry, it'll be considered need *to know only."*

"It's quite alright," said Baumann. "I'm a solitary man. I'm perfectly happy with my books and my work. And I prefer the country."

Julian tried to process everything he was hearing. He could sense Baumann's feeling of dread, despite his bravado, and he didn't blame him. This was a mind-boggling burden on any man.

The room began to fade and he felt himself being pulled out of the memory.

Julian was back in the Shard, except he was now seated and looking up at Hans, whose menacing, scarred face was hovering above him. He could feel his hands tied behind his back. Zip ties again. Then he realized. This wasn't real. This was another of Baumann's memories.

"SARA," said Hans. "Where is it?"

"Do you enjoy wasting your time?" said Baumann.

"Where… is… it?" repeated Hans as he brought a knife closer and closer to Beamann's right eyeball.

Julian cringed along with Baumann as the scientist closed his eyes tightly. He could feel the sharp point scraping lightly against his eyelid, teasing what might come next. Then the knife slid down his right cheek and to his neck. Baumann kept his eyes closed. Out of the blue, a surprise punch came hard upon the left side of his cheekbone, rocking his skull.

Baumann groaned. "I'm retired!" he shouted in desperation. "I don't know anything."

Another blow to the side of the face nearly knocked him over sideways.

"Where?" said Hans.

Julian had had enough. He pulled himself out of the memory and backed away from Baumann. This situation was far worse than he'd even dreamed. He could feel the blood draining from his face as he tried to process the weight of what he'd just seen and heard.

"Well," said Blaine. "What did you see?"

He stared at Baumann's face. The scientist may have been arrogant, but he was brave beyond measure. Julian weighed how to answer. It all seemed so simple. All he had to do was tell them the information they needed was at the very home they'd kidnapped Baumann from, hidden in an underground lab—that is, if it was even still there. He'd save himself, Lela's family, and maybe even Baumann. But he'd heard what Whitmore had said. SARA was the most important asset on the planet. Did he really want the fate of the world decided by his own self-interest? This was a no-win situation if there ever was one. Damn the world or damn himself and Lela's family.

"Who's Sara?" said Julian. He wanted to see how much they knew. Plus, he needed to buy time to think.

"What did you hear about SARA?" said Blaine. "Tell me."

"I only know Hans here tried to torture this poor man asking about Sara. Who is she that's so important?" He looked at Hans, whose poker face hadn't changed.

"It's not a *she* and you know it," said Blaine.

"Well maybe if you didn't torture him, I'd have been able to see more."

"I don't believe you, Julian. You're fidgeting with your gloves. You fidget when you lie. You always did."

Julian held his hands still. "What do you mean I always did?" he said. He racked his brain trying to think how Blaine would've known him.

"Never mind that," said Blaine.

Julian sighed. If he wasn't going to get answers, he at least wanted to find out how much they knew about SARA.

"How did you even know to kidnap this man?" he said.

"Julian, I'm trying to avoid using violence."

"So, what, you're going to torture me now?"

"No, we're going to torture *him*." Blaine pointed to Baumann. "Or rather Hans will. Not that I can't do it myself, but he's so much better at it. Do you really want to see this poor man suffer more?"

"He's retired," said Julian. "That's all I could see. Him enjoying retirement and then your hitman brutalizing him." He made sure to keep his hands still this time. He glanced over at Baumann, who seemed genuinely relieved for the first time.

"I told you," said Baumann, as he looked up at Hans.

"You're going to have to dig deeper, Julian," said Blaine. "If not, there are far worse people than me you'll need to worry about. Remember Lela's family. I know you can do this. I've *seen* you do this."

Julian stared at him. "Who *are* you?" he said.

For the first time, Blaine seemed to be contemplating whether to answer.

CHAPTER 20

MEETING LAURA BLACK

Laura Black was incredulous. "His brother!?" she said, standing at the coffeemaker in her kitchen. Julian's adoptive mother looked about as shocked as Lela had expected.

Last time Lela had been in this house—aside from briefly on the day of the fateful kidnapping—was to invite Julian to her party. How things have changed since then. Lela watched as Laura brought her a cup of coffee, her hand shaking from the undoubtably jarring news; she was half-expecting her to drop it. Yet, Laura Black's face was not one of shock, but of apathy. Or maybe it was disbelief. Lela needed to find out which.

"I know it's hard to believe," said Lela, taking the cup. "Thanks," she added. "And you're sure you don't remember anything about it?"

Laura shook her head as she sat at the kitchen table opposite Lela. "I would remember something like that. It doesn't make any sense."

"If you think back, what *do* you remember around the time you adopted Julian?" She took out her notebook and a pen.

"Let's start with that."

Laura thought for a moment, then spoke.

"Well, like Dr. Schaffler said, I used to work for him. I remember Julian was brought in by the state for evaluation. I don't remember much about that time, but I do seem to recall it was because of his amnesia at first." She let out a small chuckle. "I guess my memory isn't much better than his was."

"Did he know who he was?" said Lela.

"Oh, he knew who he was, at least his name. He just seemed to be in shock over something. He knew about his condition, though. His gift, I called it. We didn't believe him when he told us at first. Not until Dr. Schaffler tested him."

Lela was frantically trying to capture every word in her notebook.

"And what happened after you found out he could see people's memories?" she said. She took a small sip of coffee, which was still piping hot.

"Well, especially after that, I couldn't bear to see him caught up in the foster system. Who else would understand his issues? So, I offered to watch him until his mother returned."

"And when did you decide to adopt him?"

Laura paused to think.

"As I remember," she said, "when it seemed obvious his mother wasn't coming back, the state terminated her parental rights. That's when I officially adopted Julian. It was an expedited process. He was living with me by then, and his was a special medical case. He had no other family, so there wasn't any dispute to be concerned about. Still, it was quite an ordeal."

"But you have no recollection of going through that process with Sebastian?"

"Not only don't I recall it, but just after you called me, I looked up the adoption paperwork. There's only a record of Julian."

"Can I see that paperwork?"

Laura Black reached over and slid a folder on the kitchen table over to Lela. "By all means," she said. "I left it out so you could see it."

Lela opened the folder and perused the papers. All seemed to be as Mrs. Black described. There was nothing in there about another child. Of course, documents could've been missing, whether inadvertently or otherwise.

"Mrs. Black, I—by the way, is there a Mr. Black?"

"My husband died a few years after we were married."

"I'm sorry to hear that."

"Don't be. He wasn't a good person. I'll leave it at that. Now, what were you going to ask?"

Lela thought back to her own ordeal with Brian and could empathize with what she sensed as bitterness in the otherwise amiable woman.

"I was going to ask why you chose not to tell Julian you worked for Dr. Schaffler. Wouldn't he have known anyway if you treated him?"

"Not really. Plus, I didn't really *choose* anything. I just never brought it up, and neither did Julian. You have to understand, when Julian was brought into our office, he was in a terrible mental state. When I decide to adopt him, I left my job, except for some billing work I did from home. I had enough money from my husband's estate to live off of, modestly anyway. It was about the only good thing he ever did for me. Anyway, I don't remember a whole lot about that time. But I do remember even when I got Julian back to my house, he wouldn't talk much, he'd barely eat, and, to be honest, sometimes he just seemed like he didn't want to live. Then somewhere along the line—and I don't remember when exactly—something strange happened."

"What happened?"

"He changed. He still seemed confused about his past, but

he wasn't sullen any longer. He started eating. He started asking for video games. It was like a switch went off. He just took me as his mother after that. I did bring him back to Dr. Schaffler a few times for follow-up, but I don't even think he remembered I worked for Dr. Schaffler and I never brought it up."

"And he never brought up his real mother?"

"Never. I knew he was repressing something, but we could never get to what it was, so I dropped it."

"It does seem an extreme reaction to a mother running off, doesn't it?" Lela couldn't help but think of her own feelings about her mother abandoning her, but shrugged them off as usual.

"That was my thought exactly. But if she was murdered like you said, then he must've witnessed it. It's the only thing that makes sense. At least *something* finally makes sense. Do you really think his brother did it?"

"It's sure looking that way."

"Poor Julian," said Laura. "You know, it would break his heart to find out any of this."

"Do you think he even knows he's adopted?"

Laura's face sunk. "I don't think so. Like I said, it's never come up, and I never told him. I couldn't bear to. Not when he was finally living a relatively normal life. He never seemed curious about his past, so I figured... well... I remember something my mother used to say, 'Never trouble trouble till trouble troubles you.'"

"It's a good motto," said Lela. "Unfortunately, I'm afraid trouble's here now."

"This whole situation... I mean, who would've dreamed?"

"Did *you* ever meet his real mother?"

Laura shook her head. "No, I can't say I have."

"Not even when she brought Julian and his brother to your office four years earlier?"

"We get so many people, I'm not sure I would've remembered her anyway. But someone with Julian's ability, I certainly would have. And so would Dr. Schaffler."

Lela perused the notes she'd been taking, checking to make sure she captured everything. She added a few items she hadn't gotten to write down. For the most part, it seemed Laura Black's story corroborated with Dr. Schaffler's. She couldn't see any major discrepancies. She thought of a few random items to follow up on and jotted them down.

Check with state?
Missing Persons? Runaway?
Sabastian Galloway?

"Mrs. Black, I don't mean to bring up old wounds, but how did your husband die?" She closed the adoption folder and handed it back.

"It's okay," said Laura, taking the folder back and sliding it over where it was. "It was a car accident. He was driving drunk. It wasn't the first time. Unfortunately, two other people were killed in the car he hit. I'm curious, though. Why do you ask?"

"No reason. I'm sorry, I'm just trying to be thorough. I think I have everything I needed to know." She felt embarrassed for having asked, but she needed to rule out everything. The fleeting thought had occurred to her earlier that Laura Black herself perhaps wasn't what she seemed, but she was pretty certain that wasn't the case. Everything was still pointing to Sebastian.

"You *will* get him back, won't you?" said Laura. Lela could see a tear running down her cheek. "He's been through so much. It's not fair people are taking advantage of him."

"It isn't fair, Mrs. Black. But we're going to get him back, and I do believe he'll be okay."

"I hope so. I wish I could be of more help. And I hope you get your family back, too."

"I appreciate that, Mrs. Black. You've been a huge help." She stood up to leave.

"Where are you going next?"

"Julian's old neighbors. I'm hoping one of them remembers his brother. I'll let you know if I find anything."

"Please do."

As Lela made her way to the door, Laura said, "Come to think of it, there is one other thing."

Lela turned around.

"I don't know how I forgot it, but it could be relevant, now that you mention neighbors. I didn't think it was anything, but now I think maybe it could be."

"What's that, Mrs. Black?"

"I had a next-door neighbor. Edgar. Wonderful man, very kind. He died a few years back. Anyway, soon after I adopted Julian, I remember coming home from shopping and he was outside working on his tomatoes. He said something strange to me."

"What did he say?"

"He said, 'How are the boys doing?' I corrected him and said there was only one boy. He was clearly embarrassed. He apologized and walked away. He never again mentioned a second boy. The funny thing is, I thought he was getting senile. Now it turns out I was the crazy one. I—"

Lela could see she was suddenly visibly upset, with tears welling in her eyes. She couldn't imagine what it must be like doubting your own memory or having large chunks of it missing. She rushed up to Laura Black and embraced her, holding her tight and patting her back for comfort. They were both anxiously awaiting news of their loved ones, which was a bond closer than she could've possibly imagined. She wouldn't wish it on anyone. She cursed herself for doubting this woman, even for a second.

After she left the house and headed toward her car, she thought about what she'd just heard. It seemed Sebastian may have been here as a child after all, at least once. And he'd apparently erased part of Laura's memory as well. She swore to herself, once her family and Julian were home safe, she'd see to it that he paid for all of it—all the heartache and trauma he'd caused.

CHAPTER 21

THE ASSET IS A LIABILITY

J ulian stared at Blaine, waiting for an answer. Somehow, Blaine knew more about him than anyone, and he was quite sure he'd never met him. Nor was it the type of detail Blaine could've dug into or obtained anywhere else.

"I'm family, Julian. That's who I am."

"What kind of family?"

"The kind of family you don't really want."

Julian couldn't argue that point. "I don't remember you," he said. He glanced over at Hans, who was standing near Baumann like a zombie, probably listening.

"You wouldn't."

"You're not going to tell me, are you?" said Julian.

"As soon as you tell me what you really saw."

Julian threw up his hands. "I told you. Nothing other than your man torturing him. How do you expect him to remember anything else after that?"

Blaine ignored him and walked over to a nearby armchair and sat down. He reached toward a wheeled swivel chair and sent it rolling toward Julian. "Take a seat."

Julian grabbed the chair and sat opposite Blaine while Hans continued to stand guard by Baumann just twenty feet away.

"Julian, I know what your face looks like when you've seen something surprising. Shocking even."

"Like torture?"

"No, I said surprising, not painful. You saw something that blew your mind. I could tell by your face when you came out of it."

"I don't know what you're talking about, I—"

"You're lying, Julian."

This tack wasn't working. He had to buy time to decide how to get out of this. Not to mention the jetlag was starting to hurt his head.

"I need a break," he said. "I can't even think."

Blaine seemed to be studying his face. "Alright," he said. "Follow me."

Blaine rose from his chair and headed to the door they had entered from, which was partly concealed in the paneled wall. He entered a code into the keypad and pushed the door open. Julian followed him toward a side door to the left that led toward the interior of the building. As soon as Blaine opened the door, a tough-looking, stout, bald man in a charcoal suit was waiting for instruction. He looked like he'd been guarding the door.

"Kenneth, take Julian to the break room, would you? Be sure he gets back here."

Julian followed the man through a hallway, noticing he had his hands in his pockets. No doubt he was hiding at least one weapon.

Unlike the rest of the building, which was mostly all glass walls and windows and cheerfully bright, this seemed more like a service corridor. As they passed the WC, Julian noted a small green exit sign pointing to the right that showed a symbol of stairs. He glanced up the right corridor as they passed. He spotted a white, metal emergency door.

As they continued, he tried to think about what to do. He knew he couldn't give them the information they wanted. That was out of the question. He thought about other options and then realized his best chance was to get among people. Lots of people. It would give him a chance to somehow get to the police and tell them what was going on. Blaine wouldn't dare do anything to Lela's family if there was a police search going on. His pulse was starting to quicken with the thought of taking such drastic action as they approached another door. But it was now or never.

He stopped and turned to Kenneth, nonchalantly holding out his right hand.

"By the way, I'm Julian," he said. "I don't think we've properly met."

"Cheers, Julian," said Kenneth in mock friendliness, as he lifted his left arm out of his pocket and waved his black leather gloved hand to show Julian. "Now, what say you get movin'?" he added, in his gruff English accent.

So much for distracting the guy. These people were well informed.

They came to a door straight ahead that was just past a cleaning cart in the hallway. Kenneth went through it first as Julian waited in the open door.

Then Kenneth turned around. "What yer waitin' for?"

"Sorry, gotta run," said Julian, as he backed out and slammed the door shut. He hurriedly slid the cleaning cart in front of it, then turned and raced back toward the emergency exit. Behind him, he heard Kenneth crashing through the cleaning cart almost immediately. As he turned left at the WC to go to the emergency exit, he noticed a fire alarm on the wall and pulled it. Immediately a deafening alarm sounded. He rushed though the exit door and into the stairwell, hoping the alarm would lure more people. Frantically, he scooted down the stairwell as quickly as he could, almost tripping on the steps. As he'd hoped, a few other people entered the stairwell down below, probably thinking it was a fire drill. He glanced back and saw that Kenneth wasn't far behind him.

Running for his life, Julian sped downstairs, occasionally looking back to see Kenneth still in pursuit. As he darted past a few men and women, he approached a sign for the tenth floor, making a mental note that Blaine's offices must've been on the eleventh. He ducked behind the people entering and scurried through the open door. Just as he entered the main hallway, with its sleek, blond-wood walls and fancy marble floors, the alarm stopped. He continued running down the hall until a woman came out of an office just in front of him to see what all the fuss was. He bent over, half out of breath, and asked her where the elevators were. She shot him a strange look and pointed down the hall. "The lifts are straight ahead," she said.

He turned and didn't see any sign of Kenneth, but still, he proceeded as quickly as he could to the lifts. Finally, he saw the lift waiting area. To his great fortune, a group of lifts had just arrived, signaled by the sound of loud beeping. He couldn't help but notice the massive moving image above his head depicting a glorious painted ceiling by one of the old great masters, which, as he glanced up, he could see extended the length of the lift area. Just as the image started to change to a futuristic glass roof, he rushed into an open lift and pressed the *close door* button. Two other men in sport jackets and casual slacks were already in the back of the lift. They didn't seem to be a threat, so he just stood in front of them.

The lift was mirrored on all sides. But it wasn't until it began to move that he felt as if he were in a spaceship. Majestic, spacey music began playing, and more moving images appeared above his head, reflected in the mirrors around him. It created the magnificent effect of the London sky receding and the seasons changing, with eye-opening interludes on the streets of London. Any other time, it would've been quite a Disneyesque experience, but he had more pressing things on his mind.

The lift stopped on the seventh floor and the two men stepped around him and exited. He was tempted to get out with them and tell them what was going on, but he figured there'd be more people in the lobby—and hopefully some guards. As the lift doors closed, he was beginning to second-guess that decision and was suddenly feeling isolated and vulnerable.

The lift continued and then stopped on the second floor. As the door opened, he prepared to run out, but a smartly dressed businesswoman entered, so at least he wouldn't be alone. Besides, he was close to the first floor. He decided to stay put.

Finally, the lift arrived at the first floor. He let the woman exit first, and then he stepped out into the marbled hallway. As he made his way past the lifts toward the lobby, a hand grabbed him by the arm from behind. As he turned, his heart sunk. It was Hans.

"It would be a mistake to leave," said Hans, revealing a holstered pistol under his jacket.

Julian noticed Hans wasn't wearing gloves. It gave him an idea, but he'd have to be quick about it. Things could go horribly wrong in a hundred different ways.

Without warning, he grabbed Hans's left hand.

Immediately, he was thrown into a horrendous nightmare—a rapid succession of stabbings and shootings, and worse. He was forced to participate as Hans decapitated a pleading Italian-looking man with one swipe of a long, curved-blade instrument—ducking as the blood splattered toward his face. He had a front-row view of a beautiful young woman's panicked expression, watching her visage turn lifeless as Hans strangled her to death. He felt like a tiger stalking its prey as Hans quietly watched a hooded man run desperately into a forest, and then chased him endlessly, only to eventually stop and throw a knife into the man's back. And he was unable to turn away as Hans aimed a gun at a frightened boy of about twelve and pulled the trigger, despite the kid's heartbreaking pleas. Memory after memory, Hans ruthlessly killed people from all walks of life. How many were innocent?

Finally, Julian managed to get the strength to remove himself from the vision.

He was staring up at Hans, who had no idea his memories had just been read—until he looked down at his hand.

"All those people," said Julian. "How did you feel killing them all?"

Hans gave a crooked smile. "Delighted," he said, without any sense of shame.

"Even the kid?"

"Especially the kid."

Julian shook his head in disbelief.

"There was one other memory," he said. He was tempted to bring up the only memory in which Hans showed any emotion whatsoever, the one that gave him his scar. But he thought the better of it.

Hans gave him an inquisitive look.

"Oh, never mind," said Julian.

One thing was certain. After seeing all those visions, escaping Hans wasn't an option. It had been a valiant effort trying to escape, but now he had no choice but to go with him.

♦

"Welcome back," said Blaine, as Hans led Julian back to the brown leather couch he'd been sleeping on earlier. Blaine was seated at his desk, lighting a cigar. "I never took you for a runner."

Julian took a seat on the couch, as directed by Hans.

"Should I take him for the usual treatment?" said Hans.

"What's the usual treatment?" said Julian. He could feel his palms start to sweat as he thought back to Hans's treatment of Baumann.

"No, Hans," said Blaine. "That'll be alright."

"What are your plans?" said Hans.

"I'm taking Julian for dinner at the Ritz."

Julian looked up at Hans, who was stonefaced. Then he shifted his attention to Blaine to see if he was kidding or not. He didn't appear to be.

"The Ritz," said Hans, as if he'd doubted what he'd heard.

"I'm a traditionalist," said Blaine, shrugging his shoulders. "You can go, Hans. I'll fill you in later."

Hans didn't seem happy. He turned in a huff and left the room.

"No offense," said Julian, "but I don't want to go anywhere until I know Lela's family is safe. You owe me that."

"It seems to me I don't owe you anything yet," said Blaine. "But if it makes you feel better..."

Blaine turned his computer monitor around to face Julian. A video feed showed Angel Mars, Lela's stepmother Shelly, and Lela's sister all sitting in what looked like a luxury suite and watching TV. Two guards were in the room as well. One was sitting in a chair opposite them and the other was standing by a cocktail table pouring himself a drink.

"See?" said Blaine. "One big, happy family."

"How do I know that's not a recording? How do I know they're still alive?"

Blaine pressed a button on his desk.

"Sylvan," he said. "Wave into the camera, would you?"

Just then, the seated guard turned toward the camera and waved.

"Satisfied?" said Blaine.

Julian nodded. He was relieved to see Lela's family in good condition. Now the trick was to not let things change for the worse, while somehow not putting the whole world in danger in the process.

♦

Hans was livid as he waited for Olga to pick up his call. Finally, she answered. He immediately shared with her that Blaine was foolishly taking Julian out to dinner in a public place.

"His recklessness will expose us all," he said.

"It seems Blaine's talent has gone to his head. What do you know of the asset?"

"The asset is now a liability," he said. "He refuses to cooperate. He almost escaped. And now it seems he is family."

There was silence on the other line for a few seconds.

"You were right to call me," said Olga. "It is now time to act. Did you do what I told you?"

"I did."

"Good. We have waited long enough. It has become clear what we must do."

Hans listened as Olga filled him in on the plan.

CHAPTER 22

SAPPHIRES AND EMERALDS

L ela wasn't having much luck searching for Julian's old neighbors. She had brought De Luca with her, and they'd knocked on the doors of four of the homes near Julian's old house. Two of the neighbors had recently moved in and didn't know anything. At the third house, the woman looked to be at least ninety and was hard of hearing. She'd kept thinking Lela was saying she was looking for bouillon.

"What kind of bouillon?" the woman kept saying.

Finally, De Luca had tried articulating each syllable, impatiently yelling, "Jool-ee-an!"

"I don't know any Julie," the woman had replied, looking at him as if he'd had two heads.

"Oh, I've had enough of this lady," De Luca had said, throwing his hands up. That's when they'd given up and gone to the next house, where nobody was home. Or at least nobody had answered the door.

Now they were running out of options.

"One more house," said Lela, motioning to the house next door.

"I hope they can hear at this one," said De Luca. "One don't answer. The other don't hear. Maybe this one'll be blind."

They approached the front door of the next house, a freshly painted white door with an antique brass knocker. The house was on the opposite side of Julian's old house and a few doors down, but maybe they'd get lucky.

Lela tapped the knocker against the door and they waited.

"Did it ever occur to you," said De Luca, "maybe the mother and the boyfriend weren't the only ones that that kid buried?"

"Let's not even go there," said Lela. She hadn't even thought about that. Leave it to De Luca to bring it up. That's all she needed, on top of all this, was a serial killer.

After about ten more seconds, the door opened and a seventyish woman, about five feet tall with short gray hair, appeared.

"Can I help you?" she said.

Lela flashed her badge.

"I'm Detective Mars, ma'am, and this is Lieutenant De Luca. Let me start by saying nothing's wrong. We're just asking a few questions in the area."

"Sure, I'm Jackie Stanton," said the woman. "Anything going on in the neighborhood?"

"Not above ground," said De Luca. Lela elbowed him.

"No, nothing bad," said Lela. "I'm just wondering if you remember a neighbor who used to live across the street. Her name was Eve Galloway."

"Who *doesn't* remember Eve Galloway?" she said. "She had a real winner of a boyfriend. And by that, I mean loser. One day they pick up and leave, just like that. I always suspected foul play. Then, wouldn't you know it, they turn up dead just behind their house."

"So, you remember that?" said Lela.

"Of course. I don't know what shocked me more, that they were found dead or that he wasn't the one who did it."

"Who's *he?*" said De Luca.

She looked at him like he was crazy. "The boyfriend, who else? He was a low class... pig of a man. I still think he was responsible somehow—some kind of trouble he must've gotten himself into. Those poor boys. I always wondered what became of them."

Lela looked at De Luca, whose eyes were about to pop out of his head. She was so choked up she could barely speak. Finally, someone remembered—someone Sebastian hadn't gotten to. She'd been so exhausted, and now it felt like an ocean of pain was about to be lifted off her shoulders. De Luca patted her on the back.

"Are you okay?" said Mrs. Stanton.

"I'm sorry," said De Luca. "Did you say *boys?*"

"Yes, there were two boys. Hey, would you like to come in?"

"No that's alright," said De Luca.

"We'd love to," said Lela, wiping her eyes. "If you don't mind."

"Not at all," she said. "I asked."

They followed Mrs. Stanton inside and both took a seat on the Victorian-style upholstered couch in the living room, which was elegantly appointed and immaculate. On the mahogany coffee table was a small tray of decorated Faberge-style eggs and a beautiful stone sculpture of figures dancing in a circle. Mrs. Stanton took a seat opposite them on an armchair.

"I saw you admiring that," said Mrs. Stanton, motioning to the statue. "It was sculpted by a Holocaust survivor. I wish I could remember her name. Klara somebody. Oh yes, Klara Sever. I'm very good with names. Can I get you anything? Tea? Coffee?"

"No thanks," said Lela, as she took out her notebook.

"I'll take a coffee," said De Luca. "Black."

They waited while Mrs. Stanton went into the other room.

De Luca picked up one of the expensive-looking decorated eggs.

"Hoity toity," he whispered, probably louder than he realized. Lela shushed him and he clumsily put it back down, clinking it against another egg.

Finally, their hostess returned with a mug of coffee for De Luca and put a coaster down in front of him.

"Mrs. Stanton," said Lela, "what can you tell us about the boys, from what you remember?"

"Well, they kept to themselves mostly. And they always wore gloves, even in the summer, which I thought was odd."

"They had a skin condition," said Lela.

"A really bad one," said De Luca.

"Such a shame," said Mrs. Stanton. "I thought as much, but I didn't want to pry."

"Do you remember anything else about their appearance?" said Lela. "Hair color? Any special markings?"

"Nothing special that I recall. They seemed well cared for. They both had brown hair. The older boy's hair was darker."

Lela jotted down the hair color while De Luca sipped his coffee.

"Anything else?" said Lela. "I know it was a long time ago so it may be hard to remember."

Mrs. Stanton thought for a moment. "Oh wait," she said. "How could I forget? There was one thing, now that you mention it. The older boy had sectoral heterochromia. Are you familiar with what that is?"

"No, I can't say I am." She was surprised to hear such a technical term coming from Mrs. Stanton.

"It sounds painful," said De Luca.

"Are you a doctor?" said Lela.

"I was an optician, before I retired. So, I always pay attention to people's eyes. I still do." Mrs. Stanton leaned forward to explain. "Sectoral heterochromia," she said, "is a condition in which the iris is multicolored."

"I was gonna say that," said De Luca.

"It's quite rare. It occurs in less than one percent of the population. And his, I noticed right away in both eyes. They were a beautiful mix of blue and green—like sapphires mixed with emeralds. As soon as I saw... oh, I forget the boys' names. They were English-sounding names if I recall. Their father was English."

"Julian and Sebastian," said Lela.

"Oh yes, that's right. Well, anyway, as soon as I saw Sebastian—he was the older one—it was the first thing I noticed."

"Mrs. Stanton," said De Luca. "You said the kids' father was English. Do you mean Eve's boyfriend? Jack?"

"Oh no, I mean their real father, Howard. He was almost as bad as the boyfriend. A real drug addict. They divorced soon after they moved in. The younger boy was just a toddler. Such a sad life."

"Was his last name Galloway?" said Lela.

"I don't remember. No... wait. I do remember. When they first moved in, they had a gorgeous sign on their mailbox with their last name. I remember complementing them on it. It was a beautifully carved wood. A dark wood. It was—"

"Jesus," said De Luca. "What was the name?"

"Blaine," she said. "Eve and Howard Blaine."

"SB," said Lela. "Sebastian Blaine."

"Yep, that's our guy," said De Luca.

"I beg your pardon?" said Mrs. Stanton.

"We've been trying to find Sebastian," said Lela. "He left a note and signed it SB. It sounds like he may have taken his father's last name after he disappeared."

"Disappeared? That's terrible. I always thought the boys ended up with family."

"It's… complicated," said Lela.

"That's the understatement of the century," said De Luca.

"Unfortunately," said Lela, "we can't go into more details. Do you know where Howard Blaine is now? We'll want to have a talk with him."

"You'll have to talk loud if you want him to hear you," said Mrs. Stanton. "He died about five years ago. It was a drug overdose if I remember. I can't say I was surprised when I read it in the Inquirer."

Lela tried to digest what she'd heard, as she updated her notes and De Luca sipped more of his coffee.

De Luca put his mug down on the table, then realized his faux pas and moved it to the coaster.

"Well, I think that's everything, Mrs. Stanton," said Lela, as she rose from the couch. De Luca rose with her.

"Thanks for your help," said De Luca.

Lela thanked her profusely and headed toward the door with De Luca. To think that a half hour before, she thought she'd reached a dead end. Now she had enough information to operate with, and, more importantly, she had a plan. Or at least the beginnings of a plan.

"I hope you find him," said Mrs. Stanton, opening the door for them.

"Don't worry, I will," said Lela.

"And thanks for the coffee," said De Luca.

Lela walked to her car with De Luca, half-dazed, though the fresh air was starting to clear her head.

"That was like my grandmother's coffee," said De Luca.

"That good?"

"No, the opposite. My grandmother was known for one thing. Absolutely horrible, stinkin' coffee. This was just like it."

Lela chuckled as she climbed into the driver side of her SUV, the first time in a while she found humor in anything. But then reality set in. She was more hopeful than she had been, but the future was still up in the air. She wouldn't rest until Julian and her family were back safe.

As De Luca settled into the passenger seat, she took one last look at her notes.

"If Howard Blaine was a Brit," said De Luca, "it makes sense that his son might've gone to London and taken his last name. And if the dad was as bad news as this lady says, then it sounds like it's a case of 'like father, like son.'"

"It's amazing Julian turned out as stable as he did," said Lela.

"Yeah, thanks to Laura Black," said De Luca. "No wonder the kid repressed everything."

"At least now I know who I'm looking for," she said. "Sebastian Blaine, forty years old, with dark brown hair and blue-green eyes. That narrows it down pretty good."

"So, what's next?" said De Luca.

"Next I look up flights."

"You serious?" he said. "You're gonna go to London?"

"Damn right," she said. "Sebastian Blaine won't know what hit him."

CHAPTER 23

RASPBERRY SURPRISE

T he private, ruby red William Kent Room at the Ritz was so regal that the first person to hold a party there was the Queen herself.

Julian was in awe as he entered the opulent, Renaissance-inspired dining room, with its rich, red velvet walls and chairs, magnificent golden ceiling with ornate details representing Greek mythology, and a long banquet table that sat elegantly under a glorious chandelier.

"Are we expecting the Royal Family?" he said. It looked like it could sit at least eight or ten people on either side.

"No, just us," said Blaine. "I wanted somewhere we could talk in private. I think you'll like it. Oh, and I took the liberty of ordering a custom menu. Nothing fussy."

Blaine led Julian past the table and motioned for him to take the end seat on the near side, where a place setting was already prepared. Julian unrolled the white cloth napkin and took out the unusually heavy silver utensils while Blaine sat opposite him.

"I feel underdressed," said Julian, who was wearing a navy

sport jacket over a cream, pullover sweater, both of which Blaine had lent him. Blaine had changed into a gray flannel suit.

"Nonsense. It's a private room. Nobody's coming in here. Besides, the jacket fits you. Good thing you're my size."

Almost immediately, a tall, dark-haired waiter in a black tuxedo arrived with two glasses of white wine and two small, white bowls of what appeared to be lobster meat rolled with a colorful mix of tomatoes and delicate greens, all artistically arranged like a culinary masterpiece. Julian didn't know whether to eat it or take a picture of it.

"Merci, Jacques," said Blaine.

"But of course, Monsieur Blaine," said the waiter, before leaving quietly.

"So much for nothing fussy," said Julian.

"We're having Beef Wellington for dinner," said Blaine. "It's comfort food. I ordered us a bottle of 1990 Margaux to go with it."

"I'd like to say I'm impressed, but I don't know wine. I wouldn't know the difference between a Margaux and a Manischewitz."

"About fifteen hundred dollars. Twice that in taste buds."

"Listen," said Julian, "if you're trying to bribe me with expensive food and drinks—"

"I'm not trying to bribe you with anything, Julian. Except maybe this."

Blaine produced a flat, gift-wrapped box from under the table and pushed it toward Julian.

"This doesn't mean we're engaged," said Blaine. "Open it."

Julian carefully peeled open the blue giftwrapping to reveal a rectangular black gift box. He opened the box and looked inside to see couple sheets of a flat, skin-like material. He picked it up and realized what it was. It was a pair of gloves.

"They're prosthetic," said Blaine. "Now you can take off

those silly white things."

Julian peeled off his white gloves and put on the new ones. As he held his hands out in front of him, he was in complete awe.

"I can barely tell these are on," he said, as he looked at both sides of his hands in wonder. He grabbed a fork and marveled at the sensation. He could feel every nuance of the cutlery and the coolness of the metal against his skin, the same as if his hand were bare.

"That's the idea," said Blaine. "I don't want to tell you how much I spent over the years getting the formula perfected. They're waterproof, too."

"These are incredible."

He was so excited, he ate the rest of his appetizer just to feel the sensation of the fork. He didn't realize how hungry he was.

"Life-changing, aren't they?" said Blaine. "They're yours."

Julian loved the gloves, but then he remembered what was at stake. He put his fork down and looked at Blaine.

"I don't know how or why you created them," he said, "but I can't do this." He started to peel off the gloves.

"Keep them, Julian. No strings attached. I mean that. Like I said, we're family."

"I don't understand you," said Julian, thinking back to what he'd seen in Baumann's memory, not to mention seeing his own mother lying on the floor unconscious. The more he thought about it, the angrier he got. "You keep saying we're related, but you don't say how. You take us to this fancy dinner, but you have Lela's family kidnapped, just like you kidnapped me. And now you want me to help you destroy the entire world while we sit here like kings!" He banged his hand on the table for emphasis. "You think this is all a joke. Let's fiddle while Rome burns."

The waiter startled him, coming to take the plates away and

replacing each with a large, white, gold-rimmed platter that showcased a small, rectangular piece of white fish covered in puff pastry, resting on a mixture of olive oil and balsamic vinegar, accompanied by a semicircle of green grapes.

"Voilà, the Turbot Véronique, monsieur."

"Destroy the entire world?" said Blaine, as the waiter left. "It's not as dramatic as all that, and I doubt you'd want to hear me play the fiddle. But you *did* see something, didn't you? What did you see?"

"I saw enough," said Julian. "But I'm not telling you or anyone else a damn thing. There's too much at stake and I won't be part of it. And I'm keeping the damn gloves."

"I already said you could keep them. Listen, how can I make you trust me?"

"Okay, you could start by telling me what you know about my family."

"You want to know about your family, Julian?"

"Please," said Julian. "Enlighten me." He wasn't sure he'd believe whatever Blaine said anyway, but he was curious what his story would be.

"Eat. I'll tell you."

"I don't feel like eating."

"Okay, then *I'll* eat." Blaine started digging into the second course. How he could eat during all this was a mystery.

"To start with," said Blaine, in between bites, "your father was a drug addict. Or I should say *our* father."

"What are you talking about?"

"We have the same father, Julian. We're brothers."

Julian laughed. "And you expect me to believe that?"

"It's true."

Blaine lifted his hand and began peeling off a prosthetic glove, just like the ones he gave Julian. He dangled the glove in his hand and smiled.

Julian was never more confused. Either Blaine was telling

the truth, he was an ingenious manipulator, or he was certifiably insane.

"I don't get it," said Julian. "*You* can read people's memories, too? If that's even true, then what did you need me for?"

"No, *you* were always the memory reader," said Blaine, as he slid the glove back on. "My gift was different. I could make people forget. So, believe me, I'm the last person anyone wants touching Max Baumann. See why I need you now?"

Julian watched dumbfounded as Blaine finished his fish. Could he have been making all this up?

"In other words," said Julian, "you're saying you made me forget my own childhood." He was still trying to digest whether it was even true.

"That's quite a reach, Julian. I don't recall ever saying that."

Julian was relieved.

"But yes," said Blaine. "You happen to be right. Think about it, you have no memory of your mother or father. Didn't you ever wonder?"

"My father, maybe, but I live with my mother—which I know you know, because your man Hans knocked her out."

"Laura?" said Blaine. "She's not your mother. She used to work for Dr. Schaffler until she adopted you. You were nine years old, Julian. If you don't believe me, ask her when you get back."

Julian felt a deep chill run through his veins at the thought of his whole world being a lie. He was speechless. He buried his head in his hands to think. The woman he's called mother all his life. How could she have not told him? All of this was so hard to believe. But then again, why couldn't he remember anything before he was nine? How did Blaine know so much? None of this could be a coincidence.

"Do you believe me?" said Blaine.

Julian was still in a daze. He lifted his head from his hands and looked at the man who was claiming to be his brother.

"Why didn't my mother ever mention a brother?" he said.

"You mean Laura? Think about it."

Just then, the waiter came with a bottle of red wine and two covered platters.

"Ah, the Beef Wellington," said Blaine.

As Blaine sampled the wine, Julian tried to digest everything he'd learned and why he was never told about a brother. Maybe it was to protect him. But from what? Then it dawned on him.

"She didn't know," he said, as the waiter lifted the lids to reveal the Beef Wellington. "She never knew I had a brother."

"She didn't remember," said Blaine. "It's complicated."

Julian thought about it as the waiter left. Complicated? That was putting it mildly.

"Let's say for a moment I believed you," he said. "What happened to my real mother?"

"I don't think it would do either of us any favors if I told you. Why don't you eat before it gets cold?"

As if he could eat anything now. "I want to know," said Julian. "I have a right to know."

He couldn't get a read on Blaine's face. Then Blaine reached in his jacket pocket and pulled out what looked like a newspaper clipping and slid it across the table.

"Read it and weep," said Blaine. "But don't weep too hard. It's not worth it."

Julian examined the article. It was about two bodies being discovered in the Pennypack woods behind some house—Eve Galloway and Jack Rimshaw.

"Who are they to me?" he said.

"Eve Galloway was our mother. And Jack Rimshaw was the worst kind of human being you could imagine, if you could even call him that. He made Hans look like Mister Rogers."

Julian studied their photo. Eve Galloway looked slightly

familiar. She had blonde hair and looked to be about forty in the photo. He could tell from the picture she had a warm personality. He didn't recognize Rimshaw at all, but he had dark hair and beady eyes.

"And Jack Rimshaw, he was our father?"

"He thought he was. No, our real father may have been a drug addict, but he wasn't a bad guy. Rimshaw? He's right where he belongs."

"And our mother?"

"She made a bad choice."

He stared at Blaine. Everything he was saying sounded absurd, but he seemed sincere. He still couldn't tell for sure if Blaine was the world's greatest con man or if there was some actual truth to what he was saying. What frightened him most was that he was starting to believe the latter.

"Something's not right about all this," he said. Something still felt like it was missing. He didn't have the whole picture.

"What's not right, Julian?"

"Why did you make me forget?"

Blaine was silent and seemed to be contemplating a reasonable answer. But would it be a truthful one?

"Was it the trauma?" said Julian.

"Yes, it was the trauma. Can we put it behind us now?"

Julian thought about it for a moment.

"Who killed them?" he asked.

"Julian, does it really matter? I don't know who killed them. Why don't you eat your dinner? We still have the Raspberry Surprise coming."

"But it *does* matter. My whole life has been a lie. I need to know why you made me forget." As he looked around at the ruby red walls and the ruby red chairs and the ruby red curtains, his head started spinning. Brief flashes of distant memories suddenly flooded his brain. He took a glimpse at the woman's face in the photo and, almost immediately, the red from the room permeated his vision. That's all he could see. Red. A pool of blood. A pistol in a young hand, followed by a deafening gunshot. More blood. Bodies being dragged. It was all a jumble. A crimson jumble.

"Julian," said a male voice, startling him out of his stupor.

He gasped as he shook the memory off and came back to reality. He stared down at the juicy red meat in his Beef Wellington.

"Are you okay?" said Blaine. "You went into a bit of a daze there."

Julian's heart started pounding as he came to the awful realization that he'd witnessed his mother's murder. He could feel the blood rushing to his face with the thought he was sitting opposite that man who'd killed her—a man who was making jokes out of everything, and who'd been living a life of luxury.

"You!" he said, staring at Blaine. "I saw it. I saw the murder. Now I know why you made me forget. *You* killed them! You killed them and then made me forget about it."

Blaine looked shocked by the accusation. Then his shock seemed to turn to anger and indignation as his lips flattened, and his eyes grew fierce. He no longer looked like the nonchalant, devil-may-care man of a few minutes ago.

"Is that what you think, Julian? You think I killed our mother?"

"I don't think it," he said. "I know it."

Blaine glared at him, his face turning red.

"No, Julian, you're wrong. *You* killed her."

CHAPTER 24

TRUTH AND CONSEQUENCES

J ulian wasn't sure what kind of game Blaine was playing. "I don't believe you," he said as he stared across at Blaine. He couldn't fathom the thought of hurting anyone, let alone killing his own mother. It was impossible. Blaine had to be trying to either shift the blame or play head games.

"I was hoping not to resort to this," said Blaine.

Blaine reached into his jacket pocket and pulled out what looked like a small hypodermic needle in a silver tube. Julian clenched his legs and looked toward the exit. He inched back from the table and was about to make a run for it.

"Calm down, it's not for you," said Blaine. "It's for me."

Julian exhaled in relief and settled back into his seat. He was more confused now than afraid. He gave Blaine an inquisitive look.

"It's so when you touch my hand, you don't forget even more," said Blaine. "It dulls my abilities. It's amazing the little tricks you learn when you grow up with a drug addict."

"Why would I possibly want to touch your hand?"

"You wanted to know what happened? Well, now you'll

see it all—a front row seat."

He wasn't sure he was ready for this. He remembered a fortune cookie he once got that said: *It's good to know the truth, but sometimes it's better to speak of palm trees.*

"Don't look so glum, Julian. I'm giving you back your memories."

He watched as Blaine jabbed his own neck with the needle. Blaine took a few deep breaths and then peeled off the glove of his right hand and extended it across the table.

"I believe it's your move," said Blaine.

Julian hesitated. He wasn't sure he still even wanted to know what happened, but if what Blaine said was true, he had to find out for himself what details he was leaving out.

He took one last look around the room, if only to experience his current world one last time without the knowledge that would change his life forever. Resolute in his decision, he peeled off the glove of his right hand and slowly reached out toward Blaine's open palm. He paused for a moment, and then took hold of Blaine's hand.

Within seconds, he was no longer in the Ritz. Nor was he Julian. He was Sebastian—middle-school-aged Sebastian, with a folded piece of paper hidden in his hand. He was standing in the kitchen, watching his younger brother in the adjacent dining room pleading with his mother to listen to him. Julian recognized the younger brother. It was him—at nine years of age. And he recognized his mother. She *was* his mother. He knew it now. How could he have forgotten that golden blonde hair and sparkling blue eyes? He even remembered the house and the musty smell of the hardwood floors.

The nine-year-old boy stared back at him as if to seek approval, and he nodded—or rather, Sebastian did. It seemed otherworldly to be staring at himself as a child.

From the kitchen, he could hear every word they said.

"What do you mean he did it again?" said his mother.

"I saw it, mom," said young Julian. "In your memory. You can't lie. Why do you let him do that to you?"

"You need to keep your gloves on," said his mother, looking both annoyed and embarrassed.

"You don't even care about us, do you?" said young Julian, as he swiped his hand and knocked over the pile of schoolbooks that were resting on the dining room table.

"Of course, I do," said his mother.

"If you did, you'd get rid of him. He hates us, you know."

"He doesn't hate you. He just doesn't know how to deal with your gifts."

"Julian's right," said Sebastian, walking into the dining room. "He thinks we're freaks."

"That's nonsense, he doesn't—"

"Then how do you explain this?"

He held up the piece of paper, which he unfolded.

"What is that?" said his mother.

"Your boyfriend's own notes. Read it. It says a 5150 hold is needed for involuntary commitment of a minor. Jack wants to have us put away."

"What!?" she said. "Give me that."

He handed it to his mother, who grabbed it and began reading. Her face went pale as she studied the note in horror. A tear rolled down her cheek as she lifted her head and absent-mindedly dropped the note to the floor.

"I didn't know," she said, looking at him and then young Julian. "You have to believe me, I didn't know." The aching sorrow was evident on her pallid face. She knew she could no longer defend that horrible man. Not that she seemed to have any great love for him; she had just been too afraid to leave him.

"Now do you believe me?" said young Julian.

She nodded.

"You know what I can do, mom," said Sebastian. "I can make him forget all about you."

She looked at him through watery eyes, her face growing red; he couldn't tell if it was shame, anger, or both.

"Do it," she said, nodding. "Do it."

As the room faded away, Julian now found himself in a new place—a different memory. He was still fourteen-year-old Sebastian, but this time he was standing in the living room, waiting for Jack to come through the front door after work. The clock on the wall said six. His mother was standing in the dining room. He could see she was afraid to come in, and looked nervous. He turned and saw young Julian sitting on the sofa, his knees curled up in his arms. Then he heard the car door slam outside.

"He's coming," said Sebastian.

He backed away from the door and peeled off his wool gloves, tossing them onto the sofa.

He heard the key in the latch and waited as the doorknob turned.

The door opened. Jack entered and glanced at Sebastian, then looked over to Eve standing in the dining room.

"What the hell's going on?" he said.

"Nothing," said Eve. "We were just talking about what to have for dinner."

"It's already six. Just make something. They'll eat what you make."

"Jack," said Eve. "I need to talk to you about something."

"Not in front of them you don't." He whistled to Sebastian and young Julian. "Get movin'," he said.

Sebastian meandered slowly toward Jack as young Julian got up from the sofa. He'd been hoping to be able to grab his hand by surprise, but now he'd have to rely on speed. The timing would have to be perfect.

"And put your damn gloves on," said Jack, pointing to the wool gloves on the sofa.

Now what? He had to make a move, because if he went back to the sofa to put his gloves on, the whole plan would be delayed. No. It was now or never. He was tired of waiting.

Sebastian lunged forward and reached for Jack's hand. Immediately, Jack grabbed his arm, and in the same motion pulled a gun out of his jacket with his other hand. Sebastian's heart was pounding as he backed away for his own safety. The plan was blown.

"Just what the hell are you trying to pull?" said Jack, pointing the gun toward his face.

"Jack!" screamed Eve. It was the first time she'd ever raised her voice toward the man. "Just go," she said, rushing forward to push him out the door. He kept the gun pointed and didn't budge. "I need you to go," she said. "Now."

Sebastian watched in horror as Jack elbowed her in the face and she stumbled backward.

"You planned this whole thing, didn't you?" yelled Jack, turning to face her. As she held her hands over her face, he punched her in the stomach. "Didn't you!?"

Sebastian was about to explode watching her double up in pain.

Just as Jack swung the gun back to hit her with it, Sebastian leaped forward and grabbed the gun before Jack could hit her again. Jack turned and pushed him hard against the wall as the gun went flying onto the hardwood floor.

Dazed, Sebastian slid to the floor. His head was pounding from hitting the wall, but he turned just in time to see young Julian staring at the gun. Jack was about to dive for it, but then Eve jumped on his back from behind and held her arms around his neck. While Eve struggled to hold onto Jack, young Julian made a mad dash for the gun and picked it up, aiming it at Jack.

Jack stood firm as Eve was still holding onto him for dear life.

"Julian, no!" yelled Sebastian.

A deafening sound rattled his ears as Julian fired the weapon and missed, shattering the chandelier in the dining room behind them.

"Julian, stop!" said Eve. "It was my mistake, honey. I made a bad choice. Just let him go." She said to Jack, "You'll go, won't you?"

"Yeah, sure," said Jack. "Just let go of my damn neck."

Just as she released her grip on him, Jack rushed toward Julian.

"Give me that goddamn gun."

Julian fired. Then he fired again.

Everything happened so fast, Sebastian wasn't even sure it was all real. The hairs on his arms stood up. He watched in fear as Jack held his chest and fell to the floor. That's when he noticed his mother. She was lying on the floor behind Jack, a pool of blood running from her head.

In that moment, Sebastian knew she was gone, but he didn't want to believe it. Time seemed to stand still, just to tease him. For that horrifying second, he wished there was a way to reverse the moment; to rewind and change what had happened, but he couldn't.

"Mom!" he yelled. But he knew she wouldn't answer. He looked at his little brother, who was standing in shock.

Julian pulled himself out of the memory and jerked his hand away from Blaine's. He couldn't breathe. He tried to gasp for air, but he wasn't getting any. He was hyperventilating. Sweat was pouring down his face. He forced himself to breathe in through his nose, a trick Dr. Schaffler had taught him. It was working. He started to calm down.

"Don't stop there, Julian," said Blaine. Before he could react, Blaine grabbed his hand again.

He was back in the same living room, facing young Julian and grasping him by the shoulders.

"Julian, you have to calm down."

Sebastian glanced over at the two bodies wrapped head to toe in blankets. That's all they could be to him now—bodies. He refused to process that it was his mother rolled up in that blanket. His main focus had to be to protect Julian. It was an accident. A horrifying and tragic one, but an accident. The police might not see it that way, though. Even worse, both their fingerprints were on the gun. No matter what happened now, they'd both be known forevermore as the kids who murdered their mother. They'd be judged, even if it was in self-defense. And maybe they

*deserved it. Though it was Julian who'd pulled the trigger, Sebastian knew
he only had himself to blame for throwing the plan in action when the risk
was too high. Because of his impatience, they were both cursed.*

*But he could change all that, at least for Julian. It would be one way
to atone for his sin—for getting his little brother into this mess in the first
place.*

*"Julian, listen," he said. "I'll help you. We have to get rid of their
bodies. I'll dump the gun in the river. I just need your help moving them."*

*Young Julian couldn't even respond. He was crying, and clearly in
shock.*

*"It's okay, Julian. If we don't do this, you could end up in juvie, or
worse. It has to look like they ran away and left us."*

*Finally, young Julian nodded and mindlessly followed him to the
blankets.*

*Before long, they'd made their way out the back door, stopping every
so often to catch their breaths. Soon, they were dragging the bodies into the
woods. It was dark, and the blankets kept unraveling, and the shovels
he'd rolled up with the bodies kept falling out. Young Julian remained
silent the whole time, though he paused every so often to cry.*

"This spot will work," said Sebastian, as they approached a clearing.

*He took out the shovel and began digging. Young Julian just sat on
the ground, silently.*

Julian felt like the shoveling would never end, but
thankfully, he now found himself in a completely different
place. He was sitting on a boulder by the Delaware River,
comforting young Julian. It must've been late in the evening,
as nobody was around.

"It's okay," said Sebastian. "It was an accident."

*Young Julian shook his head, sniffling. "Why did she have to die?"
he said.*

"She was still trying to grab him from behind. It wasn't your fault."

"It was!" said young Julian. "It was."

"I can make you forget, you know."

"No. Don't."

He felt tears well up in his eyes as he reached for his younger brother's hand.

Julian pulled his hand away from Blaine's. He was back at the Ritz.

"Seen enough?" said Blaine.

"You made me forget everything," he said. "You took it all. Even the good stuff. Even her."

"Not exactly, Julian. Unlike you, I have a little control over my gift. If I focus on something hard enough, I can make people forget it, with a little collateral damage maybe. In that case, I only made you forget that day."

"Then why can't I remember anything else?"

"I was getting to that."

"Well, please do."

"Alright. How about I start with after that godawful night? I tried having us live in the house ourselves. As you could guess, soon the mortgage came due and I realized pretty quickly we couldn't stay there forever. Stupid idea anyway, but what did I know? I reported our mother missing and we ended up both being processed by the state."

"That must've gone well."

"Yes, they took quite an interest in our hands. I told them we both had neurological conditions, so we had to wear gloves. Wish we had *these* back then." He raised his hand to show the prosthetic glove.

"Between that," he continued, "and your obvious lack of memory, they wanted to send us to a neurologist, so I gave them Dr. Schaffler's name."

"So, you knew Dr. Schaffler?"

"Mother took us to him when we were younger. He always seemed to take to you better than me. I think I frightened him.

I liked his nurse, Laura, though. And so did you. She even wanted to adopt us. The social worker loved the idea, too."

"You're telling me she adopted us both?"

"Not quite. Unlike you, I didn't have amnesia. I couldn't get the memory of that night out of my head. And as much as I hate to say it, I resented you for it. Anyway, I knew then and there what I had to do."

"You made us forget you."

"I made *all* of you forget I ever existed. I walked out of that office and never came back—at least not to your knowledge. The social worker got in a bit of trouble for that if I recall, since I made her forget me, too. If you research runaways named Sebastian Galloway, you'll see me listed as a missing person."

Julian wasn't sure what was more outlandish, Blaine's story or the fact that he believed it. But something Blaine had said was needling at him.

"What do you mean 'at least not to my knowledge?'" he said.

Blaine tapped on the newspaper article.

"This," he said. "After the bodies were found, the whole damn issue resurrected itself. You can imagine I wasn't too thrilled about that. I didn't want to take any chances, so I went back and made you all forget that, too. I'm sure you don't remember me knocking on Laura's door and trying to sell you windows. I've checked in on you over the years, Julian."

"How nice of you," he said, hoping Blaine recognized the sarcasm. "So, if you didn't stay, where did you go?"

"That's a story in itself. Are you sure you want to hear it?"

"Well, you can't stop there. I want to know how a fourteen-year-old kid ends up like... well... like you."

"So do I. Anyway, after I unceremoniously left Dr. Schaffler's, I took our mother's address book and looked up Howard Blaine. He was our real father. Turned out he was living in a farmhouse in Bucks County, so I headed up there and surprised him. I told him our mother ran off."

"I don't remember him either. Why'd you make me forget *him?*"

"I didn't," said Blaine. "He left when you were about three. I barely remembered him myself."

"Didn't he ask where I was?"

Blaine laughed. "He wouldn't have cared. He didn't even want *me.* He was completely and utterly paranoid. He told me I should find somewhere else to live. It just so happened, some drug lord's hit man came knocking on the door when I was there, making some pretty heavy threats. So, of course I shook the fella's hand and introduced myself. Wouldn't you know it, the fool forgot why he came and got back in his car. I guess dear old dad found me useful. He said I could stay for a week."

"Where'd you go after that?"

"How about we stop talking about me? Our dinners are getting cold."

"I really want to know."

Blaine took a few bites of his Beef Wellington, and Julian took the opportunity to try some of it himself. It was delectable, but he no longer had much of an appetite.

"If you must know," said Blaine, "that 'week' I was there turned into years. More drug lords came visiting, and I had to send them packing too. There must've been a lot of confused drug lords wandering around back then. I can't say I'm sorry. Anyway, I tried to get him cleaned up, but it was like trying to keep a squirrel away from nuts. Instead, he pushed drugs on *me* to manage my so-called gift. All it did was make me sick until I found the right mix. But it wasn't for me. Luckily, things calmed down for a while after that. It was a bit of good fortune that things were pretty uneventful. Until they weren't."

"What happened?"

"Bad fortune. I came home from a boring day of shopping

and the door was busted open. I ran in and found him lying on the floor. He was beaten to a pulp. Then I had some good fortune."

"How so?"

"One of the things I was out shopping for was bandages. I cut myself shaving earlier that day. Anyway, after I patched him up, my new career got started."

"Robbing drug lords?"

"You're more right than you realize. Our father was short on money and long on fantasy, so he concocted this idea that I could use my talents to steal from rival drug lords so he could pay off his debt. I won't bore you with the details, but it turned out he was smarter than he looked. Damn if it didn't work. I won't get into how I managed it, but he ended up paying off his debts and we both had more money than we knew what to do with. He even used his contacts to get me a fake ID and passport. I was Sebastian Blaine after that."

"Ready to take on the world."

"You could say that. I realized I had a whole world to explore. I was nineteen and full of energy. I had a new talent, or at least a new use for it. I was hooked."

"I suppose college was out of the question."

"And give up all that fun? No, a normal life just wasn't going to cut it for me, and it was only a matter of time before our father got himself into trouble again. But he was debt free and rich, and I figured he'd be okay. Plus, the more people I stole from, the more danger I was putting him in all over again. So, I did what I thought was right. I made him forget all about me and left."

"Yeah, you're good at that."

"I'm good at a lot of things, Julian, especially stealing valuable things from people who don't deserve them. I've been doing it for twenty years. Something about the adrenaline rush, the thrill of the hunt."

"Well, drug lords I can understand," said Julian, "but this is different."

"I only started out with drug lords. Then after a while I added the super-rich to my menu. I'm talking billionaires who were born into money, not Marv and Esther Bibblecock who inherited a few hundred thousand from a long-lost aunt. Drug lords and trust fund billionaires. You get to realize after a while they're both the same. They'd kick their mother if got them higher on the ladder. I once dated a girl who was a trust fund baby. Loaded with money and didn't do a thing to earn it. I could tell you stories about her. And don't get me started on greedy corporations. I have no love lost for any of them. And none of them pay taxes. Well, consider me the taxman."

The waiter came in to check on their meals, but noticed they were still eating and turned around. Julian took a few more bites of the succulent beef.

"Anyway," continued Blaine, "when I was twenty-five I moved my operations to Europe, where the real money was. I felt like a superhero, administering vigilante justice. But even that got old after a while. So, I started a legitimate company doing legitimate research. That's how I developed these gloves you like so much."

"But you still steal."

"I take on exclusive jobs now and then if the money's right. Sometimes, it's too good to toss up."

"You know who you sound like?" said Julian. "Those shallow, rich people you hate so much."

"If it makes you feel any better, the money goes to good use."

"But why? If you're so legitimate now, why get yourself wrapped up in all this? You must have enough to buy the Taj Mahal."

"It's not just the money, Julian. Sometimes it's the principle of the thing. I have a distaste for the privileged."

Julian looked around the room. "The irony is staggering. We're literally sitting in the Ritz."

"I've earned it."

"By stealing."

"You're missing the point, Julian."

"What point? Who even are these people you're working with?"

Blaine sighed.

"I met them through Olga. You met her."

"Yes, nice lady. She had me blindfolded and knocked out."

"Call it job enthusiasm," said Blaine, "but you got here safe and sound, and that I insisted on."

"But what kind of job? Do you even understand what they're after? Do you have any idea?"

"I know all I need to. Something about balancing the power in the world. They want to give everyone the same defense capability. That doesn't sound too bad from where I'm sitting."

"Sebastian, this could lead to a world war. You're putting innocent lives in danger." He realized it was the first time he'd referred to his brother by name. But like it or not, this was indeed the brother he'd long forgotten. He could still see the fourteen-year-old Sebastian in his eyes.

"No government is innocent, Julian. You're fooling yourself if you think so. Believe me, I've dealt with them all and I've seen the capital cronyism and corruption. One's as bad as the next, so excuse me if I don't take out the tissues."

"But I'm not talking about governments. I'm talking about innocent people. Mothers and children and grandparents. I heard what would happen if any country decided to shoot down our satellites. The US would be sitting ducks. And so would England and all of Europe. Is that what you want?"

Blaine leaned back and folded his arms.

"Nobody's taking away their ability to use the SARA

device," said Blaine. He sounded like a father telling his child there are no real monsters under the bed. "It's just that everyone else would have the same ability to defend themselves. Level the playing field and all that."

"But what if they don't just want the same capability?" said Julian.

"I'm not following."

"What if they want to reverse engineer it so they can get past it? Then they can attack at will and we'd be completely helpless. Don't you get it? If you let these people have this technology, you're opening Pandora's box. I realize this is all fun and games to you and you don't really care about how this impacts everyone, but it does. Probably really badly."

For the first time since Julian had met him, Blaine didn't have an answer. He appeared to be contemplating the implications. Julian watched as his brother seemed to be weighing what he'd said. Blaine nodded as if he finally understood, but then sighed and shook his head.

"Julian, I'm afraid it's too late."

"It's never too late. You're a man of action. I saw it in your memories. You sprang into action when all I could do was sit there in shock."

"I'm afraid it's my action that caused that whole mess. Anyway, you don't understand. These people can do anything. They're everywhere."

"What people?"

"They're called VIPER."

"Oh, that doesn't sound ominous."

"It should sound ominous. Because if we don't complete this job, the only ones who'll die for sure are you and me. Whether you like it or not, we're in this together."

"We *are* in this together," said Julian. "Luckily, it sounds like you've gotten out of worse. Think about it. We can go up against them, you and me."

Blaine laughed.

"I'm serious," said Julian.

"You know, maybe in a way, this is your payback for all the years of peace I never had."

"Peace!? You stole my whole past. But that's what you do, don't you? Steal. Do you know it's tortured me my whole life, not knowing why I couldn't remember anything? I would die for some peace."

"Julian, I didn't have a choice," said Blaine, apologetically. "Sometimes you have to make a decision that's hard to live with. About five years ago, when I heard our father died of an overdose, I wondered what would've happened if I never left. If I could've made a difference. He wasn't a bad guy inside, I knew that. It's bothered me ever since." He leaned forward. "I'm not a monster either, Julian. And I never wanted to cause you pain, I hope you can believe that. Quite the opposite."

Julian looked at his brother and could see the sincerity in his eyes. All his skepticism and doubt washed away in that moment. Despite some bad decisions and distorted motives, it was clear his brother's intent in erasing his memory was well-meaning. And he's had to live his whole life on the run, which couldn't have been easy. Both of their pasts were out of reach—a long-forgotten nightmare. Except in Sebastian's case, he was aware of it every day of his existence. All the money in the world couldn't cure that pain. Julian didn't know whether to envy him or pity him. Maybe both. The truth was, they were two sides of a coin. Just like he could see everyone's past but his own, Sebastian could make anyone forget, but he couldn't make himself forget the things that have tormented him and governed his life. But now they were reunited, and perhaps over time they could both become whole again.

He looked into his brother's eyes. "I believe you," he said.

"Thank you," said Blaine, who exhaled as if the weight of the world had been lifted. "And I take all the blame, for what it's worth."

Julian leaned forward.

"Sebastian," he said, "what happened to us was nobody's fault. We were kids. We didn't even know how to make proper decisions. The truth was, we both tried to save our mom, and when we couldn't, we tried to save ourselves. But what we do now matters. We have to do the right thing. The whole world is spinning out of control, and do you want to be the catalyst when it all burns? Because I don't. I can't, no matter what the cost. You're not alone anymore, and neither am I. We have each other. Let's do the right thing."

Blaine seemed to be absorbing what he'd said—not only absorbing it, but digesting it. Julian could tell he was considering what to do and how to do it. He could see the wheels spinning—the mastermind at work.

No sooner did Blaine nod than the door burst open to the left. As soon as Julian turned, he could see the woman from the airfield, Olga, strutting forward with at least four other men with guns. He looked at Blaine, who was visibly shocked.

"What is this!?" said Blaine, standing up.

Julian counted. There were six men.

"We can no longer afford wavering," said Olga. "We heard your conversation. You did not tell us that the asset was your brother. Why is that?"

Julian watched as Blaine frantically checked his pockets for bugs. He found one in his outside jacket pocket and threw it on the ground and stepped on it.

"Who cares if he was," said Blaine, though gritted teeth. "It wasn't relevant. Now if you want your information, I suggest you leave. Now."

"We *are* leaving. And you are both coming with us."

"That's ridiculous."

"We tolerate neither deception nor failure, Blaine. And we have sufficient doubt that you will do as you say."

"It won't work," said Julian. "You need me to read Baumann's memories. I won't do it."

"You already did," said Olga, matter-of-factly. "You said so yourself."

"I was stalling. I only saw a little. Not where the plans are."

Olga narrowed her eyes and peered at him.

"Then it is fortunate," she said, "that you will now have the chance to see more."

Julian wasn't about to give them the pleasure. He held all the cards, and they knew it. "Either way," he said. "You won't get a thing from me."

"The famous and incorrect words of many before you," she said, giving one of her fake smiles. "Hans does enjoy a challenge." She motioned to her guards. Immediately, they rushed forward and forced him and Blaine at gunpoint to leave the room.

As they made their way toward the exit, guns at their backs, the waiter entered the room carrying a tray of desserts—no doubt the Raspberry Surprise. He stopped in his tracks, looking absolutely horrified.

"Put it on my tab, Jacques," said Blaine, as they exited the room.

CHAPTER 25

LELA IN LONDON

Lela was supposed to arrive in London at two-thirty in the afternoon, but due to a delay at the stopover in Dublin, the plane didn't land until four-thirty. Finally, the taxi was heading into the city. She looked at her watch, which she'd changed to UK time at the airport. It was six.

"Saint Ermin's, right, miss?" said the cabbie. She had to get used to the driver being on the right.

"That's the one," she said. She'd chosen the hotel because it wasn't far from New Scotland Yard, not that she'd had much time to research hotels. Still, it looked beautiful in the photos, even though she might've selected something less luxurious had she had the time to look.

She watched as he adjusted his rear-view mirror. He was an older gentleman, and the whole way from the airport, he had insisted on telling her all the historic sites she should see and the restaurants she should try. She didn't have the heart to tell him she wouldn't have time to be touring. She did learn that curry was simply a British-coined term that meant sauce, which surprised her.

"You know, you're only a ten-minute walk from Buckingham Palace," he said. "And not just that, but Westminster Abbey, Big Ben, and the London Eye. I'd say you picked a good location. Get started bright and early tomorrow."

"I'll do that," she said.

"Let me try something," he said. He made a quick left and then glanced again in his rear-view mirror before redirecting his attention to the road.

"I'm taking you up Kensington High Street," he said. "It's just a minute out of the way, but it's where Kensington Palace is. You can't see much now, but it's worth checking out in the daytime."

After he turned right, he pointed out various landmarks. One busy pub had people pouring out onto the sidewalk. It looked straight out of a Dickens novel.

"Popular place," she said.

"That's the Goat. It's from 1695. It's the oldest surviving pub in Kensington."

She thought how different this was from the Kensington area in Philadelphia, which had become a billion-dollar open air heroin market, the largest on the East Coast.

After they made a right at the next traffic light, he adjusted his rear-view mirror again. This was the fourth time she'd seen him do that since the airport. Maybe it was an OCD thing.

"Miss," he said, "I don't mean to be impertinent, but do you have anyone you're meeting?"

"Not particularly," she said. "Why?" She thought it an odd question.

"Well, it could be my imagination—my wife says I have a vivid one—but it seems to me the car behind us has been following us ever since Heathrow. Every turn I make, he makes."

She unbuckled her seatbelt and turned around. A black

sedan was following behind them with two men in the front seat. She couldn't see who else may have been in the car with them. The driver was wearing a flat cap and the other guy had a crew cut.

"Can you lose them?" she said.

"I could make a few turns and see what they get up to."

"I would try that, if you don't mind."

She wondered. Could she have been under surveillance all this time? She wouldn't have put it past them. They seemed exceptionally organized. She hoped she hadn't jeopardized anything coming here. She'd tried to stay as discreet as possible.

As the cabbie made a few sharp turns in quick succession, she gripped the side door handles. Each time, she looked behind her, only to see that the black sedan had them turned with them.

"Deary me," said the driver. "If I can get you to a bobby, you might want to get to 'im straight away."

"I might need to," she said. "I think—"

She was jolted mid-sentence when the car suddenly hit them from behind. She turned just in time to see the guy in the crew cut stepping out of the front passenger side of the sedan.

"This isn't good," she said.

"You better make a run for it miss," said the driver. "Never mind the fare."

"Thank you," she said. She threw him a few bills anyway as she frantically opened the car door and ran into the street. She'd left her luggage in the trunk, but there was no time to stop. She turned to see the crew cut guy chasing her on foot, along with another man who'd exited the sedan from the back—a bald guy with a blond mustache and beard. She wished she had her pistol on her, but this was London, and she hadn't had time to get any special authority to bring one.

She raced across the street to the left and glanced back again. The men were gaining ground. Just past them she heard tires screech as a gray SUV pulled out from behind the black sedan and sped in her direction. It was dark, but she could see that a red-headed man was at the wheel. He must've been with them.

She kept running and then turned left into a side alley lined with shops. With any luck she'd be able to hide in one of them. She glanced back to see the crew cut guy and his bearded friend rounding the corner into the alley. Just behind them, the gray SUV stopped at the intersection. The red-headed driver stared at her briefly, then raced forward, unable to enter the alley. She turned and picked up her pace again, running past three old ladies with shopping bags. She used the cover to duck into the alcove of a hat shop on the left. The lights were on, but when she tried the door, it was locked.

"Dammit," she said, banging on the door.

She didn't have a gun, but she grabbed her cell phone and curled her right hand around it. It wasn't quite brass knuckles, but it would have to do. Just as she darted out of the alcove, the man with the crew cut caught up and grabbed her shoulder. She pivoted and brought her right elbow down over his arm and jabbed her cell phone-filled fist into his neck. As he staggered back, she pushed him off-balance, knocking him into the bearded guy. The distraction gave her a chance to turn and keep running. Stopping in stores wouldn't be an option now; they had their eyes on her.

As she sprinted as fast as she could—dodging a few pedestrians along the way—the gray SUV pulled across the exit of the alley and came to a screeching halt, blocking her escape. She turned around to see the two men running toward her with guns pointed, just as the three pedestrians stepped into a pastry shop as if nothing was going on.

She looked back toward the SUV. The stocky red-headed

man had jumped out of the car and was now aiming a gun in her direction. The rear passenger door was open.

"Duck!" he yelled.

On instinct, she ducked down and ran toward a souvenir shop on the right to get out of the way. The red-headed man began firing at the other men, hitting the one with the crew cut in the leg.

"Get in the car!" he yelled to her.

She made a mad dash for the SUV and jumped into the open rear passenger door. The red-headed man was already in the driver seat. Before she knew it, they were speeding ahead. She turned to see the two men standing at the end of the alley in frustration.

A clear, plexiglass barrier separated her from the driver, not unlike her own SUV back home, except this time it was she who was in the back seat. She heard a beep.

"Who are you?" he said, through a speaker.

"My name's Lela Mars," she said, bringing her police ID up against the glass. "I'm a police detective in Philadelphia. Those guys were following me ever since the airport. Do you know who they are?"

"I know who they are, alright," he said. "The question is what do they want with *you*?"

"It's a long story," she said. "Can I ask who you are, first? Thanks for the rescue, by the way."

The plastic barrier went down.

"I'm Charles Barrie," he said. "MI5. Specifically, I'm with the Counter Terrorism Operations Centre, otherwise known as CTOC. What do you know about VIPER?"

"I can't say I've ever heard of them."

"Well, it seems they've heard of you. They're a terrorist group… of sorts."

"Of sorts?"

"Meaning they don't do mass bombings or random acts of

violence. Nothing they do is random. We believe they're behind some of the world's biggest heists, probably for funding. Why do they need funding, you ask? I'm glad you asked. They have pretty considerable resources when it comes to cyberwarfare, extortion, espionage, and the like. We suspect they have some highly placed backers as well. And they're spread out, which makes them hard to pin down. It's not like we can threaten sanctions. MI6 has been tracking them all over the globe. Just a couple weeks ago, the Secret Service alerted us to their presence here in London. So, the question remains. What does VIPER want with a police detective from Philadelphia?"

"Oh, that's just great," she said. "So, an organization with infinite resources even you guys can't lock up—and named after a killer snake, no less—probably has my family held hostage somewhere in London, but maybe anywhere in the world. Is that what you're telling me?"

"Hostage? For what purpose? Who *are* you really?"

"It's not me they want. The real prize they wanted was a guy named Julian Black, and now they have him. He's been helping me on some cases. It's a long story, but he can read people's memories just by touching them. Apparently, they need him to do something, but I don't know what."

"Wait a minute," he said. "Putting aside the part where he can read people's memories just by touching them—which I have to say is a whole other conversation—why would they take *your* family if they want him? Were you lovers?"

"No, just friends."

"Well, pardon me, but it seems they think otherwise if they took your family. Why is that?"

"I think I know who's behind it," she said, ignoring his comment. "At least the kidnappings."

"Who?" he said, glancing at her through the rear-view mirror.

"Julian's brother. A man named Sebastian Blaine. He'd be about forty years old with dark brown hair and blue-green eyes."

"Sebastian Blaine," he repeated.

"That's right. I realize it may not be easy finding him."

"Finding him isn't the problem. Sebastian Blaine's one of the wealthiest chaps in London. Owns a company in the Shard called Worldwide Research. They're quite private but very proper. They probably donate more to charity than all of London combined. I'd be hard pressed to think he'd be behind something like this. He sure as Sherlock wouldn't have someone kidnapped."

"Can we check him out?" she said.

He laughed. "Can you imagine? Walking into the posh office in the Shard and saying we think Sebastian Blaine kidnapped someone? You may as well accuse Julie Andrews. It must be a different Sebastian Blaine if that's really his name. This one's practically a saint."

"Do you have any pictures of him?" she said.

"I'll tell you what," he said. "Why don't we go to Thames House so we can sort all this out."

"Thames House?"

"MI5 Headquarters. You can tell me what you know, and we can research all the Sebastian Blaines you want. We'll get to the bottom of it. And then we can talk more about this memory man you're just friends with."

"Fair enough," she said. She was relieved to have a partner in her search, not to mention grateful to be alive, thanks to Charles Barrie, as gratingly unsubtle as he was.

As soon as they rounded the corner, four black cars were blocking their way. So much for relief.

"Oh bollocks, what's this?" said Barrie.

Lela stared out the front window and spotted at least six men getting out of the cars with guns.

Barrie put the SUV in reverse and floored it, but then stopped suddenly. Lela turned around. More cars were blocking them from the rear.

"Shit," she said.

Barrie reached back and handed her a gun.

"You're hereby licensed by MI5 to carry," he said. "If this is our Waterloo," he said, "let's hope it has a better ending."

CHAPTER 26

NO WAY OUT

J ulian was once again in the Shard, standing in front of Max Baumann. But this time, he was surrounded by Olga's men. The rest of the office was empty, as everyone had gone home for the day. He glanced around the room at his captors. In addition to Olga and Hans, the six men from the Ritz and three other hulking goons were there. Blaine stood next to Hans to the right of Baumann. He looked concerned, but not panicked. In any case, there didn't seem to be any way out of this.

He hesitated and glanced out the window. It was a spectacular evening view of London that he would've marveled at in normal circumstances. Yet this time it was just a tease—a world out of reach that he might never see again. The London Eye was spinning in the background, carrying tourists whose futures could be in doubt if he were to carry out his orders. He was increasingly aware by the second that he'd reached a dead end—a no win situation. Maybe he could lie. Possibly give a false location. But would they believe it? Surely, they wouldn't let him go until it was verified. But it might buy him time to work out a plan with Blaine. What that plan could be, he had no idea.

He glanced over at Blaine, whose eyes kept darting around the room, scoping out the players like a card shark.

"You will take his hand now," ordered Olga. "Voluntarily or by force."

Slowly, he removed the prosthetic glove Blaine had given him. He folded it and tucked it carefully in his pocket.

"Julian, wait," said Baumann, who put his arms in front of him as a barrier. Apparently, his hands were still freed from their last meeting. The scientist seemed uncharacteristically afraid. "Before you do it," he said, "come closer."

Julian carefully leaned in, hoping Baumann wasn't going to try anything foolish. Hans stepped closer, ready to intervene. Baumann put his hands down by his sides.

"Sara," whispered Baumann, "was my wife. Please. This was to be her legacy. I named it in her honor. Save it, Julian. Save it."

"Enough!" said Olga.

Julian turned to see her nod to Hans.

The tall, blond, monster of a man reached out and grabbed his right arm, bringing it forward.

"Take his hand," said Hans to the scientist. Julian could feel Hans's iron grip squeezing tighter.

Baumann slowly did as he was told and brought his right hand up and reached toward Julian's. Julian wondered if he'd see anything new this time. He thought about what he might tell them.

Just as Baumann's hand was about to make contact with his, a tremendous force pushed Julian off balance.

As he fell to the floor, he looked up to see what had hit him.

It seemed in one move, Blaine had tackled him and grabbed the gun out of Hans's holster.

"What are you doing?" said Julian, realizing Blaine was overwhelmingly outnumbered.

"The right thing," said Blaine, winking as he grabbed Baumann's hand with his left hand while he shot several of the thugs to buy time.

Hans tried to approach Blaine, but Blaine was too quick and aimed the gun at him. Hans backed up as Blaine ducked behind Baumann.

Julian ducked low to the floor while some of the other men took cover behind a table and returned fire. He watched in horror as Olga calmly and efficiently aimed her gun at Baumann and shot him in the head—the scientist was useless to her now that Blaine had washed his memories.

Blaine used Baumann and his chair as cover as he exchanged a few more shots with the VIPER men. Then one of Olga's operatives took a chance and stood up, shooting the dead scientist through the chest.

At first, Julian couldn't tell why he did that. Then, as Blaine fell to the floor, his gun sliding from his open hand onto the hardwood, it became clear. The VIPER agent was aiming for Blaine and had hit his mark.

Julian froze, as if time had stood still. He replayed the scene over and over in his head, thinking back to when his mother had been shot. This happened in almost the same way. And now, here was his brother, taking action to save him once again. It was a cruel twist of fate. He felt his heart sink as he watched Blaine lying there. He rushed toward him.

"Hold your fire," yelled Olga to the agents.

Julian was heartbroken. He couldn't lose him now, just when he was getting to know him. He checked under Blaine's jacket and saw blood. Blaine grabbed him by the shirt, startling him.

"Julian," said Blaine, gasping for air.

"Don't talk. Save your strength."

Julian turned and yelled out to the others. "Someone call an ambulance!"

Blaine pulled him closer and said, "Forget it," before whispering a random series of numbers to him. Then he said something even stranger.

"Lela," said Blaine, weakly.

"What?" It sounded like he said Lela.

"Her family. They're…"

"I can barely hear you," said Julian.

"They're on… the thirty…" He coughed. "They're on the thirty-sixth floor… room 3620."

"I don't understand," said Julian. "Who's Lela?"

Blaine's face turned red. "Damn… drugs… wore off," he said, then lost consciousness as his head fell to the floor.

Julian heard a noise behind him and jumped to his feet. Olga had kicked Blaine's fallen gun over to Hans, who was now aiming it at him.

Julian worked his way slowly around the room toward the paneled wall while Hans kept the gun pointed. His back was against the wall—quite literally—as Hans approached.

Silence filled the room except for the sound of Olga's footsteps as she came closer and joined Hans.

"You have already seen Baumann's memory," she said. "This we know to be true. You will reveal to us now what you know or follow them in death."

Julian looked around for any way to escape. Then he realized, there was a door behind him, practically camouflaged into the wall. Blaine had taken him through it earlier.

"Do not try to run," she said. "Even if you escape us, which you will not, we have agents guarding the area."

"Let me think," he said. He was being truthful. He was trying to remember the numbers Blaine had recited to him through his labored breaths. They had to be the passcode to the door. He felt around on the wall behind him and found the hidden panel to the keypad. As he feigned contemplation, he discreetly pulled it open.

"What will your choice be?" she said.

He glanced again out the window at the city skyline, the London Eye spinning in the distance. Did he have any chance of making it out there?

His heart was beating through his chest as he prepared to act. It was now or never.

"I think I'll take door number three," he said, as he turned and quickly entered the passcode.

"You need a code to exit," said Olga, smugly.

He pushed the door. To his relief, it opened.

"Got it," he said, running as fast as he could.

"Follow him!" yelled Olga behind him. "You, stay with the bodies."

He didn't look back to see who she was talking to, but he ran to the left and made his way to the same corridor he'd nearly escaped through earlier. He could hear footsteps behind him as he turned at the WC sign and raced to the emergency exit. He quickly opened the emergency door and entered the stairwell. Frantic, he flew down the stairs to the tenth floor.

Once through the tenth-floor door, he sprinted toward the lifts. He turned to see two VIPER men rushing up the hallway in the distance and resumed fleeing. Finally, he was at the lifts.

His heart was about to burst through his chest, as he kept pounding the *down* button. The men were catching up.

"Come on, dammit," he said.

Within seconds, a loud beep announced the arrival of a lift. As soon as the doors opened, he darted inside and continuously pressed the *close door* button until the lift doors began to shut. One of the operatives nearly managed to get his hand between the doors, but they closed with not a second to spare.

He felt it difficult to breathe as he watched the level

numbers descend. Immersive videos surrounded him with starry skies and then an evening street scene of London with people bustling back and forth while majestic music played in the background. What a slow, torturous way to anticipate one's impending death. The slickly produced entertainment only boosted his sense of pure terror, not to mention it distracted him from contemplating his next moves.

At each level, he prayed the lift wouldn't stop. He stared at the LED screen in anticipation.

Sixth floor.

Fifth floor.

Fourth floor.

Then, his worst fear came true. The lift stopped at the third floor.

Thinking about who might be waiting for him, he backed up against the rear of the lift. He was prepared to dash toward whoever it was in hopes of surprising them, realizing the chances of it working were slim.

The doors opened. Nobody was there.

He stepped forward and peeked out. There wasn't a soul around. He made a spur-of-the-moment decision and ran out into the hallway and headed back toward the stairwell, pausing only to catch his breath. He made a promise to himself that if he somehow survived this, he'd spend considerably more time moving and less playing video games.

He entered the stairwell and looked high and low. Nobody was there. Then he heard multiple footsteps coming from above. He peered up the center of the stairwell and spotted several pairs of legs racing down from a few floors up. It made him dizzy. He scooted down the steps as quickly as he could, trying to stay ahead of them. As he approached the second floor, he wasn't sure if he should keep running or head back to the lifts. He decided to keep running and bolted down to the next level.

Finally, he was at the first floor and opened the door to find himself in the marble-floored lobby of the Shard.

He spotted three revolving doors that exited to the street and ran for them. Out of the corner of his eye, he spotted Hans rushing toward him from the lift area, where he must've been waiting. He heard footsteps from behind him and turned to see four other agents coming from the stairwell exit.

With Hans and the other men gaining on him, he darted for the left exit door, only to see four men dressed in black suits who looked suspiciously like VIPER agents standing outside waiting for him. He was trapped.

CHAPTER 27

A SHOT IN THE EYE

As Julian pushed through the revolving door, wondering how he was going to get past the four awaiting agents, a loud crash came from the street to the left. He froze and glanced toward the accident scene. It looked like a three-car collision. Another car—a white sedan—came right up onto the complex's platform, probably trying to avoid the accident. The four men seemed momentarily distracted by it. That split second was all he needed, and he dashed past them and headed toward the main cross-street where the accident was. They didn't follow and seemed to be tending to the vehicle.

It dawned on him they might've been Shard security staff, but he wasn't about to go back and ask.

Like a wildebeest fleeing a pack of lions, he sprinted toward the road just as Hans and his other pursuers came up behind him. He kept moving and then ran to the right onto St. Thomas Street. He didn't turn to see if they were catching up, but they couldn't have been far behind him. He could hear someone yell, "Don't let him get away!"

As he ran as fast as his legs would carry him, he came upon an intersection and raced into the street. He nearly jumped out of his skin when a car to his right screeched to a halt. In that frozen moment in time, he realized he'd looked to the left on instinct, despite the painted sign below his feet that said *Look Right*. He leaped forward again, narrowly missing another car, and kept running. After a few minutes at a frenzied pace, he was exhausted and had to stop for a breather. He spotted a sign pointing to London Bridge to the right. That was exactly what he needed—to get to the River Thames. Then he could get his bearings. He caught his breath and then jogged across the road and headed toward the river. He turned to see Hans and his other cronies in hot pursuit. He hadn't lost them yet.

As he approached the river, he maneuvered to avoid a few pedestrians and almost knocked over an elderly man, which he felt bad about. When he finally got to the river, he ran to the left along the famed Bankside of the Thames.

Winded, he stopped again for a pause, but then forced himself to keep moving, looking for any signs of a police officer. He passed two lovers looking out over the river and then spotted a gray-haired man in a gray suit who was watching him run by with great curiosity. To his surprise, the man took out a gun and began chasing him. Soon another agent joined the fray, an Asian man who was holding something to his ear. These VIPER agents were everywhere.

Finally, he could see a gathering of people up ahead, which would be a perfect place to try to disappear. He used whatever energy he could muster to get to them. On the verge of passing out from exhaustion, he pressed ahead, but the closer he got, the further away they seemed. He knew he had no choice but to get there, so he pushed himself into an extra gear.

At last, he was approaching them. He could see they were congregating around a pub called *Swan at the Globe*, which he now realized was adjacent to Shakespeare's original Globe

Theater—something he never thought he'd see in his lifetime. With no time to fantasize, he pushed his way into the group, surrounding himself with as many people as he could. He used the opportunity for a respite as he nudged his way to the center of the gathering. A few of the people congregating seemed put off by his assertiveness, but most were wrapped up in conversation and holding their drinks. He noticed something peculiar. They were all dressed in Shakespearean garb. It must've been a theater troupe having a post-show celebration.

He craned his neck to see if any of the agents had caught up to him, and that's when he spotted Hans looking for him in the throng. He scanned the crowd for any others and observed the gray-haired man further back, pushing through the people and looking annoyed as he held his gun in the air. It was a wonder nobody was panicking at the sight of a weapon, but they were likely either too preoccupied or too drunk to notice it. He turned again and saw that Hans was now staring directly at him with fierce eyes, like a tiger who'd just spotted its prey.

In a hurry to escape, Julian impatiently forced his way through the group, pausing only to grab a knife out of the sheath of one of the actors.

He found his way out of the mob and resumed his escape along the Thames. As he picked up his pace, he felt the blade end of the knife with his fingers to test how sharp it was. The dull blade immediately retracted. He should've known. It was a theater knife. Annoyed at himself, he was about to toss it into the river, but instead stuffed it into his pocket. Then he remembered the old saying: Never bring a knife to a gunfight. Least of all, a fake knife. Maybe he'd get lucky and someone would think it was real.

After another ten minutes of alternating between walking, jogging, and sprinting, the riverbank wound around to the left. It occurred to him it was a good thing he rode his bicycle on occasion to clear his head or he wouldn't have even made it this far. Maybe there was some benefit to not driving after all. Still, he was beginning to get side stitches and had to pause for a break.

As he looked ahead, he could see the London Eye observation wheel in all its illuminated glory, shining bright red in the evening like a beacon as it circled around hypnotically. He had to get there; he was only about ten minutes away. All he needed to do was blend in with the awaiting tourists until he could get on the ride. He had an idea in his head. It was a longshot, but it was all he had.

As he ran with renewed energy, he noticed steps that led up to a pedestrian bridge that extended across the Thames, which, as he looked, was attached to a much larger bridge. He'd always been fascinated with bridges. He remembered from his game a pair of footbridges called the Golden Jubilee Bridges, which ran across the Thames and bordered the Hungerford Bridge at the center, a rail bridge more commonly known as the Charing Cross Bridge, due to the station it led to. This must've been it. He was tempted to climb the steps to the footbridge, but he thought the better of it and kept to his plan. He kept moving and proceeded under the enormous bridge. As expected, he spotted another set of stairs to the other footbridge, which bordered the Charing Cross along its left side.

He kept going and finally spotted a crowd of people up ahead, the iconic London Eye towering above. He was almost there.

After one final push, he made it to the throng of people waiting to get on the ride and pushed his way past the oblivious tourists. He raced to the ticket booth and nudged ahead of the queue, wondering if Hans had spotted him. Trying to ignore the angry grumbling behind him, he clumsily grabbed several bills out of his pocket and purchased a ticket.

Once he received his ticket, which took achingly long, he ran as fast as he could to the queue for the ride.

Again, he pushed through the eager tourists, constantly saying "Excuse me" and "Sorry," not that it did any good. People were yelling and cursing at him incessantly. One elderly Asian man pulled his grandchildren closer to keep them out of harm's way and a stern-looking red-haired woman gave him a nasty look.

"Hey, what are y'all tryin' to do?" yelled an oversized pasty-looking guy wearing a Dallas Cowboys jacket. He shoved another guy who'd bumped him while trying to get out of the way, and the two started fighting with one another.

After annoying just about everyone in line, Julian finally made it to one of the pods, but there were at least ten people ahead of him. A ride attendee was standing just ahead, directing passengers onto the awaiting capsule.

"Mind your step," said the attendee to each family.

Julian ducked down to avoid being spotted by Hans or anyone else. Finally, it was his turn.

Though his legs were about to buckle, he boarded the illuminated capsule, which extended out over the Thames. The interior of the giant, oval-shaped glass bubble was surprisingly large, at least big enough for twenty or thirty people. The sole wooden bench in the center was already filled, so he worked his way around to the far end and stood with his back to the observation glass. As more people entered, he glanced outside through the window to scan the platform. He could see the gray-haired man standing by the river, looking up and scanning the capsules for any sign of him.

Julian redirected his attention to the people boarding his capsule, anxiously counting every second until the door finally closed.

"Mind your step," said the ride attendant for at least the twentieth time.

He glanced out the window again. The gray-haired man was staring directly at him through a pair of what looked like night-vision goggles, clearly well-prepared for a manhunt. The Asian man with the earpiece came up beside him. Julian looked further to the left and spotted the other four agents meeting up with yet more VIPER men.

"Well, aren't you a lucky bloke," said the attendant to a boarding passenger. "You're the last one."

Julian breathed a sigh of relief as the door finally closed and the lights dimmed. The reddish-purple glow would've been extraordinarily soothing if he weren't hiding for his life.

For now, he was grateful to have a short respite. Then he saw the new passenger making his way toward him.

It was Hans.

♦

Julian was afraid this might happen. But he'd also figured if Hans did catch up to him, this was where he needed to be. Now he was wondering if it was such a good idea.

Thinking about how the rest of the evening might play out, he remained at the rear of the capsule while Hans made his way toward him, shoving aside any unlucky passengers that happened to be in his way.

As the capsule slowly began rising backward, Julian glanced out the window toward the riverbank to see the gray-haired man still on the platform, still staring through his goggles. The man slowly raised his gun toward the capsule. As Julian bent down to get out of the way, the man put the weapon down. As if Hans wasn't bad enough, now Julian had this guy to look forward to, not to mention the other agents. That is—if he ever got off the ride.

Julian stood passively as Hans came up to him and faced him, much too close for comfort. The blond giant's lips were curled into a snarl.

"We will always find you," said Hans, scowling. "In any city. In any country. Across the world."

"So, what now?" said Julian, as the capsule began rising again.

Hans gave a slight, crooked smile. "You know what I do. You have seen it."

"I suppose you're going to do the same to me."

"SARA," said Hans, "Tell me now or you will not leave this foolish excursion alive."

Julian contemplated Hans's menacing ultimatum, and how much time he'd have to stave it off.

"I could make up something, though," said Julian. "How would you even know?"

Hans glared at him. "We will verify."

"And if it turns out I was right? You'll kill me anyway. My brother can't make me forget you anymore."

Han shrugged. "Die now. Die later. Your choice."

The capsule rose higher.

"Make it quickly," said Hans.

"Let's say I tell you. What would you do with the information?" He didn't even care about the answer. He needed to stall.

"That is not your concern," said Hans.

"But it is. If I know I'm not putting the world in danger, I might feel more comfortable telling you."

The capsule began rising again, offering a spectacular, birds-eye view of the Thames and all the glittering lights of London.

Hans was getting impatient. "You are out of time."

"I know," said Julian. "I'm trying to remember. It's hard to think with all this pressure."

"Be quick." Hans was beginning to sweat.

"Okay," said Julian. "But one thing I don't get. All those

people you killed. You really didn't feel a thing? Honestly?"

"Focus!" said Hans, who was partially distracted, glancing toward the other passengers.

As the capsule moved again, the ride was approaching dizzying heights. He could see Hans was getting more and more preoccupied.

"Oh wow," said Julian as he looked out. "Look at this view." He was feeling a little queasy himself.

Hans glared at him, wiping the sweat from his forehead.

"Okay," said Julian. "I think I'm starting to remember."

Hans snarled in defiance and angrily opened his jacket to reveal the pistol in his holster. "By the time we reach the top," he said, grimacing through his teeth, "you will be dead."

It was now a battle of wills. Julian was pretty sure they still needed him, but he couldn't rule out Hans killing him either. He had to play his cards right and he only had one move—a gamble, but an educated one.

He shifted his attention toward the other passengers.

"Watch out!" he yelled. "He has a gun!"

At once, everyone began screaming and pushing to get to the opposite end, shaking the capsule slightly. But not enough.

"Remain where you are and be quiet," yelled Hans to the passengers. "None of you will be harmed."

As the chattering slowly ceased, Hans glared at Julian and gave that annoying crooked smile, though he was sweating profusely now.

"Did you think someone would be a hero?" said Hans. "Unlikely."

Julian watched anxiously as Hans started to open his jacket for his gun. Fortunately, the ride began moving again and Hans nervously reached for the guardrail behind him.

"I know how you got that scar, Hans."

In an instant, the arrogant defiance and confidence vanished from Hans's face, as Julian knew it would. He looked like a scared child.

"That was a long fall from a high building," said Julian. "It was the only memory of yours where I saw any fear whatsoever. It's amazing you survived."

The capsule rose once more. They were nearing the top. Hans was practically trembling as he reached again for the guardrail behind him.

"That's your only fear, isn't it Hans? Heights. It's why you wouldn't go near the windows at the Shard."

Hans was too frozen to answer.

Now was the time.

Julian grabbed the knife out of his pocket and plunged it into Hans's chest.

Hans grimaced and his eyes grew wide—it was the telltale face of one who didn't know how seriously injured he was and was afraid to look. Clearly worried, Hans grabbed Julian's hand and slowly pulled it away. The retractable knife extended.

The ruse was up.

Julian yanked his hand away and let the theater knife fall to the floor.

As the ride began its descent, Hans started to laugh—a full, hearty laugh. It was the first time Julian had seen him truly let loose.

"It's a toy," said Hans, still chuckling. Julian could see the relief on his face as Hans glanced down at the fallen prop. "It's a toy," he repeated, his voice cracking with delight. He looked up and the expression on his face suddenly changed.

"But this isn't," said Julian, aiming Hans's pistol at him.

The look of sudden realization on Hans's face was priceless as the blond giant felt his holster, only to find it empty. He backed up against the glass, realizing Julian had used the prop as a decoy.

As the ride descended, Julian could see the confidence returning to Hans's face, despite being on the wrong end of a gun barrel. Hans came forward and puffed out his chest.

"You won't use it," he said, standing boldly.

"Not if I don't have to," said Julian. "You're my ticket out of here."

"Stupid," said Hans, as he quickly reached forward and wrapped his enormous palm around Julian's pistol hand.

The passengers started screaming again as the two of them wrestled over the gun. He gripped it as tightly as he could, feeling it slipping from his fingers as Hans tugged at his hand. Julian grabbed it with his other hand for added leverage, keeping his finger on the trigger while trying to avoid putting pressure on it. Hans clenched his other hand around Julian's wrist and began twisting it. Through the panicked screams of the passengers, Julian heard a loud pop and felt his whole hand vibrate. Somehow, the gun had gone off. He could feel Hans's iron grip on his hand and wrist begin to weaken. He jumped back in horror as the menacing henchman with the telltale scar fell to the floor dead, blood pouring from his neck.

On instinct, Julian held his hands up to indicate he didn't mean anyone else harm, but the passengers were still unnerved and piled toward the front end of the capsule. He realized he was still holding the gun but was too afraid to let it go.

Just then, a recorded voice came over the speaker cautioning people to stand clear of the opening doors and to ask for wheelchair assistance if needed.

As soon as the capsule door opened, the ride attendee said, "I hope everyone had a lovely r—"

The passengers drowned him out with their screams as they ran past the poor man, shouting, "He has a gun!"

Julian threw the pistol down and tried to blend in with the group as he nudged his way through. He darted to the main walkway. It was blocked to the right, so he ran to the left, back toward the bridges. Without looking back, he kept running, but then froze when he saw the gray-haired man ahead in the distance waiting for him. Trapped, he glanced toward the river and spotted the steps that led up to the Golden Jubilee pedestrian bridge, cursing himself for throwing away his only weapon.

He made a run for the steps, but when he got there, he could see they were blocked off by a rope. He leaped over it, nearly falling, and then rushed up the stairs. He heard a ruckus behind him and turned to see at least seven or eight men in black outfits chasing after him. When he got to the top, he ran onto the empty pedestrian bridge and raced across the Thames, looking back to see how far they were. He was surprised to see they had stopped and were lined up behind him across the bridge, blocking him from turning back.

As soon as he turned and started running again, he understood why they'd stopped.

About fifty yards ahead, Olga stood waiting for him, flanked by four VIPER agents.

CHAPTER 28

THE WOMAN ON THE BRIDGE

J ulian strode slowly toward Olga as a light breeze blew across the Golden Jubilee Bridge. As soon as he got within earshot, he stopped as she spoke.

"You see our resources," she said, gesturing to show the emptiness of the bridge and the threatening group of agents blocking his escape from behind.

He glanced around, wondering where the police were.

"Come with me now," she said. "We can put an end to this folly… without incident or injury."

He shook his head. "It won't matter," he said. "You know I can't give you what you want."

It was her move. She stood silent for a moment. In the shadow of night, he couldn't read her expression.

"And your mind is made up?" she said.

He knew it couldn't be this easy. He imagined himself saying yes and then her walking away empty-handed. If only. He wondered what kind of torture they'd put him through if he did remain firm, but he also knew Olga wouldn't settle for any more delays. Either way, they were going to take him, and then, who knows what they'd do? He thought back to what he'd heard the Permanent Secretary tell Baumann—the sheer danger of the technology getting in the wrong hands, as well as his cautionary advice that SARA was the most sought-after asset in the world. He recalled Baumann's final words before his unfortunate death, pleading with him to protect the legacy of his wife. Now, as he faced an obviously malevolent woman who was part of an unfathomably powerful and deadly organization, who was *he* to be the weak link in the line of defense? This was far bigger than him.

He took a deep breath and answered.

"Yes," he said, knowing it meant they would take him back by force. "My mind is made up."

"Very well," she said, as she lifted a gun toward him. Shocked, he dove to the ground as the deafening gunshot echoed in cool air. Then he heard another shot.

So, this was what the final seconds of a life felt like—numbness… time standing still. He could feel no pain as he curled up trying to protect himself with his feeble and vulnerable flesh and bones. Was he hit? He opened his eyes and looked toward Olga. She was lying on the bridge, dead. The other four agents had their hands up.

Two people stepped forward from behind them—a beautiful, young Latina woman who still had her gun drawn, and a stocky red-headed man in a suit. They must've been with the police or secret service or something. As their fellow officers got busy handcuffing the other agents, the woman and her red-headed companion approached. He watched as she tucked the gun into her inner jacket pocket. Then he quickly looked behind him. The other VIPER agents were busy getting handcuffed by an impressive gathering of police.

He redirected his attention to the Latina woman, who came forward with open arms as if she was about to hug him. He stepped back.

"Julian," she said. "Thank God you're safe."

He stared at her, wondering where he knew her from. Her face looked familiar. He shook off the feeling of déjà vu and simply said, "Thank you."

"My family," she said. "Do you know where they are?"

"Your family?" he said. Then it dawned on him. "You must be Lela."

Her face looked like she'd seen a ghost.

"Oh my God," she said. "Blaine. He did this to you."

"No, he's okay. Well, not okay, sadly. He's dead. But he saved me. He had a message for you."

"For me?"

"He said to tell you that your parents were on the thirty-sixth floor. Room 3620."

"Of what building?" she said.

"Oh, sorry. The Shard."

She and the red-headed guy looked at each other with wide eyes, as if there was some inner secret between them. The red-headed guy picked up his phone and seemed to be giving instructions to someone.

Julian studied Lela's face. "Did we know each other?" he said.

Lela glanced down, her expression a combination of apprehension and sadness. Then she raised her head and held out her hand, waiting for him to take hold of it.

"See for yourself," she said.

He realized he still had his glove in his pocket from before, so he reached out to take her hand.

As soon as he gripped her palm, he was immersed in her world, driving at full speed in hot pursuit of a Percy's Catering van on I-95 in Philadelphia. He remembered that van—it was the one he'd been in, taken captive by Hans. It was starting to come back to him now.

As he weaved in and out of traffic trying to catch up to the van, he could feel Lela's palpable sense of dread and her commitment to saving someone she truly cared about—him. Her relentless devotion wasn't driven by any sense of romantic attraction, but something else entirely— the heartfelt bond of what was becoming a true friendship. He remembered her now, but more than that, he understood her. As she aimed her weapon at the van's tires in desperation, he knew at once she had never been trying to just use him for his talents—at least not once she'd gotten to know him. No, she'd been rooting for him, wanting him to succeed. Her vested interest was sincere, and she needed to help her friend.

As he was daydreaming, his heart nearly jumped out of his chest when he saw himself being pushed out the back of the van up ahead. He was one with Lela as she gripped the wheel tightly and hit the brakes hard, nearly hitting the man she was trying to save.

As he bore witness to his own shocked face, everything got blurry and then he found himself in a completely different place—London, sitting in the back seat of an SUV. The red-headed guy from the bridge was in the driver seat. The car was still, but he could feel the same intensity and desperation as before, if not more so, as Lela gripped the side handles. Up ahead was a row of cars, with armed VIPER agents standing outside and blocking the way. As Lela turned and looked out the rear window, he could see more agents behind them. They were trapped.

"Are the windows bulletproof?" she said.

"They are," said the red-headed man, but there's still nowhere to go."

Lela spotted an alley to the right, beyond some trees.

"If you drive up on the sidewalk past those trees," she said, "there's a small alley. You seem to be good at blocking alleys."

Just then, the agents in front of them opened fire. Lela ducked down, her heart thumping. The pops against the window were deafening. Above the din of the bullets, she could hear police sirens in the background.

"Hold on," said the red-headed man, as the car jolted to the right. She thought the car was going to tip over as it tilted on its left side. Then it leveled out as the vehicle turned and jumped over the curb. She lifted her head to see cracks on the front and left windshields. More bullets hit them

from the rear as the car clumsily shifted to the left. She wondered if this is what it felt like being on the battlefield in a war.

"Let's go. We're here," said the red-headed man.

Lela hastily opened the door to her right, trying to stay down as she rushed into the alley. The red-headed man did the same and wasn't far behind. More sirens filled the air behind them as she heard the sound of tires screeching. She glanced back to see the VIPER agents taking off in their vehicles.

"Well, that was a bloody near run thing," said the red-headed man.

They continued up the alley and emerged from the other end, just as a blue and yellow police car pulled in front of them.

"Hello Charles," said the awaiting officer from the open car window. "Hop in."

Julian pulled himself out of the memory and looked at the hopeful expression on Lela's face.

"Well?" she said.

"I remember," he said, his eyes starting to water.

She came forward at once and he wrapped his arms around her. It felt good to have his friend back, and he knew in his heart she felt the same.

Over her shoulder, he noticed the red-headed man staring past them at the other end of the bridge. Julian let go and turned around to see what he was looking at. Then his mouth fell open.

While the police were wrapped up with securing the VIPER agents, the gray-haired man had walked right past them and was now headed in his direction.

"Look out!" yelled Julian. "He's one of them."

"No, he's one of *us*," said the red-headed man.

Julian was dumbfounded as the gray-haired man approached and extended his hand.

"Simon Beech," said the gray-haired man. "MI6." He had the clear, British dialect of a professor from an old 1940s movie. Julian quickly pulled the prosthetic glove out of his pocket and slipped it on, then shook the man's hand.

"I don't understand," said Julian. "I thought you were trying to shoot at me."

"No, as a matter of fact I was trying to get at Hans Goring, the man who was chasing you. We've been after him for some time, but it seems you did my job for me. I do have one bit of advice though."

"What's that?"

"Next time you're running for your life, don't get on an amusement ride. It makes the whole thing rather complicated."

"Thanks," said Julian, smiling, "but I hope there's not a next time."

Julian looked back to see the Asian man with the earpiece giving the police instructions.

"So, *he* was with you, too?" he said.

"He's the one who coordinated this whole operation," said Beech. "That is, once your friend Detective Mars gave Charles the tip about the Shard. We did some investigation and to our good fortune, Hans Goring was outside. Unfortunately, he was chasing after you. You probably didn't even notice the helicopters overhead."

"Julian," said Lela, bringing over the red-headed man. "This is Charles Barrie. He's with MI5. It's the British equivalent to our FBI. If it weren't for him, I wouldn't be here."

"Nonsense," said Barrie, shaking Julian's hand. "If it weren't for her, neither of us would be here."

"It's a pleasure to meet you, sir," said Julian.

Beech came over and patted Barrie on the arm.

"A job well done once again, Charles," said Beech. "How long has it been, a year?"

"At least that," said Barrie.

"And you too, detective," he said to Lela. "I hear from Charles you've been quite resourceful." He walked up to Olga's body and gazed down at it. "Yes, very resourceful, indeed."

Beech turned around and rubbed his hands together. "Well, as they say, that's that. Now, Charles, you and I have a lot of notes to compare." He shifted his attention to Lela. "And you, Detective, have a family to see."

"I'd appreciate if we could do it quickly," she said. "We still don't know if they're safe."

"Oh, don't worry. They're safe. Charles called me as soon as he heard the room number. Our man is with them now. They were in quite a posh suite at the Shangri-La hotel in the Shard. We've relocated them to another suite, just to be safe. Their guards are already in custody."

"You acted fast," said Barrie.

"We always do. Now, are we going in your car or mine?"

"I think yours is in better shape."

"Mine it is," said Beech, as the emergency crew came to take Olga's body away.

◆

En route to the Shard in Beech's massive BMW, Lela listened as Julian recounted his adventures. She was flabbergasted when she heard how he'd ingeniously thought to lure Hans up on the London Eye. It occurred to her he'd make a good cop—no, a *spectacular* one, given his other talent. Then he spoke of Blaine, how his brother had given him back his past and saved his life in the end—not to mention making a bold sacrifice grabbing Baumann's hand. With that one move, there went any chances of VIPER getting anything out of Baumann. Unfortunately, it cost Baumann his life. Between Julian's horrific childhood experience and the untimely death of his brother and Baumann, the whole tale was one tragedy after the other. Now would come the healing.

It wasn't lost on her that if she'd never involved Julian, then her family wouldn't have been kidnapped, and he'd never have had to go through any of that. But then he'd never have known about his past, and who knows if VIPER would've found another way to get at Baumann.

"When all is said and done," said Beech from the driver seat. "I should be quite eager to learn more about your abilities, Julian. And your brother's too. It's remarkable. I wonder if you would be so kind as to stay another day—at our expense of course."

Lela looked at Julian, who was glancing in her direction for advice. She nodded.

"It's the least I could do," said Julian.

"Splendid."

"I'd like to sit in on that discussion as well," said Barrie, who was sitting in the front seat with Beech.

"Yes, of course, Charles," said Beech.

"I'd like to stay too, if it's okay," said Lela.

"That can be arranged," said Beech.

"I have my reasons," she said. She looked over at Julian, then toward Beech. "Julian and I were wondering if you could do some research for us."

"What did you have in mind?"

"Howard Blaine."

"My father," added Julian. "Well, mine and Sebastian's."

"Apparently, he was British," said Lela. "Aside from being a drug addict, we don't know anything about him other than that he died five years ago. I'm wondering if it might offer any clue as to Julian's ability. And Sebastian's, of course."

"Interesting," said Beech. "And what about his mother?"

"It wasn't anything to do with my mother," said Julian. "At least I don't think so."

"Plus, she was American," said Lela.

"Very well," said Beech. "I'll see what I can dig up. Maybe we'll *all* learn something."

◆

After they had arrived at the Shard, Julian took the lift with Charles Barrie. Lela had joined Simon Beech to retrieve her family. He would have liked to have been there to support her and see their reaction, but it was a private matter and he didn't want to be the awkward bystander while they all rejoiced. Besides, he needed to say a final word to Sebastian—that is, if they hadn't taken his body away by now.

As the immersive videos played on the ceiling of the lift, along with the inspiring orchestral music, Julian counted the levels as they flashed up on the display. He was thankful Blaine's offices hadn't been on the seventieth floor or something. Not to mention, running down the steps wouldn't have been an option.

"I stayed in the Shangri-La hotel here once," said Barrie. "It was quite dear."

"I'm glad you liked it," said Julian.

"No, I mean it was expensive."

"Oh! Right." He still had to get used to British terms. He felt like an ignorant tourist.

"Still very nice though," said Barrie, clearly trying to make him feel better.

Within practically no time at all, the lift stopped at the eleventh floor and the doors opened.

Julian tried to get his bearings. He led Barrie to the left, away from the stairwell he'd been on earlier—which seemed a lifetime ago.

Soon they came to set of glass office doors that were unmarked, except for a small WRL logo at the top, barely visible.

"This is it," said Barrie. "Worldwide Research, Limited."

Barrie tried the door, but it was locked. He reached in his pocket and took out the key he'd gotten from the hotel security staff on the way in.

"Remind me to give this back," he said.

Once Barrie opened the door, Julian spotted a lighting panel on the wall. He flipped on the lights and led Barrie to the right, past Blaine's office. They passed through the endless rows of white desks and glass-enclosed conference rooms. To the left, Julian could see the breathtaking vista of the illuminated city through the floor-to-ceiling windows, with the London Eye in the background—just a small, red, spinning circle from this distance. All in all, it had probably taken him about a half hour to run there, but it seemed like a lot longer. He imagined what look must've been on the ride attendant's face when he'd discovered Hans's body lying in the capsule. He wondered if it would make the evening news.

They continued through the office until they came to the concealed door that was built into the paneled wall. Julian found the keypad and opened it. He entered the passcode Blaine had given him, which he somehow remembered. As he'd hoped, it worked, and the door opened.

As they entered, the room was completely empty, except for some construction. Then he remembered. There was another room past this, which is where Blaine and Baumann would be. He led Barrie to the next door and entered the same passcode, taking a deep breath. He knew what awaited beyond the door.

He slowly opened the door and proceeded into the room. As he feared, it was a gruesome sight. Baumann was still tied to the chair, hunched over with a hole in his forehead and blood everywhere.

"Good God!" said Barrie.

Julian turned away, but he knew he had to get to Sebastian. He summoned the courage and headed toward Baumann, stepping around the pool of blood. He was almost afraid to look.

As he stepped around Baumann to the left, he didn't see any sign of Sebastian.

"Where's Blaine?" said Barrie.

"I don't know," he said, confused himself. "Last I saw, he was right here, unless they moved him." Baffled, he looked behind Baumann and there was still no sign of a body.

"Look at this," said Barrie.

Julian walked over to where Barrie was and saw he was gazing at the hardwood floor. There were drops of blood leading toward the door they'd entered from.

He looked at Barrie. "Could the police or medics have taken him already?"

Barrie shook his head. "They wouldn't have left the scientist here, that's for sure."

Barrie headed toward the door, which had shut automatically.

"Allow me," said Julian. He rushed ahead and opened the keypad and pressed the code. The door opened.

"Look, more drops of blood," said Barrie, pointing to the floor to the left.

"This way," said Julian. He led Barrie up the corridor he'd escaped from earlier. Several more drops of blood could be seen in the hall, leaving a trail toward the area where the stairwell was.

As they approached the cross-corridor where the emergency exit was, he heard faint groaning coming from the WC on the right.

Gun pointed, Barrie rushed in first and Julian followed him.

One of the VIPER guards was laying on the floor with a

bullet wound in his leg. Julian's heart sank. He was hoping it was Sebastian.

"I swear, I didn't do it," said the guard, holding his leg and wincing.

"Do what?" said Barrie. "Do what!?"

"That man in the chair. I didn't kill him."

"Who's the man in the chair?" yelled Barrie.

The guard didn't answer.

Barrie whacked him across the face with the butt of his gun.

"Who is he!?"

Julian tapped Barrie on the shoulder. "It's M—"

"I know who it is," said Barrie. "I want *him* to say it."

"I don't know. Just some random bloke."

"Bloody hell, like my nan used to say," said Barrie. "The thing is, I don't believe you, now, do I? Now who is he!?" He lifted the gun again and the guard held his arms in front of his face in defense.

"His name was Max Baumann!" yelled the guard. "That's all I know. He was some kind of scientist. But I don't remember what we needed him for. It's all foggy. I've lost a lot of blood. I need a doctor."

"Who shot you?"

"I don't know."

"What do you mean you don't know. What did he look like?"

"That's the thing," said the guard, wild-eyed and distraught. "I don't remember. I felt pain and next thing I knew I was on the floor with my bloody leg shot up and there I was, looking up at the bloody scientist. I thought maybe he did it."

"There was someone else in the room with him," said Barrie. "Where's Blaine?"

The guard looked up at him with a confused expression.

"Who the hell is Blaine?" he said. "I don't know any Blaine."

Barrie looked at Julian. "Do you believe this knob? He's lying again."

Julian smiled, as a rush of hope filled his veins. "No, he's not." He knew that somehow, somewhere, Blaine was still alive. He had to be.

CHAPTER 29

THE IN AND OUT CLUB

L ela awoke and glanced at her phone. It was six in the morning. Her phone alarm was set for six-thirty. She'd slept off and on, probably because her system was still operating on Philadelphia time. It was her first time overseas and now she knew what jetlag felt like. She had to remind herself she'd only arrived in London a day ago, though the day felt more like a week.

Still in bed, she glanced around the spacious, well-appointed single suite. Beech had put them all up in a stately mansion whose name implied a much different kind of place—The In and Out Club. According to Beech, it was "quite a legendary private club," as he put it. The formal name was the Naval and Military Club, but it was known everywhere as the *In and Out*, a nickname bestowed upon it as an homage to the prominent 'In' and 'Out' signs on the carriage gates. According to the brochure she'd picked up downstairs, the club once had a different location, in Piccadilly, but in 1999 it moved to its current location at No. 4 St. James Square. Built in 1679, it was the former home of Nancy Astor, the first woman to sit as a Member of Parliament in 1919.

She thought about her parents and sister. They were probably home by now. They'd been so overjoyed to see her last night, and she was just as thrilled to see them. It was the first time she'd seen her father shed tears. All he kept saying was how proud he was of her and how wrong he'd been about Julian. He was anxious to get back to work and they hadn't exactly had time to pack any belongings, so he decided to fly the family home right from the Shard. Barrie had kindly paid for their tickets. After they'd left, Beech had driven her and Julian to the club while Julian updated him on his and Sebastian's unique abilities and how he and his brother had come to be reunited. She recalled how Beech kept saying, *"Extraordinary. Absolutely extraordinary."*

The phone alarm finally rang, startling her. She quickly turned it off and sat up. Eager to meet the others, she climbed out of bed, took a much-needed shower, and then got dressed. She was surprised how refreshed she felt, even though she had to put her worn clothes back on, which she'd left to air out overnight. Beech had thoughtfully arranged for a bag of toiletries to be supplied to her and Julian, along with silk pajamas. Hers had been a little loose but she didn't care. Giving her hair one last brush, she headed downstairs, where a concierge directed her to the Coffee Room.

As soon as she entered the blue-carpeted Coffee Room, she marveled at its elegance. Golden chandeliers hovered over round banquet tables that were covered in white tablecloths and prepared with formal place settings. Magnificent old oil paintings adorned the burgundy walls, and, to the right, a row of tall rectangular windows offered perfect views of St. James Square. The sizeable, gold-framed mirrors that lined the room made the dining hall look even larger than it was. At a table at the far end of the room, two elderly gentlemen were having breakfast. Slightly to the left at another table, she spotted the back of Beech's head. As she proceeded to the table, she could see Julian was with him, too. Behind them along the wall, a beautiful buffet breakfast was set up.

"Ah, you're awake," said Beech, turning as she approached the table. "Charles will be joining us after breakfast. I take it you slept well."

"I did, thank you," she said, lying through her teeth.

"Go get your breakfast," said Beech.

She walked past an elegant, golden statue of a cherub and stepped up to the buffet, filling her plate with plain yogurt, berries, a multigrain roll, and a small helping of scrambled eggs. She was hungrier than she realized.

She carried her plate back to the table and took a seat next to Julian, who was engaged in conversation with Beech.

"So, you knew all along he was afraid of heights?" said Beech.

"That's right," said Julian. "Especially once I saw him shy away from the windows in the Shard. I figured it was my only chance to get an upper hand."

"Then I retract my prior advice," said Beech. "It was great thinking getting on that ride, though I might've considered the viewing platform of the building you were in."

"I thought about that," said Julian, "but I wanted to be around people."

"Quite right," said Beech. "As I said, absolutely splendid thinking. The both of you impress me."

Lela noticed Julian didn't have his gloves on.

"No gloves?" she said, turning to him.

He smiled and held up a hand, stretching out the skin-like material. "Sebastian gave them to me," he said.

"That's incredible," she said. She could barely see they were there, though, now that she looked, she could see a slight shimmer on his palm.

"Looks like something our technologists might have

created for you," said Beech. "They've done some wondrous things. Nothing like exploding pens or anything you see in the movies, but wondrous all the same."

"Can you give us some examples?" said Lela.

He smirked. "Oh, I think you know the answer to that."

"You can't blame a cop for trying," she said, smiling.

For the next ten minutes or so, everyone was silent, focusing more on eating their breakfast. Lela noticed that Julian's toast was sitting in a vertical bread rack, which she thought was ingenious. She'd never seen one before.

After they were nearly finished eating, Beech broke the silence.

"I was just sharing some interesting bits of trivia with Julian earlier," he said, stirring his coffee. "Are either of you familiar with Operation Mincemeat?"

Lela shook her head.

"I can't say I am," said Julian.

"Ah, well you might find this of interest. Back in the Second World War, the Allied Forces were planning the invasion of Sicily, which would have been a far more difficult task than it turned out to be. That's because a Naval Intelligence Officer named Ewen Montagu came up with the clever idea to deceive the Germans into believing we were invading elsewhere—specifically, Greece. The idea was to take a dead man, dress him up as a Royal Marines officer with false plans on him, and then transport the body by submarine to the southern coast of Spain."

"That's brilliant," said Lela, "but why Spain?"

"Simple. It was a known congregating spot for German spies. Anyway, the body—the fictitious Captain William Martin— was found by a Spanish fisherman. Of course, the documents we planted ended up in German hands, as we knew they would. In reality, the so-called decorated captain was a homeless man who'd died of rat poison. In fact, one of the credentials planted on him identified him as a member of this very club."

"Did the Germans fall for it?" said Lela.

"They bought the story, hook, line, and sinker. So, while they were headed to Greece ready to fight the British Twelfth army, we were able to liberate Sicily with ease."

"So, the Twelfth Army was really in Sicily," said Lela.

"The Twelfth Army," said Beech, "didn't exist. We made up the name. In fact, the deception also included a supposed diversionary attack on Corsica and Sardinia by US troops under General Patton. None of it was real."

"How incredible," said Lela. "It puts my operations to shame."

"Ah, but just as interesting is where the idea came from. There was quite a useful memo floating around the intelligence community called the Trout Memo. Very creative. It listed fifty-four ways that the enemy, like trout, could be tricked or lured in. The credited author of the memo was Rear Admiral John Godfrey, the Director of the Naval Intelligence Division. But it was a well-known fact that it had all the signs of being actually written by his personal assistant. A man you might know of. Ian Fleming."

"The Bond author?" said Julian, whose face lit up. It dawned on Lela that as a writer, this would've particularly interested Julian.

"The same," said Beech. "I tell you this story not just to amuse you, but because we're using some of these same methods in dealing with the VIPER threat. We're a creative lot. We've only begun to scratch the surface, but last night's activities got us further than we've ever been, thanks to you both. The good news is that I spoke with my opposite number in the States last night. Fortunately, it was still five o'clock there. It seems they've made some good progress in tracking down their cells on the East Coast. At the very least, they now know they're being watched."

"That's great news," said Lela.

"Does that mean we should be safe when we get back?" said Julian.

"Safe is a relative term, but if you mean do I think you run the risk of them coming after you again, I think for the time being they wouldn't risk it."

"I can tell you in my district, we'll be very aggressive on this," said Lela.

"I was hoping you'd say that," said Beech. "As a matter of fact, I think the CIA would be quite interested in your participation. Joining the cause, so to speak. In fact, I would expect they'll reach out to you both when you return. My counterpart was quite impressed with both of you, from what I told him."

"What did you tell him?" said Lela.

"Enough. Incidentally, you'll be more interested in why I called him."

"Why did you?" she said.

"To talk about Howard Blaine. You see, I did a little research last night and found something peculiar. Enough to make me curious, anyway. So, I called my CIA contact to see what they knew on their side of the pond."

"What did you find out?" said Julian.

Beech looked around. "Not here," he said, stirring his coffee and taking another sip. He looked at his watch. "Oh dear," he said. "Charles will be waiting for us in the boardroom."

♦

When they got to the boardroom, Charles Barrie was already there, standing by the conference table. Against the grandeur of the Coffee Room, this room was more modest, though still traditional, and the pale-yellow walls, ivory shutters, and the marble fireplace gave it a touch of English charm. Until this trip, Lela had only seen rooms like these in period piece television shows.

Once everyone had exchanged pleasantries, Lela took a seat next to Julian on the right side of the conference table, while Beech and Barrie sat opposite them.

"I briefed Charles already," said Beech. "So, now it's your turn. First I must make it clear that nothing I say here leaves this room."

Lela nodded.

"Of course," said Julian.

"Good. I did some research last night, as I mentioned. As you can expect, there were quite a few people named Howard Blaine. Actors, writers, singers, janitors, farmers, and all sorts of men. Most were from the States, though enough were British. But only one was listed in our database and it just so happens I found it shockingly relevant."

He paused for a second and pulled a printed sheet of paper and reading glasses out of his jacket pocket. He placed them on the table and then looked at Julian.

"You claim you father was a drug addict," he said.

"It's what my brother told me," said Julian.

"And a neighbor confirmed it," said Lela.

Julian looked at her, confused.

"I'll explain later," she said.

"Then I propose to you," said Beech, "that he wasn't *only* a drug addict, and he had good reason."

"I don't understand," said Julian.

Charles Barrie cleared his throat. "It will all make sense, I assure you."

"The Howard Blaine in our records," said Beech, "happened to be a research scientist. And not just any scientist. He was a neurogeneticist in Her Majesty's Civil Service who was on loan to an American program—quite a top-secret one at the time. It was called Project Stargate. Most of it has since been declassified. Are you familiar with it?"

"No," said Lela, shaking her head. Immediately, she thought back to what Dr. Schaffler had said about Julian's DNA being altered. A neurogeneticist would surely seem to be someone who could do that.

"I never heard of it," said Julian.

"In short, it was a program that started in the seventies and ran for twenty-three years. The idea was to research the ability to psychically view objects and activities from afar. Remote viewing, they called it. They'd gotten wind that the Soviets were already delving into that territory, so clearly there was some urgency to it. It fizzled out in 1995 after it was declared an impractical waste of time... more or less. I suspect some at the defense department considered it an embarrassment. But it wasn't without its successes."

Lela glanced at Julian, who returned the knowing look. She turned back to Beech.

"What was Howard Blaine's role in it?" she said.

"To explain that, I'll need to explain a little more about the program."

Beech put his reading glasses on and picked up the sheet of paper.

"This is from a declassified abstract. It says, 'Recent work in both US and Soviet laboratories indicated mounting evidence for the existence of so-called *parapsychological* or *paraphysical* processes, sometimes called *psychoenergetic* processes.' That's the term to remember, psychoenergetics. The document goes on to list four conclusions from their work, in which they had psychics and laypeople alike attempt to view objects from afar. I've paraphrased here. First, the ability was not constrained by distance, and was proven to work across thousands of kilometers."

"It's mindboggling to even think of," said Julian.

"Indeed. Second, Faraday cage electrical shielding did nothing to degrade the accuracy of the viewings. Third, most of the correct results pertained to shapes, colors, and materials, not specific functions or names, indicating that it was primarily a right-brain activity. And last, the principal difference between experienced subjects and inexperienced volunteers was merely that the results of the latter were somewhat less reliable. But with time, much of the ability could be learned, meaning everyone has it to some level."

He looked up from his paper.

"So, it actually worked?" said Lela.

"To a degree. For every success, there were probably a hundred failures. But the successes were notable. They were able to locate Soviet weapons and technologies, including a nuclear sub. Later, they allegedly helped find lost Scud missiles in the Gulf War, and plutonium in North Korea. In a report from the Chinese Institute of Atomic Energy, one gifted individual claimed to be able to manipulate objects at the molecular level. To the researchers' surprise, he was able to not only identify material—written and otherwise—in a sealed envelope, but actually make a coin enter the envelope without opening it."

"That's unbelievable," said Julian.

"It *is* unbelievable," said Beech. "And personally, I'm not sure I do believe it. And I'm not sure the CIA did either, but there you have it. And this takes us to Howard Blaine."

He tucked the paper and glasses back into his jacket pocket.

"I would say, over the years at least twenty psychics joined the program, plus I don't know how many volunteers. From all accounts, the work was exhausting and relentless. Some of them ended up in psychiatric hospitals. Some became obsessed with aliens and crop circles. And some turned to drugs. Howard Blaine's story was different. You see, he wasn't a psychic. He was a researcher."

"I don't understand," said Lela.

"Howard Blaine, according to the records I have access to, joined the program in 1981. He felt the program wasn't broad enough. As a neurogeneticist, he felt the ability to read people's minds would have immense tactical use, and he began to do more research in that area. He challenged the idea that remote viewing was primarily a right brain activity, and he felt the authors of the research were making untested assumptions. According to the records, he wanted to bring the fields of…"

Beech took a small business card out of his shirt pocket and glanced the back of it. "… biogenic neurotransmission and quantum coherence into the field of psychoenergetics. How's that for a mouthful? Anyway, he felt strongly it would take the program to the next level. Now, I'm not a scientist and don't claim to understand all of it, but that's the gist of it. At any rate, when he couldn't get his proposal authorized, he was said to have conducted experiments on himself. It doesn't say how far he got or what he actually did, only that he was eventually terminated from the program for—I quote—'erratic behavior.' There's no evidence he ever returned to the UK."

"When did he do all this?" said Julian.

"It doesn't say. At least not in the records I can access, and I did a full scan. But we can assume he started soon after he joined, which would've been just before your brother was born. He likely continued through the eighties. You would've been babies, or toddlers at most."

"Can we find out more?" said Lela. Surely, there had to be records of his research.

"I said most of the program has been declassified," said Beech, "and it has. You might be surprised to learn there are some twelve million documents available. But some documents remain classified and are even above my level, not to mention that of my CIA counterpart, who I might add is fairly high up. Getting access to that information will—well, I won't beat around the bush—it'll be impossible."

"So, what do we do with all this?" said Lela.

"Well that's the rub, isn't it?" interjected Barrie. "There's not much you *can* do."

"I would agree," said Beech. "If Howard Blaine is Julian's father—and from the looks of it, he undoubtably is—it seems clear Julian's and his brother's abilities came from him."

"If anything," said Barrie, "it raises more questions than answers."

"Precisely," said Beech. He looked at Julian. "You see, there's so much we don't know. Did he experiment on you and your brother as babies? One would hope not."

"Dr. Schaffler did say Julian's DNA had some anomalies," said Lela.

Julian gave her another surprised look.

"I'll explain that later, too," she said.

"Well, that's useful information," said Barrie.

"Still," said Beech, it's hard to say if the anomalies were put there manually, or inherited naturally, which I assume would've come to a surprise to all involved, not the least, Howard Blaine. And if that was the case, was he so distraught to learn about it that he left his wife and took to drugs? Or did his self-experimentation lead him to take the drugs to dull his own senses?"

"Or both," said Lela.

"Or both," echoed Beech.

Lela thought of another peculiarity. "Why would Julian have ended up with the opposite ability from Sebastian?" she said.

"Excellent question," said Beech. "I thought about that

too. It could've been a singular coincidence. Or it could've been Howard Blaine trying to compensate after seeing what happened to Sebastian. Unfortunately, I'm afraid we'll never know."

"I feel like we're back where we started," said Julian.

"Not really," said Beech. "You now know your gift is courtesy of your father's scientific discoveries, through one way or another. All you can do now is use it wisely. Both you and your brother, despite his misgivings, have used it to save Her Majesty's government, your own country, and probably the entire Western civilization. Thanks to you both, SARA is now safe and secure, and the safehouse in the Monkton Combe no longer exists. Baumann's gone, but his legacy will live on."

"And his wife's," said Julian.

"I don't follow."

"He named SARA after his wife."

"Ah, I see. Then we all owe a debt of gratitude to the original Sara."

"Julian, how do you feel about all this?" said Lela. She was concerned how all the startling revelations would affect him.

"It's a lot to take in," he said. "But I'm not alone anymore, so that's something."

"That's more than something," said Barrie.

"And if you think I'm going to just disappear and stop hounding you," said Lela, "then—"

"I know you won't," said Julian, smiling.

"Right, then," said Beech. "As I said, I'd expect to hear from the CIA at some point after you return. I'm sure they're busy trying to root out a mole, as are we. Of course, I personally wouldn't be too upset if the two of you decided to lend your efforts from this side of the pond and help the cause from here. What say *you*, Charles?"

"We'd be delighted to have you," said Barrie.

Lela glanced over at Julian, who was smiling nervously. As generous and enticing as their offer was, she didn't see it in the cards for either her or Julian. At least not anytime soon.

"Thanks," she said, looking at Barrie. "I think first we have to get back to our lives and sort everything out."

"Understood," he said.

"Godspeed," said Beech, standing up.

♦

After the British Airways flight landed at Philadelphia International Airport and the seatbelt lights went off, Julian waited while the other passengers ahead of them pulled their luggage down from the overhead bins.

"There was a time I didn't think I'd ever see Philly again," he said.

"You and me both. Did you tell your mother… um, Laura, you were safe?"

"I did," he said. "And as far as I'm concerned, she's still my mother. She always will be."

"That's good," she said. "On both counts."

Finally, it was their turn to get up. He was on the aisle seat, so he got out first. They didn't have any luggage to collect. He'd been forced to leave his carry-on bag in the car before departing for London, and Lela had apparently left hers in the taxi in her rush to flee the VIPER agents. All they had now were the small carry-on bags of toiletries and pajamas Beech had kindly provided.

As they deboarded the plane and continued up the jet bridge to the Arrivals lounge, his legs felt like jelly. It was good to be on Philadelphia ground again, though it occurred to him he wouldn't mind having a chance to see London under better circumstances.

He walked with Lela into the Arrivals lounge, and to his

surprise, his mother was standing up ahead. She noticed him immediately and came running.

"Julian!" she said, rushing to hug him. "I was so worried."

"I told you I'd bring him back, Mrs. Black," said Lela.

His mother hugged Lela next.

"Oh, I brought you both Tastycakes," she said, pulling two packages of cupcakes out of her handbag. "I realize you're not foreigners, but I figured you'd want a taste of home as soon as possible."

"How sweet!" said Lela. "Literally."

"Mother, you really didn't have to come all the way here," said Julian.

"Of course I did. You didn't think I was going to wait one extra minute to see you, did you?"

As they made their way to the Baggage Claim area where the exit to the parking lot was, Julian felt grateful to be back home. Despite all that had happened, he made a vow to try to live a little differently now. Lela had been encouraging him on the flight, and she'd given him a bookmark she'd kept as a talisman with a quote from a French author, André Gide.

He took it out and looked at it as he walked. It said, "Man cannot discover new oceans unless he has the courage to lose sight of the shore." As he thought about it, he really did want to see some of those oceans.

CHAPTER 30

NEW BEGINNINGS

J ulian was so wrapped up in his own thoughts that he hadn't noticed the red Maserati parked half a block away as he jogged up the steps to Lela's family's front door.

"I'm glad to see you so eager," said his mother, who was lagging just behind him. He was grateful to Lela's family for inviting her.

He smiled. It had only been a week since London, and it already felt like a new beginning. He even made arrangements to meet Cassie in person once she returned from a bachelorette party weekend in Key West.

As he opened the unlocked door, he had a completely different sense of anticipation than his last visit. This time, the party was to celebrate the return of Lela's family, and his and Lela's role in bringing it about. As soon as he walked in, a roomful of people applauded him. The first one to approach him was Lela's father, who immediately shook his hand. Lela's stepmother came to greet Laura Black and proceeded to drag her off to introduce her to the other guests.

"We owe you a great debt of gratitude, my friend," said

Captain Mars. "I'm glad to hear you decided to join our district."

"I'll help where I can," said Julian. "I appreciate the opportunity."

"You're doing *us* a favor," said Mars. "I just hope the big guys don't steal you."

"Me too. I hope they're done kidnapping for now."

"Ha! I meant the CIA. But they may kidnap you, too." He laughed.

Just then, De Luca and Lela came over. The rest of the cops were wrapped up watching the first Eagles game of the season, whooping and hollering in the background. Captain Mars excused himself to tend to the guests.

"Look at this!" said De Luca, pointing to Julian's hands. "No more Michael Jackson. I'm impressed."

"They're new," said Julian.

"I heard," said De Luca. I guess now I'll have to call you Cool Hand Luke." He laughed and patted him on the back.

"That definitely has a better ring to it," said Lela.

"Good for you," said De Luca. "I mean it. Good for you."

"Thanks, I appreciate it," said Julian. He was surprised how genuinely supportive De Luca was.

"I guess the two of you heard the news," said De Luca. "We got Woodburn to confess."

"What!? No!" said Lela. "How?"

"The old-fashioned way. I lied. I managed to get in to see him, just to sign some 'forms.'" He made quote signs with his hands. "Anyway, while I was there, I told him Monica Hilson's phone recorded everything. I got him to understand it was very clear from the recording that he knew damn well it was a phone and not a weapon. Got him to admit it in exchange for a plea bargain."

"You got him a deal?" she said.

"Hell no. What do I look like, a lawyer? I have no idea how

he'll plead. The phone didn't have squat. But I got the asshole to sign a confession at least."

Julian laughed along with Lela. He was glad he was on De Luca's good side.

Just then he spotted his mother waving at him and smiling. She was chatting with Lela's sister.

"She must be happy about taking her old job back with Dr. Schaffler," said Lela.

"She's happy about a lot of things," he said.

De Luca pardoned himself and headed off to join the others watching the game.

"That's good," she said. Julian noticed she seemed slightly preoccupied.

"Anything wrong?" he said.

"Let's take a walk."

He followed her out to the white gazebo in the back yard and joined her on the bench. The same crow from last time was cawing away from the oak tree. At least he assumed it was the same crow.

"I was thinking more about Howard Blaine," she said. "You told me your brother said he learned from your father how to drug himself to dull his senses."

"That's right."

"Let's assume your father tried dulling his own senses before that. My guess is he ended up resorting to opioids, considering the hit men and how much trouble he had getting off it. I keep thinking about what Beech said. Were his experiments making him crazy? Or did your father develop some kind of gift like you and Sebastian and that's what he was trying to suppress?"

"I'm not sure it matters at this point," said Julian.

"But it does. Because if it's inherited, then it could spread to your children, too, if you decide to have any."

He nodded. He hadn't thought about it, but it was

something he'd have to consider when the time came.

"Even if he experimented on us," he said, "if it's in our DNA, couldn't that be passed down anyway?"

"Good point," she said. "I guess those are questions for a geneticist. You may want to take Dr. Schaffler up on his suggestion. It's the only way you can be sure if you can have children."

"Maybe I should start with a girlfriend," he said, smiling.

"On that topic," she said, "how are things with Cassie? Did you call her yet?" On the plane ride from London, Lela had given him a lecture about making things happen and creating opportunities.

"Um…"

"You promised me you would."

"I did, as a matter of fact," he said, smiling.

"You did!? What happened?"

"We're finally meeting in person. Next week, hopefully, after she gets back from Key West."

"That's great!" she said. "I'm happy for you! Lucky her, going to Key West."

"Tell me about it," he said.

"I just want you to know," she said, "I'll always have your back. You're not in this alone. We *will* get answers."

"I know we will," he said. "Really, if it weren't for you, I'd still be holed up in my room playing video games and writing my never-ending novel. Which I'm still going to finish, by the way… *after* I experience life a little."

"Now you're talking," she said.

Just then a bunch of yelling came from inside the house. The Eagles must've won.

"Care to go check it out?" she said.

"Sure."

Julian followed her inside where De Luca and the others were celebrating the Eagles' victory. Captain Mars grabbed De

Luca to head with him downstairs to get more beer.

Just then, Lela's sister Crystal brought Lela and Julian small plastic cups of wine. "Drink," she said. "It's a party."

"To new adventures," said Lela holding up her cup to toast.

"To new adventures," repeated Julian as they clinked their plastic cups.

As he took a sip, the four o'clock news came on the TV.

"Our first story in today's news," said the anchorwoman, "involves an unusual drug bust involving a mass case of amnesia."

Julian nearly choked on his drink.

"Wait, everyone quiet," said Lela, no doubt thinking the same thing he was.

Through the suddenly hushed chatter of the room, he focused on the broadcast.

"In Westchester, New York," continued the anchorwoman, "police received an anonymous tip about a major drug deal involving half a billion dollars' worth of cocaine. Except when police got there, they had quite a surprise. Here to tell us about it is Captain Lewis Marconi."

A split screen feed appeared on the right, showing a heavy-set cop with thinning hair and a white uniform standing outside in front of a building.

"What can you tell us, Captain?" said the anchorwoman.

"Well, it's truly the strangest thing I've ever encountered," said Marconi. "When we arrived on the scene, all the perpetrators were engaged in what appeared to be a drug deal in progress. Some of them we knew from priors. The odd thing was, every single one of them looked... I would call it shaken... confused, to say the least. I'd say they seemed less concerned about us than their own mental wellbeing. All the cocaine was there. All the players were there, as far as we know. The only thing that wasn't there was any sign of money.

None of them had any recollection of where the money went or who took it, or how the cocaine even got there."

"Captain, could this be just a case of bad actors pleading the fifth?"

"It sure makes a convenient excuse, but the fact is, no money was at the scene and these men were, in my opinion, baffled and afraid. Were they drugged and robbed by someone? We don't know. The only clue, which is strange in itself, was a large note scribbled in black marker left at the scene of the crime with one of the perpetrators. But all it said was, and I quote, 'The answers are at the farm.' What that means or what farm it's referring to is anyone's guess. We urge anyone with information to come forward, including the individual who left the anonymous tip. That's all I have, as we're still investigating, including the possibility of a digital transaction."

"Thank you, Captain. One last question. Could these men have been set up?"

"Again, we don't really know at this point. There are still some complex circumstances we have to dive deeper into. Like I said, we're still investigating."

"Thanks again, Captain." The split screen went away, and the anchorwoman resumed. "If anyone has any information on this case, please call the number at the bottom of the screen."

"It's an unusual case, to say the least," said her co-anchor, a silver-haired man who looked like a game show host.

"I'll say. It sounds like something from a Batman movie." She turned to the camera. "In other news…"

Julian looked at Lela with a knowing grin as everyone resumed their conversations.

"It's him," she said. "It has to be. I'm just glad it wasn't in my district. But what's up with the note about the farm?"

"Maybe he was just toying with them," he said. He couldn't

imagine what it could've meant. He glanced down at his prosthetic gloves and thought of his brother, who seemed to take a whimsical view of everything. He wouldn't have put it past him to play a joke with a bogus note. As he thought more about it, he couldn't help but smile. He looked around at the joyful, familiar faces in the room and absorbed the warmth of the moment.

"I'm glad to see you happy," said Lela.

"I'm just grateful," he said. "For everything."

"Oh my God, that reminds me," she said.

"What?"

"Nothing," she said.

"Oh, come on! You can't say 'Oh my God, that reminds me' and then say 'nothing.'"

"Okay, come with me."

She seemed like she was in a hurry. He followed her to the front door and outside onto the porch.

"I wasn't going to say anything until later," she said. "What do you make of that car?" She pointed to the right on the opposite side of the street.

He tried to follow her line of sight and then he saw it. The hairs on his arms stood up. It was the red Maserati.

"I don't get it," he said. "That's Hans's car."

She took a key fob out of her pocket and pressed it. The Maserati's lights blinked on and off and he heard a chirp.

"It *was* Hans's car," she said. "Now it's yours. Courtesy of our new friends at the CIA."

He looked at her in bewilderment as she held out the keys for him.

"You're kidding."

"Nope," she said.

"But is that safe?" He was imagining all sorts of VIPER agents noticing the car—and him in it.

"The former owners are in jail," she said. "And it has new

plates. Oh, and I forgot… the windows came bulletproof. But if you want to be sure, you can always have it painted. Want to take it for a spin?"

He grinned. "Will you join me?"

"Hell yeah," she said as she tossed him the keys.

He still couldn't believe it was real. There had to be strings attached, but for now, he didn't care. He made his way to the car and used the key fob to unlock the doors. The old Julian would've been afraid to take the car out, but he had to remind himself to take positive risks. He knew how to drive; he'd just resisted it for so many years. He climbed into the driver seat and marveled at the fancy dashboard as Lela settled into the passenger seat next to him.

He took a breath and started the engine, then pulled onto the street. He couldn't believe this was his car. It made him nervous even owning something so expensive. But as he picked up speed and rounded the corner, he began to settle in. He was driving again and it wasn't too bad.

"What do you think?" said Lela.

He grinned. "I think I can get used to it."

His mind wandered as he drove up Route 532, which was fairly empty. Then a thought hit him out of the blue. How could he have missed it?

Nobody was behind him. He hit the brakes and the car came to a screeching halt.

"What's wrong?" said Lela.

"We have to go back," he said.

"Why?"

"I know what the note about the farm meant."

"What?" she said.

"We need to get Howard Blaine's last known address. He lived in a farmhouse in Bucks County. That message was meant for us."

"You're kidding me. Are you sure?"

"I'd bet anything. Whatever answers we're looking for, whatever he wants us to find, it's there."

♦

Julian pulled back into the parking spot near Lela's family's house. Thankfully, the car had a fancy screen assistant to help him park. Then he ran to the house with Lela.

"If you don't mind, I'd like to keep this to ourselves," he said, as they rejoined the party.

"Of course."

He followed her down to the basement where she had an office set up. He sat nervously on a leather recliner, fiddling with his hands as she buried herself in her laptop.

He watched silently while Lela talked to herself as she discovered one wrong Howard Blaine after the other.

"Found his obituary," she said. "It says he lived in Buckingham. That's Bucks County. Now I just have to find the right…" Her voice drifted away as she searched.

"Got it," she said. "It says he lived in South Philly and moved to Buckingham. It doesn't list your old address, but it must be him. Now to search the Buckingham address to see who lives there."

After a few minutes, she stood up.

"Arthur and Jenny Foxcroft," she said.

"Who are they?"

"No idea, but that's who lives there now. What do you say we go pay them a visit?"

"Now?" he said.

"Unless you'd rather go upstairs and talk Eagles with De Luca."

"Um… no," he said. "Let's do it."

She grinned. "I thought you'd say that."

CHAPTER 31

THE FARMHOUSE

J ulian followed the car's GPS directions as he and Lela
made their way to the Foxcrofts' address in Buckingham,
Pennsylvania. She'd insisted they take the Maserati to give
him practice. They drove up York Road and passed a variety
of shopping centers and restaurants until the townships grew
more rural, with antique shops and the occasional boutique
store serving as points of interest. Soon they passed the quaint
None Such Farm Market on the left. Julian's jaw dropped as
he glanced to the right and saw the open fields of the sprawling
None Such farm itself. With its rolling hills and rows of corn
and a red barn in the distance, it would've made a good
postcard. He continued per the instructions and then turned
right at an old colonial inn that appeared to be from the
Revolutionary War days.

"That place looks haunted," he said.

"I wouldn't be surprised," said Lela.

He continued along Durham Road, and then made several
more turns until he was driving alongside a flat, open field on
his left.

"It should be up ahead on the right," said Lela.

After another five minutes, the GPS announced the address, and he could see the old stone farmhouse on the right, set back at the end of a long, dirt road driveway. Dusk had set in by the time they got there.

"That has to be from the seventeen hundreds at least," said Lela.

"Or older," he said.

He drove up the dirt road and felt the pebbles hit the bottom of the car as he pulled onto the lawn. As he got out of the vehicle, he gazed up at the old stone house. Colonial blue shutters adorned the white-paned windows, and a white rectangular balcony supported by three matching columns stood towering over the front door. The white paint on the columns looked like it was peeling. As they approached the house, a colonial blue rocking chair that matched the shutters sat on the patio, rocking slightly from the wind.

"Well, *that's* not creepy," he said. "Do you think anyone's home?"

"There's a Toyota over by the side of the house," she said.

He glanced over at the white Toyota and followed her to the front door. He waited while she rang the bell.

"You're doing the talking, right?" he said.

"If anyone answers."

He took a deep breath as they stood there waiting, but it seemed more and more apparent nobody was coming to the door. She rang again and then knocked loudly. Then she tried the doorknob and it turned.

"It's unlocked," she said. "Let's go in and have a look around."

"Are you sure about that?" he said. He didn't like the idea of entering some stranger's home.

"Why not?" she said, as she took her pistol out of her holster. He hadn't even noticed she was wearing it.

"Famous last words," he said. "Why not?"

Lela went in first. Hesitatingly, he followed her. The empty living room was fairly dark, with only the fading rays from outside coming in through the small windows. Everything was neat and well decorated, though it looked like some of the furniture hadn't changed since the Civil War. Books lined the bookshelves on every topic from gardening to antiques to photo journals of the kings and queens of Europe.

"Mr. Foxcroft?" she called out, startling him. "Mrs. Foxcroft?"

Nobody responded. The only sound was their footsteps against the creaky hardwood floor.

"Is anyone home?" she repeated.

"In here," said a male voice from the other room.

Lela gave Julian a confused look. He shrugged his shoulders. If *she* was confused, he surely was. She readied her pistol.

He followed her into the other room and his mouth dropped.

Sebastian Blaine was sitting in an office chair behind a desk, facing them and smiling. He wore a navy blazer over a gray turtleneck. "I was hoping you'd get here sooner or later," he said. "You must be the indefatigable Lela Mars. You don't need the gun."

"Who the hell are you?" she said.

"Care to do the honors, Julian?" he said.

"Lela, allow me to introduce my brother. Sebastian Blaine."

"You're Sebastian!?" she said, putting the gun away. "Why didn't you answer the door when we came?"

"I happened to look out the window and spotted that cheerfully red Maserati. I thought Hans was here."

"Hans is dead," said Julian.

"Dead? How'd they manage that?"

"I did it. On the London Eye."

"The London Eye? So that's what all that fuss was about." He looked at Lela. "You better start paying him more. Hans is no easy target... uh *was*. Well, good riddance to him."

"I thought *you* were dead, too," said Julian. "Then we found the guard you shot."

"I didn't shoot him," said Blaine.

"Who did?" said Lela.

"After everyone left, he came to check if I was alive and I jumped up. The idiot was so scared he shot himself in the leg. Turned out I was saved by vanity." He reached into his blazer jacket and pulled out a silver money clip full of cash. "I'll have to thank Gucci for making strong money clips. Never say money can't buy you happiness."

Julian shook his head. He couldn't help but grin.

"Still gave me a nasty gash and knocked the wind out of me," said Blaine. "Cracked a rib or two."

"By the way," said Julian. "How did you know I made it out of there?"

"Kenneth. You remember him."

"The VIPER guard?"

"No, he works for me. He played his part pretty well. I have to give him credit."

"I'll say," said Julian.

Blaine looked at Lela. "You're welcome, by the way."

"For kidnapping my family?" she said, not appreciating the humor.

"Kidnapping? They dined on foie gras and lobster. We should all be kidnapped like that."

"Is everything about money with you?" she said.

"Have you even *had* foie gras?"

"I can see you think it's all a joke," she said, "but if the British authorities find you—"

"I hope they do," he said. "I helped save the world. They should give me a knighthood."

Lela looked at Julian. "Is he always like this?" she said.

"You have no idea," he replied.

"Oh, come on," said Blaine, looking at Lela. "We have a lot in common, you and I. We're both unyielding and we don't stop until we get what we want. I admire that." He leaned forward and dispensed with the airy façade. "In all seriousness," he said, "I'm on your side. Really, I am."

"What can you tell us about Howard Blaine?" she said, unmoved.

"He was my father. And Julian's. But you knew that."

"Do you know if he did experiments on the two of you, or were your gifts an accident?"

Blaine paused for a moment. He seemed to be contemplating, recalling something. Then he spoke.

"My father was afraid of us," he said. "We were a reminder of a godawful mistake he made that got out of hand."

"A mistake he made to himself?" she said. "Or to you?"

Blaine rubbed his chin and leaned back in his chair.

"It's not exactly black and white," he said. Julian wasn't sure what he was getting at.

"Try me," said Lela.

"Okay, it was natural. At least in my case. It got passed down, thanks to dear old daddy's experiments on himself. It didn't even become apparent until I was about four." He smiled. "Seems I kept making my mother forget she brought me cookies, so she kept bringing me more."

"And Julian?"

"From what I was told, Julian was born *in vitro*. Our father, who art in heaven—or somewhere—was absolutely sure he could fix Julian so he wouldn't end up like me. You can see how it turned out. It tormented him for the rest of his miserable life. *That's* why Howard Blaine became a drug addict."

"So, what he did to us… it was all done in good faith," said

Julian.

"If you call it that." He looked at Lela, "Hey, you would be a good detective. You should think about that."

"Is there anything else you can tell us?" said Lela.

"Sure, I can tell you if you keep that Maserati, you may as well paint a big sign on it that says, 'former VIPER-mobile.' If you think the CIA caught them all, I have an old farmhouse to sell you."

"Wait, this is your farmhouse?" said Julian. "Then who are the Foxcrofts?"

"Me. I made up the names when I bought this property after our father died. Call me sentimental."

"So, what now?" said Lela. "What do you know about VIPER?"

"Plenty. Enough to know they won't stop. They're not the type to quit the war because they lost a battle. They're way too big for that. No, I'd say we have to go after *them*."

"We?" said Lela.

"Sure. In fact, now that we've gotten to know each other, how would you both like to take a little trip?"

"A trip where?" said Lela, sounding skeptical.

"I was thinking somewhere warm, like Cap d'Antibes in the French Riviera."

"That's awfully specific," said Lela. "And what would we do there?"

"I don't know. I was thinking we'd relax, see who makes the best Negroni, maybe venture out and sample some Bouillabaisse in Marseilles. It would be a crime not to try the Salade Niçoise in Nice. It's nothing like what you get here. Oh yes, and I own a classic Bermudian cutter I keep docked in Cannes. We'll *have* to take that out."

"So, you're proposing we take a vacation," said Lela, shaking her head and chuckling to herself at the absurdity of the idea.

"Why not?" he said. "Maybe we can do a little VIPER hunting while we're there. Rattle a nest or two."

"Go after VIPER?" said Julian. "Seriously?"

"How would you propose to do that?" said Lela, looking suddenly intrigued.

Julian was trying to imagine the three of them traveling together. Sebastian and Lela would probably kill each other.

Blaine smiled.

"Let's just say I'm going to help you track down a man with a yacht."

ABOUT THE AUTHOR

J. B. Manas is a bestselling American author whose fast-paced, twisty thrillers are often infused with a touch of mystery, adventure, and science-fiction. In addition to The Mirror Man, he is the author of the sci-fi thriller, Atticus, and co-author of The Kronos Interference, named to the "Best of 2012" by Kirkus Reviews, which gave the book a starred review, calling it "impressively original" and "[a] tour de force."

He is also a writer for Guy Dorian Sr.'s COR graphic novel line, collaborating with legendary artists and creators from the world of comics.

He is a member of the Authors' Guild, International Thriller Writers (ITW), and the Association of Former Intelligence Officers (AFIO).

Manas writes out of his home in suburban Philadelphia, where he lives with his wife, daughter, and dog Max, a loveable mutt that looks like a cross between a King Charles Cavalier Spaniel and a Corgi, but in fact has the DNA of neither.

J.B. loves hearing from his readers and can be reached via email at jb@jbmanas.com. Visit his website at www.jbmanas.com.

Printed in Great Britain
by Amazon

17373332R00169